House of Rooms

Siri Res

Polygon
Edinburgh

First published by
Polygon
22 George Square
Edinburgh
EH8 9LF

Copyright © Siri Reynolds 1997

Set in Minion by Palimpsest Book Production Limited,
Polmont, Stirlingshire
Printed and bound in Great Britain

A CIP record is available for this title.

The moral right of the author has been asserted.

ISBN 0 7486 6230 8

The Publisher acknowledges subsidy from

towards the publication of this volume.

My thanks to Linda Anderson for her comments during the writing of the first version of what finally became this book. Thanks, too, to Angela Cran and James Robertson for all their help and encouragement, and to Catherine Johnson for her continuing enthusiasm. Alicia Stubbersfield's friendship and insight have been much valued and much appreciated – thank you, Alicia. Finally, much love to Andreas Schöter: thanks for everything.

To my friends

1

'Now, just relax.'

Helen felt cool metal, then the familiar, insistent sense of being winched open. The doctor's anglepoise lamp stared dispassionately into her as he touched something deep and distant. She wished she had remembered to shave her legs before the test; she was annoyed that it bothered her, that it even occurred to her to care what he thought. She stared back at the lamp, willing the sharp light to scrub away her awareness of the push and shove of machinery.

Institutional lino; grey squares, black squares, zig-zagging away. Clothes piled neatly, body hidden in a towelling gown that doesn't smell like her. Ankle socks and handbag as she pads to the doctor's room. Woman in a suit. Man in a suit. Woman smiles, man looks. She consults her clipboard, talks about fitting the cap, about the man's need to learn. Helen meets his eyes, eyes that know her diagrams; to be helpful to doctors, to other women, she gives her permission. The woman's hand on her belly, the other searching, fitting rubber to the unseen. Now he must feel it. His fingers scrape in her, thumb crude on her clitoris. She isn't breathing. Speech is not hers to use; learning, he looks down into her dumb eyes.

'That's lovely,' the doctor said, fiddling with the speculum. 'All done.' The alien pressure in her began to ease and the speculum slurped out in a warmed soup of lubricating jelly. 'Well, you wanted to keep hold of that,' he chuckled and handed her a tissue.

Helen fumbled for it through the light bursting like rain in her eyes. She smiled to make him feel comfortable but anger quickly grabbed her mouth. 'I don't think so,' she said. 'How would you like it?'

'My apologies. I'm sure I wouldn't.' His professional appeasing voice, designed for the troublesome woman. He tugged at the screening curtain and hid himself. 'A smear test is in your own best interest, especially bearing in mind your other little problem.'

Her little problem, she thought: little, as in baby; little, as in no baby.

Little.

The latex gloves slapped at the air as he peeled them off. She hurried back into her clothes, managing to put her knickers on inside-out but, safe inside them, she wasn't coming out again.

They were everywhere. Pregnant women invaded the parks, the pavements, infiltrating the supermarket, pedestrian crossings, the coffee shop where she sat.

Helen tried not to stare. She'd done her reading; she knew it was normal that she should notice these women, normal to feel anger and guilt and then some more guilt for good measure, since she was jealous, too. September heralded the coming crop of babies, winter nights warmed into fecundity all around her; so easy for them. She stared at the woman at the next table whose hands were folded over her growing child. The woman looked placid, bovine: she blinked sleepily at Helen and smiled, rearranging her hands into exactly the same position. So blameless.

The thought sliced through Helen: I hope there's something wrong with it.

She busied herself with denial, with shame. All better than thinking.

In Safeway inoffensive music tinkled out of concealed speakers and offended her; a man walking past hummed along. She wanted to slap him.

'I had a really bad head, you know, and she insisted on talking about her operation,' a woman pushing a pram said to another. 'I think she's responsible, you know, for my heads. She's always had it in for me.'

'Mm,' said the second woman, as she watched her child tear leaves from the plastic foliage pretending to grow around the plastic tree that denoted customers' arrival at the fresh fruit section. 'Stop that, you,' she said without conviction.

The small face in the pushchair had a chocolate outline mouth pearled with snot. Helen tried not to think it but it escaped anyway: she would do it better than those women, she would do it properly; why should they have the chance and mess it up?

She went to Hannington's department store and made her way to the crafts department. There she bought some embroidery silks she didn't need, just for their deep colours, just for the feel of them in her hands.

A tatty Transit van was badly parked outside the flat when she got home. Of course – the new people would be moving into Ivan's flat now he was away. She should go and say hello, offer them tea perhaps. She crept up the stairs and sneaked in her front door. Tomorrow; she would go down tomorrow and be neighbourly.

Ivan had been reassuring about the tenants, saying he was sure there would be no noise, they seemed very sensible. 'And no babies, so no wailing day and night either.'

Helen and Dan hadn't told Ivan about wanting a baby. He had assumed that they were childless through choice: no point in worrying him about there maybe being noise from their flat since that possibility got smaller with each red tide the moon pushed through Helen.

A burst of laughter flooded up the stairs and over her.

Crumbs and curls of fluff on the carpet. Books striping the table, the chair, the windowsill. Dan's chin spiky with bristles neat as mown grass. Her face wet from the laughter that had pulled her to the floor; her breathlessness flickers on the edge of more. His warm weight steadies her; she feels the newness of him inside her. Unsure mouths gain confidence. Finally, after the suddenness and greed and hurry of flesh, they look at each other again. Things are different. 'You're squashing me,' she says. 'What were you laughing at?' he asks. It wasn't any one thing in particular, but a spark that lit inside her; they were never explainable. 'It wasn't that funny,' she says. 'I just got helpless. You're still squashing me.' He eases his weight onto his elbows; their thighs peel apart a little, stick together again.

The laughter echoed around the hall again; a woman.

Other people's happiness going on all around. Self-pity lapped at Helen; she crushed it. The thoughts always came together: that she had no right to it; and that it was her fault, after all. Her fault.

2

'Now then, Dan, come off the fence. Are women drivers crap or are they crap?' Greg inched the car forward precisely the same amount as the car in front had moved forward: precisely negligible, thought Dan, and not worth taking the handbrake off for.

This was Greg's favourite subject for morning conversation. 'Well?'

'You know what I think. It seems a bit pointless to me to keep saying the same things over and over again.'

'Get enough of that at work, eh? No, but seriously. Take this morning, for example. Three incidents: pulling out in front of me, turning without indicating, and, the cream of today's crop so far, that silly cow doing her make-up in the mirror. All women. I rest my case.'

'I think she had something in her eye actually,' said Dan.

'*Jesus!*' Greg banged the steering wheel. 'Did you see that? Did you?'

'It's a man, though.'

'It bloody isn't.'

'How many women do you know with a beard?'

'Excluding my mother-in-law?'

Dan looked out of the window. Helen was lucky to have a part-time job ten minutes' walk from the flat. He'd stopped complaining to her about these rides, partly because he felt like Greg while he was doing it, and partly because he was sure she wasn't listening even though she made comments that sounded like she was. Maybe the same complaints deserved the same comments.

'And I don't f-feel that we're being taught the right kind of things, real

world things I mean. I don't mean to say it's your fault but . . .' She flicks unnaturally black hair back over her shoulder.
'It may seem a little pedestrian, Lesley, but once you've got the basics out of the way then you can build on them.'
Her face is powder-pale, her mouth a sudden, bloody red; grey eyes in a stark black outline. She purses her lips. 'I thought you'd say s-something like that.'
'Sorry to be so predictable, but I can only say what I think.'
She sits back and scrutinizes him, black-clad arms folded tight against her chest. 'So, what are you going to do about my – our – c-complaints?'
Aggression undermined by her stammer, she waits.
Realization spreads like a stain in him. He desires her. His embarrassment silences him.
She waits.

'Dan! It's good to see you!' Mick charged across the coffee room.
'How was the sabbatical?'
'Completely brilliant. Didn't do any work on the book of course but my guitar playing's coming along nicely. How's Helen? Still . . . ?'
'Yes, still.'
'Never mind, things will work out – you'll see.'
The trouble with Mick's platitudes was they were heartfelt. Dan couldn't resent him. 'How's Caroline?' he asked.
'In the pink. The kids are great, too. And I have done some work on the book, only I began a rewrite so it's all taken rather longer than I'd planned. Can the world wait much longer for this startling insight into statistics, we ask ourselves?'
'I'm sure it will be fine. Not that I'll understand a word of it, but I'll be expecting my signed copy.'
'Fine, as long as you buy it. Then I can guarantee sales of at least two, as my mum says she'll buy one as well. Her on a pension, too – still, who needs food when you can have esoteric knowledge instead?'
'Sorry, Mick, I've got to go. Tutorial at two. How about lunch tomorrow?'
'Half twelve?'
'Fine. I'll buy you a pint and you can tell me what it's like to sit around on your arse for a year.'

'A year and a day at least – I won't rush into any work, I might put my back out or something.'

Orangey sunlight slipped around the edges of the blind and ran across the floor. Lesley's legs tangled with the light. She wore thick black tights. She'd worn those a lot in the summer as well, thought Dan: she must have got very hot.

'It's only two weeks into the term. Don't you think you should give it a while longer?' he said.

'Two weeks plus all of last year. That s-seems quite a long time to me.' Her gaze was steady; too steady. He felt like a specimen. 'I think a change to a different course is the solution,' she said.

'All the work you've put in up to now would, effectively, be wasted. And there would be funding problems, too. Have you seen your personal tutor about this?'

'I only just decided when I came in.'

'Then you should think on it. Who is your personal tutor?'

'Lexington. He's an old f-fart who doesn't have a clue about anything.'

Dan wanted to agree with her: the man seemed to be held up solely by the starch in his shirt and the iron crease of his trousers. 'Well, you can change your personal tutor, you know.'

'Could I have you?' She was still giving him that steady look. He was sure she hadn't blinked.

'In principle. But that probably wouldn't be wise, given that it's my course you're trying to dump.' And given that he kept thinking about her, this edgy, angry child-woman.

'But I want you.' She blinked. It was slow, deliberate, and a hundred per cent effective.

'Then you must go through the proper procedures. Apply through the departmental office. Felicity will give you the form. You'll have to explain why you're dissatisfied with your present tutor and, if you want to specify the replacement, why you want that particular person.'

She slunk out of his office, a long black cat in Doc Martens. She didn't stop at the secretary's office.

His cheeks were glowing. He went to the toilets and washed his face. He looked at himself in the mirror. Dark hair, receding slightly, with plenty of grey; beard; brown eyes: a thirty-four-year-old man. Not good-looking, not bad; not tall, not short; not fat, not thin – Mr Average personified.

'I can see them anyway,' says Helen.

'But I'm only twenty-one,' he says.

'They're there, laughter lines, very faint. They're going to look great when you're older.'

'Go for older men, do you?'

'Not yet. But give it a few years when you've had a chance to catch up . . .'

She's sprawled on his bed, writing an essay. A half-eaten pizza in a box on the table; a cup of coffee steaming on the floor by the bed. And Helen, dressed in papers and books.

He tries out the phrase in his head. 'My wife.' How bourgeois. 'I'm Helen's husband.' 'This is my wife.' My wife.

Dangerous stuff.

'What are you thinking about?' The words get mangled working their way past the pen she's chewing on.

'Nothing. Drink your coffee.'

3

ALL USHA COULD see were Jaz's legs supporting the pile of boxes and the blue point of his turban showing over the top.

'You've overdone it a bit, haven't you?' she said.

'Just tell me where to put them, will you.'

'Anywhere.'

Jaz walked unsteadily to a corner and set the boxes down. 'What's in these?'

'Books, I think.'

'How do you know where anything is? You haven't written on any of the boxes. I'd like to see *you* running a business.'

'You're starting to sound like Dad,' said Usha. 'You want to watch that.'

'Yeah, right. Anyway, there's one more lot of stuff and that's it.'

'And then I'll get us something to eat.'

'What? *You* make something? Usha-I'm-allergic-to-kitchens making food?'

'A sandwich.'

'I don't think Mum would be very impressed.'

Usha picked invisible lint from her trousers. 'Does she ever say anything about me?'

'She misses you.'

'She says so?'

'It's obvious. You know what Dad's like. You're not to be mentioned.'

'She's just doing what he says, as usual.'

'She's doing what she thinks is right. So is Dad. You can't blame them. After what happened, what did you expect?'

'More, I suppose. "Do what we want," they're saying, "and we'll love you; don't and we won't." That isn't love – it's acting out parts, saying and doing the right thing.'

'Well, no one could accuse you of that.'

'I miss them, Jaz. I'm so angry – but I miss them.' Tears stabbed behind her eyes. She willed them away but they crowded in.

Jaz knelt beside her. 'Poor Usha.' He put his long arms around her and the heat from his body comforted like a fire. His familiar smell was like a pillow. 'Poor little Usha.'

The supermarket is vast; shelves run away in all directions, glittering with colours. A baby sits in a trolley; vacant blue eyes focus on her and he smiles. He turns his head to the shelves and smiles at them.

Jaz holds her hand, leads her. She follows. Jaz always knows what's best. They're at the motorbike now. 'Look.' He shows her a coin. 'We can go on it.' It has lights that flash on and off, on and off. Jaz lifts her on; he's not much bigger than her but he does it easily. Jaz is strong. He puts the coin in and climbs on.

The motorbike growls and sways. She clings on to his back, her hands meeting in front, her cheek pressed against him. He's warm. The motorbike vibrates through her body and she can hear it through his. He's talking to her. His voice vibrates inside her, too. She laughs and laughs and when the ride stops he gets off and the air she lets herself fall into becomes straightaway the safety of his arms.

'Come on,' he said, 'let's get this finished.' He released her; she felt small and exposed. She watched him leave, noticing the fine hair on his neck was darkened with sweat.

The last time she had moved was with Alex; they had crammed their things into the tiny two-roomed flat whose air was restless with the sound of the sea and they couldn't stop smiling. His eyes were a clear green and she thought she could see everything.

'This is it, then,' said Jaz, bringing in the last of the boxes. 'Where's that food?'

'I've got them here.'

'That was quick.'

'Not really – I got them in Marks and Spencer this morning. Cheese and celery, or cheese ploughman's?'

'Cheat. No chicken tikka?'

'You're the worst vegetarian I've ever seen, Jaz.'

'I'm the victim of cultural conflict, that's all. I'm confused.'
'You're useless, you mean.'
'Fair enough. I'll have the ploughman's. But I want a cup of coffee with plenty of caffeine,' he added. 'I've got a lot on this afternoon.'
'But you're the boss – shouldn't you delegate?'
'Would *you* delegate to Subash? Anyway, I've got to fetch that suit I told you about to see if you can fix it.'
'I am useful for something, then.'
'An O-level in needlework isn't anything to get big-headed about, you know.'
'What about the A-levels, and three-quarters of a degree?'
'They're not really *useful* though, are they? Especially not to a woman.'
'I sometimes wonder if you're joking when you talk like that,' said Usha. 'I bet when you get married it'll be to some submissive little miss who'll be your servant.'
'I certainly hope so.'
'I hate you.'
'I hate you, too. Can I eat my sandwich now?'

Usha looks at his profile in the fading light. It seems frivolous to turn on the lamp. 'Alex, what's wrong?'

The clock's tick busies in the still room. It seems very loud. He takes a drink from the glass of whisky and she senses rather than sees the shudder.

'I've said something that's upset you?' *she asks.*
'Christ, can't you leave it alone?'
'You're unhappy. I want to help.'
'My being unhappy – if I am unhappy – messes up your little world, is that it?'
'That's not what I said. If you think I've done something wrong I need to know.'
'Funny how we seem to end up talking about *you* in these little chats which are supposed to get me talking about me.'

The neck of the bottle rings on the edge of the glass but he doesn't spill any as he refills it. She wants him to stop. It's taking him away. She has to say it.

'Haven't you had enough?'
'Apparently not.' *His voice has furred over slightly.*

'It doesn't help.'

'That's a matter of opinion, Miss Squeaky-Clean, never-touch-a-drop. Is being a tight-arse part of your religion or is it your personality?' She gets up. She wants to be anywhere else. 'Not deserting me, are you?' he says. 'Just when we were getting around to talking about something important.'

'We'll do it when you're sober, when –'

'You're doing it again! Controlling me, telling me when to talk, how to talk.'

'I'll see you later.' She picks up her bag. He gets to the door ahead of her and flicks on the light. His eyes are bloodshot. 'Let me leave,' she says.

'Such a regal princess, ordering your minion about.' He digs about in his pocket. 'You know about worms, don't you?'

'Worms.'

'Worms and a certain activity known as turning.' He produces a key, the deadlock key for the front door, which he proceeds to lock. He can see her thinking about her own key. 'Don't bother trying. You couldn't get past me.'

Her heart is pounding.

What does she do now? 'Stop messing about. Unlock the door. I'll stay, but unlock the door.'

He goes back into the living room. She hears him open the bottle, hears him waiting for her.

Jaz returned a couple of hours later.

'You know, if Subash wasn't a cousin . . .' He shook his head. 'I mean, there are two deliveries while I'm out and he leaves them right in the middle of the shop. The punters are squeezing past loads of boxes and he just sits behind the till listening to bhangra on his Walkman, bobbing about like he's got some kind of nervous condition.'

'Perhaps he's not cut out for life in retail.'

'I think he isn't cut out for life in general. I don't know how Auntie's coped with him for all these years.'

'She knew one day that he'd be out of the house for hours on end annoying another close relative – that must have helped.'

'Here it is,' said Jaz, putting a plastic carrier bag down on Usha's lap. She pulled out the steel-blue suit. 'And the the rip's where?'

'Left leg, near the bottom.'

She poked her finger through from the inside. 'How did it happen?'

'I caught it on a pallet in the stockroom. Funnily enough, Subash was supposed to have moved it but was too busy doing whatever it is that people like Subash do instead of work.'

'I'll have a go but it looks like some of the material's missing.'

'Whatever. If you can't do it, chuck them out.'

'What? This is a nice suit. I hate to think what you paid for it.' The material was soft under her fingers. 'If I can't fix it I'll give it to an Oxfam shop. But I'll see what I can do.'

'Tidy this place up a bit first, eh?'

'Oh come on, Jaz, I've just moved in. You can't expect it to look great.'

'It's hard to tell with you. It looks like your last place to me.'

'I like a home to look lived in. A little untidiness is a good thing.'

'A little! Come on, Usha, you're messy, admit it.'

'I'm not the same as you, so you think there's something wrong with the way I do things.'

'Housework not being one of them.'

She snorted. 'What does it matter? There won't be any husband to complain, will there?'

She and Jaz looked at each other. Usha began to put the suit back in the bag.

'I'd better go,' he said. 'There's a rep coming in at four and he might think Subash knows what he's talking about.'

She followed him to the door. 'Phone me.'

'I will.' He kissed her cheek. 'You know, I found Subash dancing in the changing room in front of the mirrors. I think he's very fond of himself.' He waved his arms and legs about, smiling vacantly. He look uncannily like Subash, and completely ridiculous. She laughed and pushed him into the hall. He danced down the hallway, partnered the door, and waved goodbye as she laughed again.

Back inside the flat she looked around at the boxes and bags that covered the floor. Jaz's carrier bag sat on the table. She took the suit into the bedroom and hung it in the wardrobe among the tinnitus of empty hangers. The material smelt faintly of Jaz; she buried her face in the jacket and breathed him in.

4

'It's a couple. Dylan – I think that's what Ivan said they were called.'

Dan's voice became muffled as he walked to the bedroom to get dressed. 'We're to call the letting agent if there's trouble with noise or anything. He's a friend of Ivan's.'

Helen didn't answer. She hated conversations that carried on despite the fact that the participants were in different rooms. When she was at home her mother used to shout up from the living room while Helen was in the toilet and then get irritated when she didn't reply.

Dan appeared with his tie undone, carrying his shoes. 'He's a lucky bugger, that Ivan, getting to fly off to the sunshine for a year,' he said. 'I should have got into computers when I had the chance.'

'When was that?'

'Well, at university, I guess. Psychology was definitely the wrong choice.'

'But you love it. And besides, you're a complete Luddite.'

'True.' He pushed the knot of his tie up against his throat. It was crooked. 'Still.'

She watched him tie his shoelaces, noticing, again, that his hair was beginning to thin. He stood up, slightly pink in the face now.

'I have to go,' he said. 'Mustn't keep Greg waiting.' He put on his jacket. 'Did I tell you? Mick's back, looking very chirpy. He asked after you.'

'I don't need protecting, you know,' she said.

'What?'

'Don't pretend you don't know what I mean. He asked if I'd conceived yet, didn't he?'

'Not quite like –'

'Same difference.'

Dan sighed. 'Yes, all right, same difference.' He looked at her. 'Whatever I do is going to be wrong. And what was I supposed to say?'

'It wasn't your answer I was objecting to, just the fact that you were pretending he asked a general question when it was a quite specific one.'

'I wasn't pretending anything, it's a figure of speech: "He asked after you". Which he did. Look, I don't want to argue. Especially when there's nothing to argue about.' He picked up his briefcase. 'I'm going.'

He looked . . . baggy. She felt a rush of remorse. 'I'm sorry,' she said. 'I'm a bit tense. There's a big meeting at work today. I have to get the project more money if I can or we'll have to lose someone.' She straightened his tie.

He patted her on the shoulder. She wanted to hit him; what was she, the family dog?

'I'll see you tonight. Try to relax. You'll be fine at the meeting, I know it.' He kissed her forehead.

She tried to smile, feeling only that she was contorting her face at him.

She closed the door and went to look at the list that she had written for herself of things to do, all things she had been putting off. She read through it, then read it again. What difference would it make to put them off for a little longer? She sat down in the big padded armchair in the living room and took out the cushion cover she'd been working on. Its texture bubbled under her fingers, the colours heaving together. She wasn't sure she liked it. She had to finish it, though; it had pulled and pulled at her since she started it, growing almost of its own accord. She watched her fingers working, surprised at their certainty. They could have an hour, then she would go and see if the new people were at home.

She'd stolen an extra hour for herself: the flat wouldn't get vacuumed today. She picked a few bits of fluff off the carpet and put them in the bin. She read her list again and filled the kettle; it was time to go downstairs.

Helen could hear music coming from inside and someone – a woman – singing along. She rang the bell. The door opened and music, half-reggae, half-Indian, snaked out over her. A young Asian woman in a crimson satin dressing gown looked enquiringly at her; she was taller than Helen, with long black hair and curiously light-brown eyes that made Helen feel she was looking through a window of brown glass to another window of lighter brown glass beyond.

'I'm from upstairs – I'm Helen, Helen Clifton.'

'Is it the music?'

'Sorry?'

'The music – it's too loud?'

'No, no, it's not that. I've just come to say hi, really. I thought perhaps –'

The young woman smiled. Helen thought how lovely she was; sleek, like a skein of silk.

'I'm Usha. Would you like some tea?'

'Well, that's what I came to ask you actually.'

'Now you're here, you might as well come in and save me the trip. The place is a mess but there you go.' Usha closed the door behind Helen, and danced over to the ghetto blaster and turned it down. Her feet were bare. 'One of my favourite tapes. You're bound to get familiar with it, the volume I play it at.' She laughed. 'Only joking.'

Helen felt pale as a grub. She was completely beige. Her hair, her skirt, her skin. She felt resentful for a moment, as though Usha had taken something away from her.

'Have a seat,' said Usha. 'I'll put the kettle on.' She went into the kitchen.

Helen looked around. There was nowhere to sit. Ivan's suite was covered in bags and clothes and boxes that might have contained anything.

When Usha reappeared Helen smiled apologetically. 'I'm sorry, I don't seem to be able to –'

'Oh, just move it out of the way.' Usha pushed a pile of clothes onto the floor. 'There.' Usha herself sat on the floor. 'So, we're neighbours.'

'That's right.'

'Have you lived here long?'

'I've always lived in Brighton – I was born here – but we've been in this flat about five years.' That's how long she and Dan had been trying. Time split into two: before and since. 'My husband – Dan – is a lecturer at the college.'

'What in?'

'Psychology. He specializes in child psychology.' Helen wanted to tell Usha how ironic that was. She smiled and dragged out an old line instead. 'Quite appropriate for a man, really.'

'Depends on the man,' said Usha, burrowing under some clothes. 'There's one here somewhere – a tray, that is, not a man.'

'And your husband?'

'I'm not married.' There was the slightest change in Usha's posture.

'I'm sorry, I thought – Ivan, that is, the man who owns the flat, he said that –'

Usha turned back to Helen. 'It's alright, don't worry.' She waved a green plastic tray. 'Found it.'

'Partner is what I should have said. Significant other. It's presumptuous to . . .'

'The kettle's boiled.' Usha got up. 'It's okay. There's only me.'

'Right.'

'I've got coffee, ordinary tea and herbal tea – raspberry or apple.'

'Regular tea will be fine. No milk, no sugar.'

'That's easy. Even I can handle that.' Usha padded out to the kitchen.

Helen picked her way over to the bookshelves. Books on law, mainly: undergraduate books.

'Here we are.' Usha put the tray on the floor. 'There are some biscuits somewhere,' she said, looking about vaguely.

'I'm fine.'

'But I haven't had any breakfast yet. I wonder where they are.'

'Are you a student?'

'Is that the sort of breakfast you'd expect a student to have?'

'Not necessarily, but the books . . .'

'Oh I see. I have been a student and will be again next year. I'm not one at the moment. I'm . . . taking a break.'

'I don't blame you – I thought of it when I was a student,' Helen said. 'That was about a hundred years ago, of course.'

'What was it like being one of the first women allowed to take a degree, oh wise one?' Usha grinned at her over the steam from her cup.

'Well, alright, it wasn't quite *that* long ago. It just seems like it sometimes. What are you studying?'

'Law – though, as I said, not at the moment.'

Helen wanted to ask why. She and Usha looked at the bookshelves and back at each other. The unsaid budded between them. Helen sipped her tea too quickly and felt it draw a burning line down through her chest.

'I don't think I can face this lot,' said Usha. 'I wish it would do itself and then leave me a list of where everything is.' She poked a bulging black bin liner. 'I wonder what's in here.' She began to open it. As she leant forward her dressing gown gapped and revealed most of a breast. Helen took in the suddenness of the red against the soft brown flesh. That's it, she thought, that's the combination for the final section of the cover. She saw Usha seeing her looking and unaccountably felt ashamed; she wanted to explain, but the moment was added to the unsaid.

'It's more washing,' sighed Usha. 'I think it must reproduce when I'm not looking.'

'Well ...' Helen put down her cup. 'Time for me to go to work. Perhaps when you're more sorted out soon you'd like to come up one evening for a meal with me and Dan.'

That smile warmed Helen again. 'I'd like to – thanks.'

Helen made her way upstairs. She had a little time before she had to go to work and returned to the padded armchair, where she picked her way through the box of silks, looking for the colours she had stolen from Usha.

'I thought it went very well,' said Maggie, peering with suspicion into a coffee cup. 'This one's nearly clean – you can have it.'

Helen closed the filing cabinet drawer. 'I hope you're right. I thought he seemed a bit of a miserable bastard.'

'Well, he is, but he loves opera – the more tragic, the better – so he's sort of on our side.' Maggie freed her very red and very wild hair from its elastic tie and it sprang energetically back around her face. 'God, that's better. I thought it best to squish it down – I reckoned it would probably frighten him.' The kettle boiled and she poured water into the cups. She overfilled the second one and water sloshed out onto the desk. 'Oh bugger.'

'I'll get a cloth,' said Helen.

'No, it's okay.' Maggie opened her handbag. 'I have something I keep for emergencies.' She fished out a small plastic packet decorated with little pink flowers and tore it open. 'That's better,' she said as she pressed the sanitary towel firmly on to the water. 'Hey, this is just like an ad.' She spoke in a husky and intense voice. 'And with its unique slurp-it-up comfy-pore design this wingéd wonder is all a woman could desire.' Her voice returned to normal. 'I'd rather have a good shag, personally.'

The door of the office opened. Maggie and Helen looked at Jim, dressed in his best suit to play better the part of the boss for the money man. Jim looked at Maggie's hands.

'I'll come back,' he said and closed the door.

Helen and Maggie looked at each other and cackled themselves into helplessness.

Helen put away the shopping she had bought after work and set about making a casserole for dinner, enjoying the steady crunch of the knife through the vegetables. She saved the aubergine till last, its glossy perfection reflecting a purple-black kitchen and a mad woman with a knife. She ran her fingers over it; so smooth, like fleshy glass. She cut it up.

Once the casserole was in the oven and she had tidied the kitchen, she read through her list of things to do. It was very neat. Suddenly irritated by it, she screwed it up and put it in the bin. Looking at the calendar she remembered Dan wouldn't be back for another couple of hours; he had a late meeting tonight.

In the living room she adjusted the lamp and curled up in the big armchair with the cushion cover in her lap. Just a few minutes: it was nearly finished.

About an hour later she spread it over the back of the chair and stood back to look at it. It was dark, swirling with heavy colour, with Usha's red like a stab wound in the corner. It was different from most of the things she had done over the years; she felt a little excited – it had something, although she couldn't define it. Only a cushion cover, but it made you look at it.

She wanted to give the cover body. She found a cushion in the airing cupboard and as she tucked it into the cover the phone rang. She carried the cushion with her to the hall.

'Helen? It's Moira.'

'Hi, Moira. How are you?'

'I'm well, thank you. I'm ringing to make sure you're still alright for Sunday lunch.'

'As far as I know. Around one o'clock?' Helen caught sight of herself in the hall mirror, cushion clutched to her belly. She turned sideways.

'Perhaps a bit earlier. I thought we could have a little chat.'

The thought of a little chat with Dan's mother was far from appealing.

'That's fine.' Helen looked at the effect: seven or eight months gone?

'And how's Daniel?'

'He's fine but very busy. He's out late tonight at a meeting.'

'He works too hard to give me and his dad a ring, apparently.'

He just doesn't know what to say to you, you old witch, thought Helen.

'Well, you know how it is,' she said. 'But we'll be there on Sunday, and you'll have lots of time.'

'Sunday then. Don't forget our little talk, will you.'

'No, don't you worry, Moira.'

When Helen had put the phone down she continued to look at herself in the mirror. If she put the cushion under something, then she could get a proper impression. Another part of her watched her as she went upstairs and got out a loose summer dress from the wardrobe, knowing this was unhealthy, knowing she should stop tormenting herself, yet as curious as the hungry part that drove her.

It looked real. She rested her hand on the swell. She could feel the embroidery through the thin fabric, little bumps like acne. She was filled with a sudden fury and disgust: she struggled out of the dress and flung the cushion onto the bed.

'You're fucking pathetic,' she said. The silent room absorbed her words.

She lay on the bed. Low sun threw a shadow of the net curtains over her body, making her look as if she were covered in grey lace. She stroked at the pattern, at herself, discarded her underwear. Her body responded to her touch, legs opening to the confidence of her hand. She used no images, simply relaxed into the sensations, bathing in the pleasure that connected only with herself; no mechanics, no hope, no reason. Colours swept through her and when she came, red wavered and swelled at the edge of them. She curled on to her side and, pulling the cushion tight to her chest, she listened to her heart beating.

5

In the shower Dan began to soap himself and watched as his cock lumbered into a half-erection.

'Hello.'

His cock nodded back.

'There's not much point in you making an appearance, you know.' It would be pretty pointless at this time in the cycle. 'The' cycle – her cycle. Sex used to be pointless pleasure; way back when. He imagined the slight tension he would feel through her skin if he touched her. He watched his erection wavering. Then Lesley was there, arms folded defensively over her naked chest. 'Well?' she said. Questioning grey eyes. Skin very pale and very smooth. Mousy pubic hair curling in a neat triangle. No: no pubic hair. Lesley liked to be radical. He could clearly see her labia, pure as a child's. No child this, though, her breasts round, with hard little nipples, arms stretching back as she lies there, waiting for him. He kneels between her legs; deep glistening pink receives him as he pushes into her.

But there's something too naked, too vulnerable: he magics a condom onto his cock and goes back to the moment before he enters her. He slides into her. She exhales and fucks back a little.

The bathroom door opens. Dan and Lesley look at each other. She disappears.

'Do you want wine with the casserole?' said Helen.

'That'd be nice.' His voice sounded unnatural to him.

'Are you ready for me to do your back?' she said. She poked her head around the shower curtain. His soaped erection was mighty and unmistakable. She looked at it. 'On the other hand, if you tie the bathbrush to it you could use that.' She snapped the curtain closed and left the bathroom.

Dan rinsed himself and got out of the shower.

She stood by the armchair and gestured to the cushion.

'Well, what do you think?'

He didn't like the design at all. There was something too internal and fleshy about it. As if your hand would come away wet. It had echoes of the framed tapestry of hers he had taken to the office a while ago but never hung.

'It's . . . interesting.'

'You don't like it.'

'I didn't say that. It *is* interesting.'

'It was the pause that did it,' she said. 'Anything could have followed that – horrible, crap, anything.'

'It certainly isn't crap.'

'Ah, but it is horrible.'

'No, I didn't say that. Why do you insist on telling me what I've said when I haven't said anything?' His stomach rumbled impatiently.

'*I* think it's one of the best things I've done, if not *the* best.'

'Then what I have to say about it is irrelevant. You don't need my approval all the time.'

'What about encouragement?'

'I *do* think it's interesting, it just isn't my kind of thing. You know I liked your earlier stuff but this is different. You've evolved, but I haven't evolved with you. That doesn't make either of us wrong, does it?'

Her eyes were shiny with tears and her lips were trembling. 'I think . . . I thought . . .'

He crossed to her and held her. Tears twisted in his throat. He didn't know what they were arguing about; he felt he was always one stage behind, full of old, useless information.

Helen sniffed hugely into his shirt. 'I can hear your stomach gurgling,' she said and gulped out a laugh. 'Let's eat before you fall over.'

'She seems nice.' Helen sipped her wine. 'I invited her up for a meal, when she's sorted herself out a bit.'

'What does her husband do?'

'She isn't married. Ivan must have got it wrong.'

'But I'm sure it was a man he said he was dealing with.'
'Whatever. She's on her own, anyway.'
'What kind of an Asian is she?'
'I don't know,' said Helen. 'Think about it, though. On meeting a white person your first thoughts wouldn't be on whether they're a Catholic or a Baptist or whatever. Using your approach you define someone who looks Indian automatically in terms of religion, which you wouldn't do with a white person. Isn't that racist?'

'Maybe there's a difference between being race-aware and racist.'

'Hm.' Helen fidgeted with the stem of her glass. 'Do you want that wine?'

'You have it if you want.'

'Are you sure?'

'I said so, didn't I?'

'There's no need to be like that.'

He set his knife and fork down on the empty plate. 'I wasn't being like anything.'

They looked at one another across the table.

'What are we fighting about, Helen?'

'Are we?'

'It feels like it. But it's as though I've come in half-way through and missed the key part.'

'I don't know what you mean.' She nudged a slice of carrot across her plate with the very tip of her knife.

'Oh, come on.' He wanted to snatch the knife from her and mangle the carrot's perfect roundness. She moved on to a piece of mushroom.

They sat in silence. The dull thrum of next-door's washing machine massaged the air. Dan drank the rest of his wine down in one and pushed his chair back. 'So much for communication,' he said and stood up.

She dropped her knife heavily onto the plate. He set his plate on top of hers and began to walk to the kitchen.

Her voice was small and puzzled. 'The trouble is, I missed the beginning as well. If I could turn the clock back . . .'

His anger surprised him. Suddenly he was sick to death of it, of this habitual consideration that he refused, for the first and most frightening time, to call love. He said nothing.

In the kitchen he rinsed the plates. When he turned off the taps he could hear Helen crying. I should comfort her, he thought: I don't want to. What about me?

He filled the sink and began the washing-up, his hands stinging in the too-hot water as he scrubbed and scrubbed at the plates' featureless faces.

'Will it be possible to s-see you today?' Lesley looked anxious, even paler than usual.
'I've already told you the procedure. All you have to do –'
'It isn't about that. It's a ... personal thing.'
'Dr Lexington is your personal tutor, isn't he?'
Lesley raised an eyebrow. 'Would you want to tell him anything about yourself?' She stepped a little closer. 'Please, Dan, this is important. I c-can't talk to that guy. This needs someone from the twentieth century.'

She was the same height as Dan. Her face was close to his; her eyes were pleading, and it seemed as if she was having to look up at him. The little resolve he had packed its bags and left.

At eleven o'clock she was sitting in the saggy blue chair. She crossed her long legs and folded her arms. She looked tangled up with herself like that, knotted inside her limbs; she kept her eyes on the floor. This was a different Lesley.

She raised her eyes; cloudy grey. Anxious.
'So ...' Dan sat opposite her. 'What's this about?'
She looked intently at him. Her hands grabbed at the flesh of her upper arms.
'I'm living in this house-share. Me, Chrissie and a couple of blokes; one of them is a c-computer scientist so he doesn't count, the other is a final-year anthropology student.' She stopped.

Outside someone was trying to start a car. The engine turned over and over and finally started. There was some whooping and cheering and the blare of the engine as the accelerator was kept to the floor.

'A few weeks ago,' said Lesley, 'we had a party.' She uncrossed her arms and clasped her hands together. White dots appeared over each knuckle. 'Jesus, I don't know why I'm making such a meal of this. Bongo – that's the anthropology student, he plays the drums, you see ...' She took a shaky breath and continued. 'Bongo and I bonked.' She

23

laughed, a little wildly. 'I did it with someone called B-bongo, can you believe it?'

Dan wondered what the correct facial expression was for the current situation. He flipped up a wry smile and got rid of it immediately.

'I'm pregnant,' blurted Lesley.

They looked at each other. He'd rehearsed for this moment but it was supposed to be Helen. It was supposed to be joyous.

'Um . . .' He cleared his throat. 'I don't know what to say to you.' Her waiting was unbearable. 'I mean, I wish I did.' The engine slowed and stalled. Boos ensued. 'It's difficult. Um . . .'

'Well, I'm *so* g-glad I came to you. I knew you'd give me some good advice. Bloody hell, even I managed to come up with "oh shit".'

'I'm sorry,' he said. He waited for the inevitable cough-cough-cough of the car.

'No, I'm sorry. I d-didn't mean to be horrible.' She shrugged. 'It isn't your fault.'

The car began to hack again, sounding tired now.

'There's no need to apologize. Can I do anything to help?'

'Tell me what to do.'

'I can't do that. What do you want?'

She was rocking back and forth very slightly. 'I don't know.' It was quite expressionless. She said it again.

He didn't know what he should do. She looked at him. A tiny twitch juddered under her left eye. She didn't look like she was going to cry but her eyes wanted more from him than this politeness.

She stood suddenly. 'I'll go. I don't know why I –' She looked around. 'My coat, where's my coat? I'll be fine, I'll go and please don't worry, this is stupid. This is –'

She let him hold her. She was angular, a new shape to adapt to. He put her head on his shoulder and stroked her hair. Her skull felt unbearably fragile under his hand. She gave out a low moan; not crying exactly, but the leaching of misery.

The car had fallen silent. He could hear the wind rattling the reddening leaves outside the window. He felt obscurely happy with this unfamiliar need.

The knock at the door and the door opening happened in a single instant. Graham Lexington looked at them.

'I'll come back,' he said, and closed the door.

6

'Aren't you ready yet?' Jaz looked at his watch. 'I don't have time to wait around.'

Usha retrieved her handbag from under a heap of clothes on the armchair.

'This place is still a mess.'

'I'm getting there.'

'You are?'

Usha looked in the mirror and smoothed a hand over her hair.

'You're only going to see Veena – you don't need to preen yourself any more.'

'I've seen you at a mirror, Jaz, so I don't think you're in a position to criticize.' She looked at him. 'We all know you're beautiful but no one knows it better than you, hm?'

The handle is cold and fills her hands: she reaches up, opens the door. Over the lamp there's a silky red scarf swirling with gold stars. Everything looks warm but indistinct. A towel forms a damp heap on the floor. Jaz is asleep, facing the door. His long black hair is spread out like neat scribbling over the pillow. His nakedness is painted with red light; his body is a picture she has never seen before. 'Jaz?' She approaches him. There is shadowed roundness between his legs. He opens his eyes; he smiles.

A wisp of hair had sneaked from his turban and was nestling against his neck. Usha tucked it back in. 'You're looking very smart today,' she said. He wore a deep charcoal suit and black tie, and a shirt that looked startlingly white between the material and the glossy black of his beard. 'Matching turban, even.'

'For the bank manager. I'm being a civilized Paki today.' He waggled his head in an Indian caricature.

'He has a problem with you?'

'She – and I don't know, she's new. The last one was always ultra-careful. You know the type, bending over backwards so far to show they're not racist that they virtually disappear up their own bums.'

'At least he was trying,' said Usha. 'There's plenty who wouldn't, who are quite plain about where they're coming from. You'd prefer that?'

'"Where they're coming from?" University is supposed to educate you, not make you sound like a hippy. Some lawyer you'll make, talking like that.'

'Don't change the subject.'

'Alright. What I would prefer is that they didn't make any big deal about it at all. Just base it on the business – which, though I say so myself, is an extremely good risk. Because there isn't any risk. Because I know what I'm doing.' He looked at his watch. 'Are you ready *now*?'

'I told you I was.'

'You didn't.'

'I did.'

'No you didn't.' He gave her a gentle push. 'Let's go.'

Jaz fastened his seatbelt and started the car. 'I know you don't approve,' he said as they moved off, 'but the confused white liberal is a real gift when it comes to getting a bargain.'

'And you're the one who wanted to be treated fairly – but it doesn't work the other way round? Hypocrite.'

'Don't complain. You know the flat? Well, the guy who's renting it out was over the moon to be able to rent it to someone ethnic – next best thing to having one as a friend. And the rent only covers the mortgage, he was very keen to point that out, so he's not making a profit from your need for housing. He got the idea that it was for me and my wife. I didn't put him right, there didn't seem any point.'

'Isn't that dishonest?'

'You sound like a granny.'

'Well . . .'

'Well, nothing. The rent's paid for a year so you don't have to worry.'

'I don't know what I'd have done without –'

'You're my sister. I don't have any choice. I *have* to help you.' He glanced at her and grinned. 'When Trouble's in trouble someone has to sort it out.'

Jaz edged the car into the traffic rushing its way down the long hill of Edward Street. She picked a piece of fluff from his shoulder. The strand of hair had escaped again and waved gently at her in the warm breeze from the heater.

Jaz dropped Usha off on Marine Parade. Palace Pier glittered noisily in the autumn sunlight, the funfair ride at the far end whirling shrieking people high in the air towards an empty horizon and then snatching them back to the safety of the frenetic clutter perched on the boards below. On the corner stall, T-shirts jostled for attention, variously decorated with pop stars and Union Jacks and more or less obscene messages according to your taste. She made her way to Old Steine Gardens to meet Veena. Here the air was sharp with a familiar cocktail of salt and car fumes; water splashed from the mouths of the vast hallucinatory fish that formed the Victorian fountain's centrepiece and the wind had snatched some of the water and blackened one of the footpaths around the pool. There was a man asleep on the grass, just at the edge of the dampness; a fine film of water frosted his coat. Usha sat on the edge of the pool's dry side and listened to the burble of the fountain. As she looked into the water, a Coke tin bobbed past, closely followed by a condom.

Two youths on the far edge of the grass were looking at her. The fair-haired one nudged the one with spiky brown hair. She looked away towards North Street, the direction Veena would be coming from. Usha watched the Coke tin and the condom go round again.

The lads were coming over. Usha concentrated on the gaudy traffic crowding its way around the island formed by the gardens. Perhaps the youths would walk straight on past to somewhere empty of her.

'Hello, darling.' Blondy grinned at her and offered her his beer can. 'Want some?'

She shook her head.

'So, what's your name?' She said nothing.

'Aah, she's shy,' Blondy said.

'That's sweet,' said Spiky.

They sat either side of her, too close.

'Well, this is nice,' said Blondy. Spiky belched. She smelt the sourness from his stomach. Blondy moved closer; his upper arm briefly pressed on hers. 'You on holiday?' he said. He leaned round virtually into her lap and gazed up at her. She tried to stand but he pressed down on her shoulder. 'No, don't go yet.'

'Get off!' she yelled.

'It speaks!' Spiky exclaimed as Usha struggled to get up.

'Not very nice, though,' Blondy said. 'That's no way to talk, is it?'

She was free of them now.

'Is it?' Blondy shouted after her. 'Oi!'

Usha was almost running. She could see Veena on the other side of the road. She waved frantically at her, hating the ease with which the fear had been inflicted, with which she had submitted to it.

'I'm just furious now,' said Usha as she and Veena settled themselves at the table. 'I wish I could do karate or something. That'd show them.'

'But what would it achieve?'

'Satisfaction for me.'

Veena smiled. 'You'd look good in the outfit, too. I can see it now – Usha the avenger.' She rooted about in her handbag and brought out a packet of cigarettes.

'Oh Veena. I thought you'd given up.' She watched as Veena lit up and waved the smoke away from Usha.

'Me too.'

'Kirpal knows?'

'My dear husband smokes more than I do.'

'But it's . . .' Not right for a Sikh, she thought, pricked with greater discomfort at the thought that it was somehow worse for a woman. 'It's not good for you.'

'I know, and you're sweet to worry about me. But sometimes, Ush, you have to let people do what they're going to do anyway. You're a lesson to us all on that one.'

'Some lesson. Mum and Dad still aren't talking to me, and they probably never will.'

'You'd be surprised what they'll accept in the end.'

'Mum, yes. But not Dad. Once he's decided something, that's it.'

Veena exhaled. She smoked very neatly; even the smoke looked tidy. She sculpted the end of her cigarette against the ashtray. 'He is quite . . . forceful, isn't he? He made such a fuss when you and Alex . . . well, you know. That affected quite a few people – the garage Singhs in Kemp Town married their daughter off pretty quickly. Mind you, there's no saying they wouldn't have done that anyway. They're stuck in a fossilized version of rural India they exported with them two generations ago.'

'And it's not like it's my fault, is it? The way other people react is down to them not down to me.' Usha grimaced. 'But I still feel guilty.'

'I'm sorry it didn't work out. He seemed okay, that time I met him.'

'He was.' Usha dug around in the sugar with a teaspoon. 'Was. One day I realized I didn't like him. But I wasn't sure if he'd changed; did I start looking at him differently or was he like that all along?'

'People do change. It could have been either of you. Or both.'

'He had a nasty streak. It seemed to get wider and wider until there was nothing left. Before that, though . . .' She shook her head. 'Like a drug I couldn't get enough of.'

Alex is pissing into the sink; it drums against the steel, reminds her of the sound of vegetables draining in the colander. The thought of using the sink for washing-up shrivels inside her. Her attention returns to her own desire to piss. The toilet is downstairs and Alex has trapped her here. She has asked once to go; it is clear he won't allow it. She won't beg.

Hours and hours. She can think of nothing else now. Alex hasn't slept either. He's waiting.

The cat-litter tray they'd bought for a cat they hadn't got in the end. She is squatting over it, Alex holding her head against him, stroking her hair, murmuring. As she finally, finally, empties there is a groan that oozes from her, a voice she doesn't know.

Veena patted her hand. 'Poor Usha.'

'You know, I'd like to go home – to Mum and Dad's, I mean. It's . . . safe there.'

'You couldn't wait to get out when you went to university. You said it would be a relief to be away from all that where-are-you-going-and-who-with stuff.'

'And I had a go at you, too, for getting married and not going to college.' Usha shrugged. 'I got everything wrong. They were like that because they *care* – cared. I knew that then but it just got on my nerves. I wanted everything my own way.'

'So did they. It isn't all down to you.'

'That's what it feels like. I've been trying to figure out if I would miss me if I was them and I wonder.'

Veena stubbed out her cigarette. 'You *are* feeling sorry for yourself.

But I think they *will* change their minds. You're their only daughter, after all.'

'They have a son, don't forget. The wonderful, successful, dutiful Jaz.'

'Who also moved out of home to go to university and never went back.'

'He does everything else right. They don't really need me.'

'Jaz isn't all he might be – he's not telling them he's seeing you, is he? So, lying to your parents; not a sign of a good son, is it? And he isn't exactly pure himself – what about that married woman he was seeing last year?'

'They don't know about her.' He was too good for her, Usha thought: that pasty face and drab hair, that doughy body.

'They might think he's the ideal son, but he has got some flaws. Don't put yourself down, Ush.' Veena got out another cigarette and looked at it carefully before she put it between her lips. 'These things will be the death of me.' She lit it. 'At least when we go round to Kirpal's parents' we don't smoke, so that cuts it down. And my parents, too.'

'How is he?'

'Kirpal? He's fine. Insurance broking isn't exciting but it's steady work. I think he likes it on the quiet – all that nit-picky attention to detail. I know you thought I was mad to get married at eighteen but I'm happy. Me and Kirpal are lucky, we're well-matched. Our parents did a good job.'

'Dad – when he was still talking to me – said that the way I was behaving showed that I didn't have any trust in him. "We're not arranging a marriage for you," he said, "but we'd want to meet the boy's family first, make sure everything is right."'

'That's how we do things.'

'It felt like they wanted to choose a pair of curtains to match the carpet they already had. I don't see it so much like that now. But it's too late, isn't it?' Veena didn't meet Usha's eyes. 'Isn't it?'

Veena looked up. 'Maybe things will work out. Give it – and you and your parents – some time.'

'And then I might be lucky and get some middle-aged widower who already has three kids and needs someone to do the washing and cooking.'

'Not necessarily.'

'I'd go off my head.'

'If you want to come back you'll have to compromise,' said Veena.

'I know, I know. But *you're* still my friend. *You* haven't deserted me.'

'But, don't you see, they don't think of themselves as having deserted you, it's you that's deserted them – us, Sikhs in general. It doesn't matter much to me if we're seen together – I have a reputation for being a bit "wild" anyway, so my in-laws will probably get more sympathy. But it's different for other people. They see you as . . . possibly contagious, I suppose.'

'The Usha virus.'

'Somebody somewhere will always disapprove, no matter what you do,' said Veena. 'I have to go, Ush. I've got to shop for tonight's tea.'

'Marital bliss, huh? You're too intelligent to just be a housewife, you know.'

'Housewives aren't stupid – don't be so arrogant. I like it. It may be hard to believe, but I do.'

'It'll be kids next.' Usha smiled to cover her sudden jealousy.

'Not yet. At least we have the Pill here – imagine, if we lived in a village in India we'd be breeding like cats. The only way to stop it would be to have our equipment removed.'

'Or maybe the man could use a condom.'

Veena laughed. 'Kirpal says wearing one is like stroking a cat while you're wearing a rubber glove.'

'So major surgery for the woman is a better option, is it?' Usha could hear the anger fraying her voice. 'Or taking chemicals to interfere with your hormones and give you thrombosis and God knows what.'

'It's the woman who gets pregnant,' said Veena tartly. 'These politics of yours are all very well but they're not based in reality, in how things are.' She picked up her handbag and stood up. 'I'll get the bill. My treat.'

Usha brushed the crumbs on the table into a neat little pile. A waitress came to take the cups away, and the pile disappeared into her cloth as she wiped the table.

'Hello,' said a voice beside Usha. It was Helen.

'Oh, hi.'

'I wanted to say, "Do you come here often?"'

Usha smiled. 'I like the cakes. And on Sundays they have all the papers and you can sit around and read and eat croissants.'

'Can I get you something?'

'I was just leaving.'

Helen looked disappointed. The lines around her mouth deepened. How old was she? Thirty-five? Definitely thirty-something.

Veena arrived back at the table. She looked at Helen. 'Are you ready, Usha?'

'Well, I . . . this is my neighbour, Helen. And this is Veena.'

Helen smiled. 'Hello.'

Veena nodded. 'Nice to meet you. Usha? Or are you staying here with Helen?'

There had been the slightest of pauses before 'Helen'. Usha knew it was because Veena was irritated with her but she felt like Helen had been insulted. That wasn't fair.

'Yes, I think I will for a bit, as you want to get to the shops.'

She and Veena looked at each other, bobbing on the undercurrents.

'Fine,' said Veena.

'I'll see you,' said Usha.

Usha watched her leave.

'Bit of an argument?' said Helen with a smile.

'It was that obvious?' Usha shrugged. 'We were best mates at school. We're a bit different now, that's all.'

'What would you like?' said Helen. 'Tea? Coffee? I'm definitely going for a piece of that chocolate cake.'

They both had some. The cake was sweet and sticky and as smooth as velvet.

'Oh boy,' said Helen as she downed the last mouthful. 'Better than s –'

Usha grinned. 'It is, isn't it.'

Helen had a crumb of cake near her mouth. 'You've got a bit of chocolate . . .' Usha said, touching where her own cheek mirrored Helen's. Helen brushed at her cheek and missed the crumb. She looked questioningly at Usha.

'Further over,' said Usha and watched Helen fail again.

Helen handed her a serviette. 'You can see me better than I can,' she said. She's pretty when she smiles, Usha thought. She took the serviette and nudged the crumb away.

'Thanks,' said Helen. 'I would probably have just smeared it all over the place.' She laughed. 'So much for being a grown-up.'

Usha smiled. She was beginning to like this woman.

7

'DANIEL!' MOIRA CLUNG to her son as if she had imagined never to see him again. 'Well, you're a sight for sore eyes. And Helen, it's been ages.' She kissed the air somewhere near Helen's cheek. 'It's lovely to see you both. Come in, come in.'

They all went through to the living room. An extremely hairy and extremely old dog struggled to its feet, swayed and then plodded over to Dan, its tail wagging weakly. Eyes frosted with cataracts pointed up at him. 'Hiya, Wally.' He squatted down and played with Wally's ears. 'How's my favourite dog?'

The smell of dog clogged in Helen's throat. Christ, she thought, how can they stand it? She moved around Dan and walked over to the patio doors, and stood looking at the fresh air.

'Oh, good old Wally,' said Jack. 'Mind you, his hearing isn't much these days, either. And of course there's the arthritis . . .'

Helen watched leaves spiralling onto the perfect lawn, wondering if they wanted the dog to die. I would, she thought, I do: it's pitiful.

'He still gets a lot from life, though,' said Moira. 'He loves his dinners, don't you, Wally? Now he has that special food there haven't been any more . . . digestive problems.'

Dog shit on the carpet: sick under the table; all caricatured into do-dos and tum-tums. Dan and his parents looked at the dog; Helen looked at them. Dear old Wally would have had to go if that hadn't been sorted out. 'Put to sleep', as Moira would have it.

'Well, lunch won't be long now. Perhaps you'd give me a hand in the kitchen, Helen?'

Time for the little chat, Helen thought: time for me to run screaming through the glass of the patio doors and cover myself with leaves. 'Righto, Moira.'

Jack began to explain to Dan how he had mended the vacuum cleaner. Dan wouldn't understand but he would smile and nod and look at Jack's hands turning invisible parts in the air.

In the kitchen the steam from the vegetables Moira was overcooking made Helen feel she was trying to breathe in a pond.

'Kitchens are such cosy places, don't you think?' said Moira. 'The heart of the home.'

'Mm.'

Moira put on her apron and smoothed it down. She clasped her hands beneath her bosom. 'You're looking a little pale, if I might say so. But you look as if you've put on a little weight. That's good.'

'It's an illusion. I'm wearing fat clothes.'

'Pardon? Oh, I see.' Moira smoothed her apron some more. 'Your face is still thin.'

Helen raised her eyebrows.

'That's not good,' said Moira. 'Being underweight can prevent conception, did you know that?'

'I'm not underweight, Moira. This is called "slim" and it's perfectly normal. Don't you think one of the doctors would have mentioned it by now if there was a problem with my weight?'

'Not if they knew how touchy you were going to be.' Moira sighed. 'Look, this conversation has started off all wrong. Let's begin again.'

'Fine by me,' said Helen.

'Well, I was reading this magazine article all about not being able to have a baby.'

'Why don't you say "infertility"?' said Helen.

'You're not making this easy for me.'

'No.'

'Well, there was a whole section about the different kinds of treatment that are available. It was very interesting.'

'I'm aware of what's available.'

'Yes, but this was right up-to-date. I took the liberty of sending off for some leaflets.' Moira fetched a folder from the drawer and held it out to Helen. Helen looked at it and back at Moira. 'Well,' said Moira, putting the folder on the table and sitting down, 'there is a lot of information in here about the latest developments in IVF. That's *in vitro* –'

'I *know* what it means.'

Moira placed her hand over the folder as if she were about to swear to tell nothing but the truth. 'I'm only trying to help.'

'You're interfering,' said Helen. 'Why can't you see that?'

Moira looked pained but saint-patient. She took a breath and rushed into her piece. 'Have you considered IVF? Many couples who had tried for years and years with no luck have successfully conceived using this method.'

'Have you memorized that sentence from one of your leaflets?'

Moira swept on. 'The figures speak for themselves.'

'And do they mention any of the drawbacks? The tests, the measuring, the intensity of the treatment and how it can destroy relationships – not to mention the low success rates.'

Moira put her hands together. 'Do you want a child or not? I don't mean to be brutal but you're not behaving like you do.'

Helen felt a sudden desperation to explain, to appeal. 'There comes a point ... I don't want to be interfered with any more; on my back ...' – here Moira closed her eyes briefly as though offering up a swift prayer – '... with all that shiny metal that's supposed to reassure me of how scientific it all is; how I'm supposed to submit gratefully, how it's for my own good. I've even been spied on through my own belly button, for God's sake.' And all the while, she thought, I smiled and smiled until my face ripped away from my skull and no one, no one noticed.

'We all have our burdens,' Moira said. 'I'm sorry to have to say this but deep down, I don't think you can want a baby as much as you say you do. And this isn't only about you. What about Daniel?'

'I could conceive naturally, you know. That's what the consultant said – "Extremely unlikely but not impossible".'

'But be realistic, Helen. You've been trying for years now. And you're getting older every year.'

'Gosh, I hadn't realized that.'

'You can try and wriggle out of the subject all you want. I know what you're doing. I understand you want to avoid the hurt, that you –'

'You understand absolutely fucking nothing!' yelled Helen. I've done it now, she thought, but she was liberated. 'What you want is a grandchild. Don't give me all this shit about poor Dan, about how understanding you are. You don't have a clue, not a fucking clue.'

Moira drew herself bolt upright in her chair. 'There is no need for that kind of language. I won't have it in this house.'

'Fuck, shit, *fuck*!'

'This has gone far enough.' Moira stood up. 'This is the thanks I get. You don't *deserve* a child. God knows what sort of monster you'd bring into the world. You're an evil, twisted woman.'

'Who stole away your baby son and won't give you a replacement. Who's the twisted woman here, really?' Helen took a couple of steps towards Moira. She backed away. Helen moved towards her again. The door opened.

'What on earth's going on in here?' demanded Jack, Dan at his shoulder.

'She's having a breakdown!' wailed Moira, hurling herself into Jack's arms. 'She's dangerous!' She began to sob. 'She tried to hit me!'

'I did nothing of the kind, you old witch.'

'Now look here –' began Jack.

'Let me by. The non-functioning womb is leaving.' Her anger propelled her into the living room and swept up her handbag. She ran from the house into the soft autumn afternoon. She could hear Dan's footsteps behind her and though she ran and ran they were still there. She'd had this dream often.

'I can't, Dan. I'm not going back.'

They sat in the brand-new rustic bus shelter that seemed somehow cowed by the disdain of Rottingdean's timbered houses. A crisp packet, trembling in the breeze, purred in the corner.

Dan is talking again, she thought; I should pay attention.

'*Helen*, please, be reasonable.'

'*You* be reasonable. She'll be wanting to examine me next to make sure the doctors haven't missed something. I can see the headlines: *Housewife in infertility breakthrough – "It was just after I had strapped my daughter-in-law to the kitchen table that I realized –"*'

'Stop it.'

'You don't know what I was going to say. It might have been another of my wry observations on life. You might have laughed.'

A bus drew up at the stop. The doors shushed open. The driver looked at Helen and Dan.

'Do you mind?' said Helen. 'This is a private conversation.'

The driver rolled his eyes and shut the doors. The bus rumbled away, filling the shelter with the gasp of diesel fumes.

'Please, Helen, come back with me. It'll be okay.'

'And she'll apologize, too, will she?'

Dan exhaled. 'You know she won't.'

'Okay, okay, I'm coming,' she said wearily, wondering what the hell she was doing.

Standing with her hand clasped to her apron as if afraid her heart was about to fall out, Moira accepted Helen's apology. Helen watched herself with some amusement; humility had never been a strong point. The words struggled out and plopped unconvincingly onto the carpet. It was excruciating.

Moira bustled away into the heart of the home, taking Jack with her to collect the roast. Helen and Dan sat at the table. Moira reappeared with the mineral water Helen had asked for. She placed the glass in the precise centre of Helen's coaster.

'I put some ice in – water seems so, well, *plain* without it,' she said. Helen had told her last Christmas about how iced drinks made her teeth hurt; they had had a long conversation about sensitive teeth, the kind of conversation that only served to slow down an already tortoise-like day. Since then it seemed that Moira had given her ice at every opportunity.

'Lovely,' said Helen and looked for blood on the muzzles of the hounds in the hunting scene printed on her place mat.

'It's been ages since you've come for lunch,' said Moira, passing Dan a plate perilously heaped with a ridiculous amount of food. 'I hope you're feeding Daniel properly, Helen.' There was a slight pause and Moira made a noise something like a laugh but as though she didn't yet have the knack. They all looked at her. Helen was cheered that Moira was still afraid of her.

Moira passed Helen's plate to Jack, who handed it to Helen. She looked down at it. The mounds of food seemed suddenly obscene, the contents of someone's stomach.

She and Moira watched each other watching the men eat.

8

'I'LL GET IT,' Dan called and started for the front door.
Helen hurried out of the kitchen. 'No, I'll get it.' She smiled faintly. 'She doesn't know you.'

He hovered in the hallway. She didn't open the door fully at first; she spoke a few words he didn't catch. She was a schoolchild preventing him from copying, the door a protective arm to block his view.

She held the door open. The young Asian woman came into the hall. Her hair was long and glossy; she wore a loose shirt of brilliant green and dark green leggings. A tiny silver flower glittered in the side of her nose. 'Usha, this is Dan. Dan, Usha.'

They smiled at one another. 'It's nice to meet you,' said Dan, and they shook hands a little awkwardly. Her hand was cool and smooth.

A buzzer sounded from the kitchen. 'I'll be with you in a minute,' said Helen.

'Would you like a drink?' asked Dan as he led Usha through to the living room. 'We have all the usual stuff.'

'Um, I don't drink.' Usha smiled. 'I mean, of course I drink, just not alcohol.'

Her eyes were an interesting colour: light brown, somehow transparent, like water-colour.

'There's some real lemonade in the fridge, made by Helen's own fair hand. There's orange juice and that kind of thing, too.'

'The lemonade sounds good.'

'You didn't tell me she doesn't drink,' he said to Helen in the kitchen.

She tasted the sauce and added some salt. 'I didn't know,' she said. 'Why doesn't she?'

38

'I didn't ask. Maybe it's a religious thing.'
'Because she's Asian, you assume that's why.'
'I didn't assume anything. I was wondering aloud. You're the one making a big deal, not me.'
'I don't want to offend her, that's all.'
'You should act naturally. I'm going – we wouldn't want her to think we were in here talking about her, now would we?'

He poured Usha a glass of lemonade and handed it to her.

'Thanks. This cushion cover is stunning.'
'It's Helen's, that is, she made it.'
'The colours are unusual.'
'She's very talented with embroidery. She'll be pleased you like it.'

Usha cradled the cushion in her lap, stroking it like a cat.

'Helen tells me you're a law student.'
'I'm ... resting at the moment, you know, like an actor.' Her smile was as sudden and bright as a lighthouse beam; Dan couldn't help smiling back.

'How long for?' he asked.
'I'll be starting my final year next year.'
'What will you do in the meantime?'
'Tomorrow I start looking for a job. This is my last day of leisure.'
'Well, here's to leisure,' said Dan, raising his glass.
'Remind me what that is again,' said Helen as she came in. 'No, no, forget it, I haven't got time.' She looked at Dan. 'Ha ha. Could I have a drink as well, please?'

'What would you like?'
'Wine, I think.'
'Certainly, my dear,' he said. 'Will that be the bathful or just the bucket?'

'The bath is full of your vodka,' Helen said swiftly.
'A bucket it is, then,' he said and poured her half a glass of white.
'Usha was admiring your new cushion cover.'
'It's wicked,' said Usha. 'The colours are great.'
Helen beamed. 'Are you settling in okay?'
Usha nodded. 'But I could do with a few of your cushions. The decor is tasteful but bland. Sort of corporate, if you know what I mean.' She clapped a hand to her mouth. 'That's so rude! The landlord being a friend of yours and –'

Helen laughed. 'Don't worry about it. But I'm glad you like the cover. I may do some more on the same colour theme. It's a question of time, though. It's a lot of work.'

'But worth it.' Usha's long brown fingers lay against the colours. Dan saw that Helen was blushing. The sudden colour in her cheeks made her look like she'd been slapped. Her eyes were bright; she looked happy. He felt the punch of jealousy in his chest: when had she last looked like that because of him?

'This is delicious, Helen,' Usha said as she ladled more sauce onto her plate.

'Do you like cooking?' asked Helen.

Usha shook her head. 'I'm a lazy vegetarian. I eat lots of vegetables that are good raw so I don't have to cook them.'

'Hot food's good, too,' smiled Helen.

Usha grinned. 'That burger place in St James Street does a good veggie burger.'

Dan took the plunge, despite feeling Helen willing him not to. How could you get to know anyone if you only ever waited for them to volunteer information?

'Is being vegetarian a personal decision or a religious one?'

'Both, I guess. My family are Sikhs *and* vegetarians – though not all Sikhs are. So I grew up with it but I also feel it's right for me personally.'

'We don't eat much meat –' began Helen.

Usha laughed. 'If I had a pound for every time someone had said that to me I'd be rolling in it.'

'Well, we don't,' said Helen.

'That's fine,' said Usha. 'But you don't have to justify your decisions because I do something different. It isn't a moral judgement.'

Dan drank some wine. 'Isn't it?'

'It's a personal moral decision for me but you can't then assume that it's a moral judgement on everyone else.'

'That sounds like a fine semantic distinction – I suppose I shouldn't expect anything less from a lawyer.'

'A nearly-lawyer,' corrected Usha.

'And a natural, too, by the sound of it.'

'Dan, would you get another bottle of wine out, please?' Helen waved the empty one at him.

'We both have work tomorrow, you know,' he said jovially. 'Perhaps we should move on to water.'

'You can walk on it for all I care, please just open another bottle.' She looked at him then turned and smiled at Usha. 'Don't take any notice. We're always like this.'

'You are, Helen, you are,' he said.

Dan fetched more wine. 'Do you have any brothers or sisters?' he asked Usha as he opened the bottle.

'A brother.'

Dan poured Usha and himself some lemonade. 'Older or younger?'

'A bit older. He graduated two years ago.'

'What did he study?' Helen put her glass down neatly in the red ring bleeding into the tablecloth.

'Business and economics.'

'Ah,' said Dan. 'A captain of industry.'

'Not yet. My dad wanted Jaz to become a doctor like him but Jaz likes money more than people.'

'Doctors don't have to like people,' said Helen, pushing her plate away. 'As long as they know where all the bits are they are gods and the rest of us mere mortals.' She picked up her glass and paused. 'I don't mean your father's like that, of course. I was just . . .' She sipped some wine.

'Dad does like to help people, though, and they like him for that.'

'And meanwhile Jaz works on his plan for world domination,' Dan said.

Usha laughed. 'He's in the early stages. He owns a clothes shop in Churchill Square.'

'Which one?' asked Helen.

'First Fashions.'

'I know the one,' said Dan. 'I had a Saturday job in a tailor's. They gave me my own tape measure.'

'Jaz would persuade you to buy it,' said Usha. 'As an investment.'

'Well, good for Jaz,' said Helen. 'Getting out there and going for it.'

Dan looked at her. She was definitely a bit pissed. At least she wasn't being embarrassing.

Music heaved through the dim party air. He tripped over someone's legs and hurtled into a soft dancer who took his hands and tried to make him join in.

'Have you seen Helen?' He was having to shout so close to her ear he

could have kissed it. Lou smiled an unfocused smile and shook her head. A man with frizzy, exploded hair handed him a joint and began to nuzzle Lou's neck.

He toked on the joint; the bitter burning brought tears to his eyes and scrubbed at his throat but he held the breath. He released it slowly, feeling himself a sudden calm oasis in the frantic, jerky world. He kissed at the joint again, this time several small gentle pulls that reduced the heat.

A hand plucked the joint from his fingers. The blue of the woman's eyes seemed to spread like a stain over her lids, changing somewhere along the way into a silver hemmed in by her eyebrows. She grinned at him and danced away.

He headed for the unkind light of the kitchen. Passing the stairs he heard Helen's voice. She stood at the top, the cheesecloth shirt with a hundred tiny buttons in her hand. She was waving her arms above her head.

'This is what it's about!' The breasts he normally found so neat and compact looked half-made somehow, pitifully naked. 'We don't tell the truth enough!' She began to work her way down past the couples on the stairs. The good-looking guy from Experimental Psychology with his curly Jesus-hair and fine blond Jesus-beard nudged his girlfriend and laughed. They observed Helen.

Dan pulled her from the lower steps and wrapped her in his arms. She fought against him. 'Let me go! You don't understand. We have to have truth.'

He held on. 'Come on, love, time to go.'

'But I have to tell you . . .'

'Not now. Later. Tell me later.'

But later she says she doesn't remember and truth is subjective anyway. He sees the distance behind her eyes and holds her, waiting for her to come back.

'What I want,' said Helen, 'is a cup of coffee. That's your department, Dan. Go hunt and gather caffeine.'

'I will take plates to sustain me in my great quest.'

'And could you bring the wine bottle stopper thingie back with you? I think I've had enough.'

He didn't say anything.

He looked at their heads bowed over Helen's sketchbook. Usha's darkness seemed to wash Helen out; it was as though Usha cast a pale shadow.

'I like this one,' said Usha.

'I did that ... now let me see – after we visited Stanmer Park. It was a beautiful early summer's day, and the sun filtering through the leaves made them look like they were glowing. They were absolutely luminous. And the greens ... your top reminds me of them, actually. The sun coming through the darker leaves looked exactly like that.'

Dan yawned. 'Sorry. It just slipped out.'

'I'm tired, too,' said Usha. 'I should be going.'

'You're welcome to stay longer,' said Helen. 'Feel free to finish looking through this.'

'Well, I would like to ...'

'I'm going to be boring and turn in,' said Dan. 'But please do stay, Usha. There's no rush for you to leave.'

'Okay, thanks. It was nice to meet you. You and Helen must come to me soon and I can return the favour. The cooking won't be as good, I warn you now.'

'I'll see you soon then.' He stood up and pushed his chair under the table. 'Goodnight.'

As he left the room he hesitated in the doorway for a moment. The two women sat side by side looking at the sketches. He felt like he'd been dismissed even though he had decided to go. Helen looked up and caught his eye, then looked back at Usha. She had registered him along with the walls and the table and the carpet. He would have thought she was glad to be rid of him but she didn't seem to feel one way or the other. He yawned again and went to brush his teeth.

He dozed until Helen came to bed. He turned and embraced her, running his hands over her warm smoothness. He caressed her breast. He could feel the change in her body, a tiny fizzing of tension building through her. He stopped. 'I want to make love with you, that's all.' She sighed. He held her breast again.

'Or you want to have sex and I happen to be here.'

He let go of her. 'For God's sake.'

'It doesn't feel like making love,' she said coldly. 'It feels like you're wanking in me.'

He shrivelled away inside, reducing to a tiny, armoured knot. 'Christ, what a horrible thing to say.'

'It's how I feel. When we do it and there's a chance of my conceiving it's different.'

'Functional fucking's alright then. Making love is out, making a baby is in.' His eyes had adjusted to the darkness; the Helen-shape turned to face him.

'You don't want a child, then?'

'Not if this is what is going to happen to us. And it's having sex purely to make a baby that feels like wanking to me.'

'And I thought we were in this together.'

'Precisely – what about us? Sex is about more than the production of potential bloody babies you know. At least it used to be.'

'You'll leave me.'

'What?'

'You'll leave me. There's nothing wrong with you. You could easily find someone else to have a child with.'

'Oh, love, we've been through this. It's not *a* child I'd want, it's *ours*. And if we can't then we can't. It isn't anybody's fault.'

'That's easy to say when you know it isn't yours.'

'What do you want me to say? That you're not a real woman because you can't conceive?'

'Sometimes I want to steal them.' She paused, then cleared her throat and continued. 'I see them wandering in a shop, an aisle away from their mothers, or in a pushchair outside the newsagent. I could take them. Do you understand?' Each word dropped from her like something heaved with great effort. He imagined Helen's hand closed too tightly around a chubby little arm. 'I could take them,' she said. 'Stupid, *stupid* women! Why aren't they more careful? I could be anyone.'

'I . . .' He shut up. There was nothing he could say.

'These feelings I get – they're overwhelming, like lust. A lust that'll never be satisfied. I'll start barking eventually. You'll have me committed and visit me every second Sunday with a bunch of grapes that you'll eat while I drool propped up in bed.' She took a deep breath and exhaled slowly.

'Now come on, it's –'

She raised herself up on one elbow. 'I'm afraid, Dan. I'm afraid that this is the rest of my life. I'm afraid that I won't ever think new thoughts. I look at someone like Usha and I could spit. Everything's so much newer for her.'

'Well, I like us. I think we should be good to ourselves. Why punish yourself because time has passed?'
'I want another chance. I want . . . everything I want.'
'Beautifully put. I know exactly what you mean.'
'Oh God.' She lay down and snuggled into him. 'I've become neurotic.'
'Mm, me too. Great, isn't it?'
'At least we're in it together.' She sniffed. 'These aren't tears, they're neurosis leaks.'

He kissed her eyelids and licked the saltiness from her face. Slowly they made love and the welcome in her made him want to cry.

In the morning when he went to the toilet he found her russet mark crusting his cock. When he returned to the bedroom she had changed the sheet.

9

Usha tied her hair back. Pulling the ends forward over her shoulder she gave herself a beard; Jaz looked back at her from the mirror. She winked at her reflection and brushed her pony tail, watching the static sucking at her hair each time she raised the brush.

The doorbell rang.

'Hi,' said Helen. She looked Usha up and down. 'You look smart.'

'I'm doing the recruitment agencies today. Come in. What can I do for you?'

Helen perched on the sofa. 'It's about last night . . .'

'I had a good time.'

'Well . . . I had a bit too much to drink and I just wanted to apologize if I made you uncomfortable.'

'Uncomfortable? No.'

'Well, I was a bit sharp with Dan and I know it can be really horrible seeing couples bickering and what with it being the first time you'd both met and . . .' She paused, cringing. 'This all sounded perfectly reasonable when I thought of it and now I sound completely mad.'

'I didn't notice anything. You seem . . . comfortable with each other. How long have you been together?'

'We met at university – it's about thirteen or fourteen years now.'

'You must be about the same age as my aunt Rani. That's my mother's sister.'

'Well, that makes me feel *really* old.'

'No, no. She's much younger than my mum. She feels more like a sister to me. And you're not exactly ready to collect your pension – how old *are* you?'

'I'm thirty-three.'
'I'm twenty-two.'
'That still makes me feel old.' Helen grinned. 'I'm on the verge of telling you that young people today don't know they're born and how the twin boys in my class had to share a pair of shoes they were so poor but at least they did have shoes. That sort of thing.'
'If you start doing it, I'll let you know.'
'I hope you find something.'
'If you're free tomorrow morning you could come down and I'll let you know how it went.'
'I'll do that,' said Helen and again Usha was struck by the blueness of her eyes and by how hard it was to look away.

'You've finished, have you? Come and sit down and we'll have a little look at your typing test.' She was glossy: brown hair as shiny as plastic, nails so slick and red they looked wet, and lipstick that stretched around an unnervingly bright smile. Her shiny name badge announced that Karen is always happy to help.
'Now . . .' She glanced at the top of the form. 'Usher –'
'You pronounce it "Oosha".'
'Sorry.'
'You weren't to know.'
'These foreign names are always a bit tricky. I thought yours was going to be easy.' Karen's teeth appeared and disappeared. She tapped into her calculator. 'Twenty-four words per minute – but you were lovely and accurate. Let's see.' She riffled through a card index box. 'Nothing here, I'm afraid.' She leant forward confidentially. 'Things are a bit slow.'
'Oh.'
'Wait a minute, we do have something else which would suit you . . . Here we are.' She pulled out a card. '"Equipment Cleansing Operative". That's up at the big computer company. Lovely offices, very modern.'
'And an equipment cleansing operative does what, exactly?'
'Well, you wouldn't be based in the offices as such but in the, well, the kitchens.'
'You mean a washer-upper!'
'It's a very responsible position. You have to make sure that you do a thorough job.' Her smile flickered and went. 'People's health relies on you.'

'I was hoping for something in an office.'

Karen sniffed. 'You're not qualified.' She closed the card index box. 'If you're not interested in that kind of work, I don't think we can help you.'

'But the cards in the window . . . ?'

'You need experience.'

'I guess that's it then. Well, thanks for your help, Karen.'

'It's pronounced Car-en.' No trace of a smile.

'I'll get my jacket.'

Outside Usha headed for the café for something to eat. It was going to be a long day.

At this time of year the streets were often clogged with the last batches of Italian schoolchildren attending the local English language schools. They roamed around in droves, easily spotted by the identical rucksacks they carried. Usha saw a couple of them round the corner into Bond Street like the first spots of rain. She crossed the road to avoid them and bumped into Cara doing the same thing.

'Usha! Wow, it's been ages.' Cara's long blonde hair foamed about her face, framing sea-coloured eyes. She was beautiful but vague, and genuinely unaware of the effect her appearance had.

'How was your summer?' said Usha.

'Great. I was in Greece in July and then Mum and Daddy rented a cottage in Cornwall and the whole family went down for a couple of weeks – my brothers and my sister, her husband, my granny on Daddy's side. It was great. I even had a real conversation with my oldest brother. I don't remember that ever happening before.'

'Is he much older?'

'Let's see . . . he's thirty-one, so he's ten years older than me. Might as well be from another planet.'

Usha thought of Helen, how she didn't seem older despite insisting on the difference.

'I'm going off to the Trafalgar Street café,' said Usha. 'Want to come?'

'Great. Only keep me away from the Danish pastries.'

'And an apple strudel, please.' Cara frowned at Usha as the waitress left. 'You were supposed to stop me.'

'I couldn't tell you not to and then sit there and eat my own, could I?'

'You're one of those people who can eat and eat and not put on an ounce, aren't you?' Cara sighed. 'I won't have any dinner tonight. That should make up for it. So, anyway, how's it going?'

'I've been going around the job agencies to see if I can get some work. They're not keen because I haven't got any work experience.'

'But how can you get it if you can't get work. Yeah, I know. Well, I hope it works out. You can't be any worse off than on a grant, can you? Did you know they want staff up at the Lewes Road Sainsbury's?'

'Maybe a supermarket would be okay. You probably get a discount, that'd be something.'

The waitress brought their cakes and tea. Cara stared at her plate. 'It does look delicious, doesn't it?' She picked up her fork and cut a piece of strudel, taking a good look at it before putting it in her mouth. She jiggled slightly in her chair. 'Mmmm.'

'Where are you living this year?'

'Elm Grove, near the bottom. It's quite a nice house if a bit expensive. Aren't they all, though.'

'Who are you sharing with?'

'Well, there's Lucy, of course, and – oh shit.'

'What?'

Bright red patches had appeared on Cara's cheeks. She rolled her eyes. 'I'm so stupid. Of course, you don't know, and now I've put my size eights right in it. I do take an eight, you know. I've got very big feet.'

'*What*? What is it that I don't know?'

'Oh god. There's no gentle way of saying this so I'll be straight with you. Lucy and Alex are an item. He'll be living in the house, too. The other guy is someone called Bongo of all things. He was a last minute addition, had to move out of his place quick for some reason.'

'Alex and *Lucy*?'

'I'm sorry, Usha. I mean that I had to tell you and that I had anything to tell you.'

'When did it start?'

'It's okay, I mean, they weren't getting it on while you and Alex were, you know . . . He was very upset about the whole thing and she –'

'*He* was upset! I told you and Lucy about some of what happened. How *can* she!'

'I know you're upset, but you don't have a claim on Alex any more.'

'You don't understand! How can she get involved with him when she knows what a wally he is? She's had a first-hand, eye-witness account.'

'Maybe you and Alex didn't bring out the best in each other. It can happen like that, can't it?'

'He had more of my best than I had of his.'

'Remember what they say about not killing the messenger?'

'But Cara, I won't be able to come and visit. I mean, that's why I'm taking a year out, because of the thing with Alex, and not being able to cope with the thought of seeing him when everything turned so bitter and . . . well, shitty.'

'Not like you to swear, Usha.'

'Well, I'll tell you, I'm learning. Some things absolutely require it.' She put down her fork. 'I can't finish this. Do you want it?'

'Uhh . . .'

'Oh, eat it. It's what you want.'

Cara smiled uncomfortably. 'Yes, it is.'

Usha shook her head. 'You're *not* fat. You carry around this guilt that sits on your shoulder looking for food.' Usha softened her voice. 'You should just do it.'

'But there's a world of difference between wanting to do something and actually doing it,' said Cara.

The room is like a cave.

Usha pushed her plate in front of Cara. 'Eat the cake – please?'

Usha poured them more tea. Cara drank some of hers and grimaced. She put a teaspoonful of sugar into it and sipped again. She looked at Usha and added a second spoonful.

'He's taken you – both of you – away from me,' said Usha.

'It isn't deliberate.'

'Isn't it? He gets – got – a kick out of humiliating me. And going after one of my friends is typical of the way he thinks.'

'It takes two,' said Cara dryly.

'You know how insecure Lucy is. She's grateful for attention.'

'There's no need to be bitchy about it. I'd be hurt, too, but please don't think this is all down to Alex. Lucy has a mind of her own. She agonized about you and Alex but it *was* over between you . . .'

'And what about when Alex decides to add *yet another* dusky maiden

to his collection? I was the doe-eyed Indian; Lucy is the half-Egyptian, half-Welsh, mostly brought up in Switzerland – now that's what I call exotic. What next? It'll have to be a man, won't it?'
'But the thing with Lucy and Alex doesn't mean that we can't be friends, does it?' Cara said. 'So, okay, maybe we couldn't meet at my house but you could come on campus, couldn't you?'
'And risk seeing the lovebirds drooling over each other? No thanks. But you can come round to the flat any time you like. I'll give you the address. I've got a phone, too.' Usha wrote the details on a piece of paper and gave it to Cara. 'Don't lose that.'
'Don't worry.'
'Just make sure you're not around when Alex decides that it's time to give a white girl a whirl.'
'To tell you the truth . . .' Cara looked sheepish. '. . . I never liked him that much. He's very attractive but there's something about him I can't warm to.'
'Are you going to be okay about living in the same house?'
'It'll be fine, I expect. I mean, he's genial enough. I don't know what it is – but I don't mean to criticize you, you know. You were so happy. Him, too. I feel caught between you and Lucy but I don't want to give either of you up.'
'You don't have to,' said Usha. 'We'll have to occupy different bits.'
'Yeah, I guess. Let me buy you a hot chocolate, eh? Liquid comfort food.'
'I can't. I've got the other agencies to go to.'
'Okay. I'll walk down to North Street with you.'
They stopped at the junction.
'You take care now,' said Cara.
'And you. And don't forget to keep in touch. I know you'll be busy and everything but –'
'Don't worry. I will.' Cara squeezed Usha's hand. 'I promise.'
Usha watched her walk away. The wind caught Cara's hair and threw it around her face. Pulling the hair from her eyes she turned and raised her hand; a wave of Italians broke around her and then she was gone.

10

HELEN LOOKED AT herself in the full-length mirror and instantly rejected what she saw. She took the clothes off and threw them on the bed to join her red dress and the trousers that made her backside look big. She pawed her way impatiently through the wardrobe.

She found the blue silk shirt that intensified the colour of her eyes. But the velvet leggings she had bought to go with it were so smooth that anything worn over them rode up into a fabric tyre after a couple of steps. She knew she should get rid of them but liked to think of herself wearing them.

Even though I don't wear them because I always remember that they do that, she thought: I'm pathetic. She put on the blue shirt and fetched a pair of black leggings from the drawer. She ran her hand over the velvet pair lying beside them then imprisoned them again for being useless.

She brushed her hair and put it up in a pony tail and promptly took it down again. Pulling my hair back makes my face look droopy, she decided. She brushed her hair out. That looks fine if you like straw, jeered her inner critic. She threw the brush onto the dressing table, put on her rings and fled from her reflection. The hall mirror crept up on her and turned her to face it as she went to open the front door. A spot's angry head poked triumphantly above the last button.

Oh good, she thought, a friend for the one on my chin.

She did up a button and promptly concluded that she looked like a twit trapped in her shirt.

She left to prevent herself from going to change again.

Usha answered the door in the beautiful red dressing gown.

'Oh hi. Come on in.' She tramped like a cat over the open newspaper spread out on the floor.

'So, how did it go yesterday?' Helen moved a pile of jumpers along and sat on the sofa.

Usha sat cross-legged on the floor by the newspaper. 'No experience, that's the problem. Oh yes, and no skills.' She grinned. 'I do have a typing speed of somewhere between twenty-four and twenty-seven words per minute. I got faster during the day.'

'That's a skill.'

'Hmm. Other people can do it better. Who's going to employ someone slow, even temporarily, when there are loads of quick people?'

Helen could see the shape of Usha's nipples outlined by the red fabric. She averted her eyes. 'What will you do?'

'I ran into one of my university friends yesterday, and she suggested I try Sainsbury's. I had this idea that I could get work as a filing clerk or something but maybe a supermarket wouldn't be too bad.'

'Would you have to work evenings?'

'I hadn't thought of that. I expect you have to do some late nights or weekends.'

'Anything in the paper?'

'Nope. I've nearly done the crossword, though.' Usha looked down at the paper.

Helen saw the vulnerable stripe of her parting and wanted to run her finger along it.

'I can't get twelve across,' Usha said. '"Don't concentrate eggs here" – two, three, six.'

'In one basket,' they said at the same time, and grinned at each other.

'Where's my pen?' Usha patted the newspaper and looked under the edge of the chair.

'I've got one in my bag,' said Helen. She handed it to Usha.

'Thanks.' Usha wrote in the answer. 'That gives me nine down as well. And seventeen down. It's finished.' The blue ink stood out against the red that Usha had been using. Usha stared at the crossword for a moment then looked up at Helen. Her look was penetrating but not aimed at Helen.

'I had a boyfriend . . . once,' she said. 'We used to do the crossword puzzle together. One day I had to go out half-way through and when I got back he'd finished it, but he used a red pen for the clues he'd done.' She refocused on Helen. 'Said he couldn't find the black one but it was right there on the table. The more I got to thinking about those crosswords, the more meaning they had.' She looked very small and baffled. 'If there was a clue he knew the answer to and I didn't he wouldn't just tell me the answer. He'd keep telling me I did know it but I needed to *think* about it, like it was for my own good.' She gave Helen a tight smile. 'It didn't last.'

Helen wanted to *do* something; hug her, pat her arm. 'Oh,' she said.

'If you know the answer, say what it is, right?' She looked a little embarrassed. 'Sorry. Don't know what brought that on.'

'Did you tell him that it got on your nerves?'

'It wouldn't have made any difference. It might have made it worse – let's wind Usha up and then say she's overreacting.'

'It can be . . . damaging to spend too much time thinking you should have seen at the time things you didn't see till later or at least until it was too late.' Helen smiled. 'Did that make sense?'

Usha laughed. 'Yeah. But you have to analyse things to make sure you can spot them if they happen again.'

'True.'

'But I have a feeling that I wouldn't see it – whatever it was – even if it was right in front of my face.'

'Oh, I don't know . . . You're alert at any rate.'

'And your country needs lerts,' they said at the same time.

'We must stop talking like this,' said Usha. 'What will people say?'

'Nothing much. They'd have to get a word in edgeways first. Oh God, is that the time? I've got to go, I'm picking some stuff up from my mother before I go to work.'

Usha sighed. 'But this means I have to go looking for a job. How can you do this to me?'

'Mr Sainsbury needs lerts, too. But I'll come down later, okay?'

'Hello?' Helen closed her mother's front door. The familiar smell of the house nuzzled around her. 'Mum?' She went to the kitchen. Through the window she could see her mother by the shed. She went outside.

'Hiya, Mum.'

'Oh God, you made me jump.' Pat held a rubber-gloved hand just in front of her chest as if she were demonstrating how to look surprised.

'I rang the bell but as you didn't answer I used my key. Which reminds me, I must get one done for you.' Helen had been getting round to it for ten years and three flats.

'Mm. I wish I knew what the pigeons around here ate. It's murder to get off.' Pat dipped a sponge into the bucket of soapy water and scrubbed at the shed window.

'What on earth are you *doing*?'

'What's it look like?'

'It's a shed, for God's sake. It's not like anyone's going to see it.'

'*I* see it. This is for me not the neighbours. I can see what your father's up to if the window's clean.'

'He won't be spending much time in here, will he?' said Helen. 'It's autumn now.'

'That won't stop him. He's been "sorting out" in here since . . . let me see now . . . nineteen seventy-six.' Pat threw the sponge into the bucket. 'Ugh. I need a cup of tea after that.'

'How is Dad?' Helen asked as they got back to the house.

'Refusing to act his age as usual.' Pat took off the rubber gloves and held them gingerly. She looked perplexed for a moment. 'Umm . . . I know.' She put them in the bin. 'He could take retirement now if only he didn't feel it's an admission of defeat. But no, he's determined to stick out these last two years even if it kills him. Still, you know what he's like once he's made his mind up to something.'

'*He looks like a gonk. A rather unsavoury one at that, I might add.*'

'Oh Daddy . . .'

'Don't "Daddy" me, young lady. This . . . person is a layabout. Rock musician, indeed.'

'He's a very good guitarist. The band could make it, they really could.'

'*I* believe that makes you a groupie. That's the term, isn't it?'

'We're getting a flat together. Ranting on isn't going to change that.'

'You call it ranting, I call it looking out for my only daughter. I shall have nothing to say to you, Helen, if you persist in this mindless, adolescent behaviour.'

'It isn't mindless. This is a considered decision, Daddy.'

'Ill-considered. Ill-advised. Where is your self-respect, child?'

'*I am* not *a child!*'

'Stamping your foot harder is hardly going to help your case, is it now.' He stood suddenly, filling up too much of the air too quickly. 'Mark my words. *If you do this, I will no longer have a daughter. I haven't spent your life looking out for you to have something like this happen right under my nose. Do you understand me?'*

'Daddy, why can't –'

'Do you understand me or not?'

'I hear what you're saying, but –'

'Well then.' One stride took him to the door of her room. The windchime's little shells tinkled tinily in the rush of air as the door slammed behind him. Upstairs Bob began to practise his drum solo on the edge of the bathroom sink.

'Silly old fart, your father.' Pat sat down. 'So, what brings you here?'

'The photocopying, remember? You wanted me to run off some copies of the leaflet for the gardening club.'

'Of course. I'll get it in a minute. Glenda's husband normally does it but he's on some management course in Wales. Climbing mountains and learning to trust other members of the team, you know the kind of thing. A much cheaper way to find out if you can trust someone is to send them down to the supermarket with a list and see what they come back with. You know what happened when I had that bad ankle and your father went.'

'Ten tins of cat food and two boxes of Brillo pads.'

The old story was like a well-worn cardigan. Pat did up the buttons. 'And us with no cat and all the pans non-stick.'

'A bargain's a bargain,' said Helen.

'So,' said Pat, 'how's Danny boy?'

'Fine.'

'You'd been arguing last time we talked.'

Helen shrugged. 'It comes and goes. We had a good talk a couple of days ago, and that's cleared the air a bit.'

'He's a good man. You're lucky. At least he doesn't seem the type to turn into a silly old fart. Mind you, neither did your father. I didn't think he'd . . . age like he has. He's probably disappointed in me.' She giggled. 'I'm not dignified enough.'

'What does that mean?'

'I don't know, really. Anyway, I was talking about you, not me. I worry about you. This having-a-baby thing is going to split you up if you're not careful. And then you won't have anything – no Dan and no baby. What good is that?'

'I can't help the way I feel.'

'You put too much store by it, my love. Babies are all very well but there are other things in life. If I hadn't had you ... What I mean to say is that it – motherhood, all that nonsense – is overrated.'

Helen was offended though she tried to resist it. 'So you'd rather not have had me?'

'Oh, don't be daft. If I hadn't had you neither of us would know anything about it so it wouldn't make any difference, would it. All I meant is that there's more to life than reproduction.'

'That sounds like a contradiction in terms to me.'

'Don't pick holes.'

'It's alright for you to say that having a baby isn't that important – you've done it.'

'Then who better to judge? Look, I've seen you going through all this worry and not having any luck and thought it was about time someone put the other side to you. No one's said it, have they? They've all been really sympathetic and not told you that it isn't necessarily all it's cracked up to be. What about those women who *choose* not to have babies? They don't all end up wishing they had, do they?'

'The point is they have a choice, don't they?'

'Yes, but . . .' Pat leaned her chin on her hands. 'It's a kind of fulfilment, isn't it, having babies?'

Helen nodded. She could feel the ache of an unknown loss fretting at her.

'Well,' continued Pat, 'there are all kinds of fulfilment, aren't there? Then channel this energy into something else. You're a capable woman, why waste yourself in this ... chase, when there is so much you could do?'

'I can't explain it, Mum. You're a mother, you should know –'

'Know what? That inexplicable call of biology? The true nature of the female?' There was an edge to Pat's voice. She looked at Helen. 'Don't invest so much in it,' she said. Her voice softened. 'Don't be cruel to yourself.'

'Okay.'

Pat sighed. 'You should listen to me, you know.'

'I know. Thanks, Mum.'

'And don't think I'd babysit for you, either. I've got a life to get on with and I've no intention of becoming a doting granny. That way lies those white shoes with perforations like teabags and thinking doilies are important.' She got up. 'I'll get that photocopying.'

'Why don't you bring Usha along on Thursday?' said Maggie.

'Well, I . . .' Good grief, Helen thought: I don't want to share her. 'Maybe I will.'

'Ashamed of Lou and me, are you?' Maggie held up a piece of paper and squinted at it. 'You know, at least fifty per cent of this fax is illegible. Modern technology is a wonderful thing, isn't it?'

'Of course I'm not ashamed of you. Though you did get a little out of hand last time: a quiet drink isn't supposed to involve stealing from behind the bar.'

'Cheek! It wasn't stealing; I borrowed that trophy to give – temporarily – to the most beautiful man I'd ever seen.'

'It was a golf tournament runner-up cup.'

'I know, I know,' said Maggie throwing the fax into her in-tray. 'And yes, the landlord was very cross. And yes, the guy was gay.' She gazed out of the window for a moment and then smiled at Helen. 'He *was* beautiful, wasn't he?'

'A bit too blond for my taste. But I don't think we'd better go back to The Swan for a while. How about The King and Queen?'

'Okay. At least Lou agreed with me about that guy.' Maggie took the fax out of the tray and began to pore over it again. 'They're either trying to sell us something or trying to give us something. Or maybe we've got something of theirs they want back.'

'Lou would agree. She prefers pale people. Take Steve – he looks positively anaemic.'

'You like dark people then?'

'What do you mean by that?'

Maggie looked up in surprise. 'Nothing. Are you okay?'

Helen felt the blush heating her face. 'Mm, fine.'

'Yeah, right.' Maggie's maternal feathers began to fluff. 'What's up, sweetie? Who's been giving you a hard time?'

'Hormone rush, that's all.' And I keep stroking Usha through that dressing gown, she thought: I can feel the cool silk under my fingers and the heat of her body beyond.

'Sure?' Maggie emerged from behind her desk, determined that Helen should be comforted. 'What can I do?'

'Make us a coffee. Make everything normal.'

'You mean as normal as it gets around here. I'll tell you what...' Maggie fetched the small rucksack she always carried and rummaged around in it. 'Ah!' Triumphantly she held up a quarter bottle of whisky. 'Something to improve the coffee. Always a good idea when I'm making. God bless Dad.'

'I didn't know he was down here.'

Maggie switched on the kettle. 'He's shut the shop for a few days to come and visit.'

Duncan was a small, plump man whose love for his daughter was huge and forgiving. He cast his kindly net to include Maggie's friends, in whom he took a genuine interest. He and Helen had spent an afternoon giggling over the family photos while Maggie was delayed on her way home from a conference. He had spoken with a soft regret of his wife, Hazel, and the tumour she had hidden from him until it was too late. His stubby fingers touched a photograph of Hazel standing on a windy pier years away. 'Lovely, foolish woman,' he said and that was the end of it.

'I'd love to see him while he's here,' Helen said.

'Absolutely. He mentioned you yesterday – I think he's got a bit of a soft spot for you.'

'He's a nice man.'

'It's a genetic thing. I mean, look how nice I am. I'm so nice I surprise myself sometimes.'

'Yes, you are nice. And quite foul, too. That's why I like you.' Helen grinned. 'And it's only because I like you that I don't run off with your dad.'

'He's a poppet, isn't he. Okay, here we are.' Maggie handed Helen a steaming mug potent with alcohol and then fetched her own. 'To people of all persuasions, light and dark. Oh yes, and to hormones.'

Helen clinked her mug against Maggie's. 'To hormones.'

11

'I WANTED TO ask you a favour.'
'Are you okay?' Dan sat down.
'On and off,' Lesley said. 'I've got an appointment with the counsellor the day after tomorrow.'
'If there's anything I can do –'
'Well, there is but it isn't connected with what we . . .' She picked at the bobbles on her black woolly thigh.
He felt stronger with the desk between them. 'So what is it?'
'Well, I left some books with a friend over the summer and I have to move them. I can borrow a car but I need a hand, the boxes are pretty heavy.'
'Surely you must know someone else who could . . . ?'
'I thought you wouldn't mind,' she said abruptly. 'You know, after the way you were on – forget it. It doesn't matter.' Thunder was creeping over her forehead. She began to get up.
'Try to see this from my point of view.'
'It should go something like this: someone needs help moving some stuff. I have arms and legs; I can help.' She stood with her arms folded, her weight thrown out onto one hip.
'Of course I'd like to help you but surely you can see how it might –'
'Do you think I'm after you?'
'That isn't what I'm saying.'
'It'd be down three floors at one flat and up two at the other. I was keeping that as a surprise, of course.' She shook her head and picked up her bag from the floor. 'Don't worry about it.'

'What the hell,' he said. 'How about tomorrow evening after work? Where does your friend live?'

'Elm Grove.'

'Why don't I meet you there – about six?'

'I'll give you her address.' The scratch of her pen seemed very loud. 'There.' She held it out to him. 'See you around six then.'

He folded the paper and put it in his jacket pocket. He could hear the jingling of the key fob she kept on her rucksack recede down the corridor; then all was quiet again. A minute or so later he thought he heard the main door to the building bang shut behind her but the noise could have come from anywhere.

He put on his coat. He went to the door, reached for the switch to turn off the light and hesitated. He reached into his pocket and took out the address. No need to take it home. He went to put it in his desk and stopped. No need to leave it here either. He memorized the address and dropped the paper into a bin on the way to the bus stop.

He rode home to the rhythm of the mantra that the address had become.

The topic had come up almost without his noticing and when he found his mouth repeating past conversations he had wearied, suddenly. Recent thoughts, new words, mushroomed.

'Why don't you face it? We can't have a child. Let's just get on with our lives, for God's sake.' Dan sat down opposite Helen.

She sat bundled with her arms around her cushion, looking at him. Pink, angry as a graze, bloomed on her cheeks.

'Well?'

'I agree. That's what you want me to say, isn't it? I can't help having hope – is that such a crime? You know what the consultant said – extremely unlikely but not impossible.' She struck the cushion for emphasis. '*Not impossible.*'

'It's not impossible that I might spontaneously combust but it's hardly worth putting money on, is it? I wish we could stop all this. Now.'

'So *you* want to stop.' She shrugged. 'Fine.' She was receding: she sat there and without looking any different she was getting further and further away.

Dan got up. 'Don't! Don't get into that "I'm on a higher plane" mode.'

'Don't shout.'

'I think I've got something to bloody well shout about! I've tried everything else.'

'You *know* this isn't something that I can simply decide not to think about any more.'

'It's just hit me, I mean, *really* hit me. I have no say here. *Our* decision – hah! *Our* child – hah!'

She threw the cushion down and stood to face him. 'It's my body.'

'But it doesn't fucking work, does it!' As he threw his arms out in exasperation his fingers contacted something. He and Helen watched the crystal pear Lou had given them hurtle from the mantelpiece and shatter on the hearth; the shards shone like drops of water.

'Oh God,' said Dan.

'It's my fault.'

'Don't be silly. I knocked –'

'My body doesn't work. It's my fault.' She pushed past him and he heard the slam of the bathroom door and the scrape of the bolt. He used a postcard from the mantelpiece to brush the glass together. He picked up a piece and looked through it; broken, it was just ordinary glass.

He went to fetch the dustpan.

'Hello, I'm afraid there's no one here at the moment . . .'

'It says here that the outgoing message can be up to three minutes long,' said Helen, surrounded by the answering machine's packaging. 'Maybe we should do something interesting.'

'We could record a message while we're having sex.'

'I don't suppose my mother would want to listen to me having sex. Or to you for that matter.' She consulted the page and plugged a cable into the back of the machine. 'Do you think we could do it in three minutes?'

'We could give it a go.'

He came in two minutes and twelve seconds, and felt strangely liberated. He licked Helen to climax on the floor without timing it; she smelt of her and tasted of him.

She recorded the message over the top of their discussion about when sex could actually be said to start and surely it was phallocentric to think of sex only in terms of penetration which is when he started the stopwatch and though they sounded perfectly normal he was already snug inside her and her hair spread out against the dark carpet as rich as cream curling into coffee.

She'd been sitting in her underwear, head close to the machine to make sure the recording would be clear, a glass of wine set unsteadily on the floor. Helen, sounding bright.

'... but if you leave a message after the beeps we'll get back to you as soon as we can.'

Dan told her he was going to help a student move some boxes of books.

A headless teddy bear was slumped in the broken armchair that occupied the tiny front garden. Bubbles of stuffing that had leaked from its neck stippled the earth between the weeds. Dan went to ring the bell and saw the button was hanging by its wires. He knocked on the door.

A slim, dark woman answered. She wore her hair in tight braids that hung like bundled cords; little coloured beads clattered quietly as she moved her head and her scalp showed in neat pale rows.

'You here for Lesley?'

'That's right.'

'Come in. Why didn't you use the bell?'

Dan gestured to it.

'Oh God, it's fallen off again. Someone's pinched the blue-tack. It works, though.' She pressed it. The bell bing-bonged. 'See?'

They squeezed down the hall past a bicycle with a flat tyre. The girl paused at the bottom of the stairs. 'Lesley!' she called, in a voice so unexpectedly loud that Dan jumped.

'I'm here.' Lesley was suddenly behind them. Dan jumped again.

'Are you always this nervous?' the dark girl asked him.

'Leave him alone, Lucy. He's just not used to this place.' Lesley's hair was damp and a little straggly. Dan wanted to brush it for her.

'Alex,' said Lesley to the young man who appeared in the living room doorway holding a steaming mug, 'how about giving us a hand down from Lucy's room with these boxes?'

'I thought that's what whatsisname was for.'

'Dan,' said Dan.

'Yeah, that's right – Dan. Anyway, like I would, but my programme's on now and Lucy's made me a nice cup of coffee.' He raised the mug. 'Luce, there's no milk in this coffee.'

'That coffee is tea, and this is what you get when you don't buy the milk and coffee when it's your turn.'

'You didn't remind me.'

'Yes I did, this morning.'

'Well, you didn't remind me again.'

'Well, children,' said Lesley. 'We'd love to stand here and listen to you bicker all night but we have some books to move.'

'I'll come and help,' said Lucy. 'I'm sure Alex and I can continue our conversation later.'

Alex sipped his tea and made a face. 'Is there any sugar?'

Lucy grinned. 'Did you buy any?'

'Oh bloody hell.'

It was warm inside the car and Lesley didn't talk much while she drove. Surreptitiously he watched her. Her lips, swathed in red as ever, looked dark, almost black, in the sodium streetlights. Her bottom lip was full, giving her a slightly sulky look; he wanted to touch her mouth. Each time she changed gear the bangles on her left wrist jangled. Her black-clad legs shaded into the darkness of the footwell, her left thigh flexing with each press at the clutch pedal. Her hands emerged in sudden paleness from long black sleeves; her nails were short, ferociously bitten. That aggressive anxiety fascinated him; he wanted to feel those vulnerable fingers find certainty on his skin.

She approached a set of traffic lights, tinkling down through the gears to a stop. She turned and smiled at him and he was lost.

The lights changed and she played back up the gears. He watched her profile from the corner of his eye and waited for her to tell him they had arrived.

'This is the last one,' said Dan.

'It's a shame there's no one else in – they could have helped us. You look hot. Why don't you take your jacket off?'

'I'll be fine. Well, I'll get going now – I'll soon cool off outside.'

'Don't be daft, I'm giving you a lift – why don't you catch your breath first?'

'It's getting late and –'

'Late?' Lesley laughed. 'Late for what? I'll make us a coffee – coffee and milk both available, I promise – and you can cool down and then I'll drive you home. How's that for a plan?' She lowered her voice confidentially. 'I have chocolate digestives.'

'Ah, biscuits, eh? White, no sugar, please.'
'You stay right here.' She paused in the doorway. 'Sit down, make yourself at home.'
Then he was alone in her room. He took off his jacket and hung it over the back of the chair that was pushed in under the desk; the seat was occupied by a neat stack of papers topped with three coloured highlighter pens. A folder was placed exactly square to the edge of the desk and a ruler, a pen and a pencil lay lined up side by side. Silk scarves of aquatic blues and greens framed the dressing-table mirror, reflecting the room in the centre of a pool. A mobile of tiny silver fish swam with its twin shoal on the other side of the mirror. Little bottles and jars were ordered by size on the dressing table, standing on a pelt of grey velvet. He picked up a bottle and unscrewed the lid.

The seminar room is warm, too warm. Sun dazzles off a window on the other side of the square. Annie, the student doing her presentation, is softly-spoken; the overhead projector hums like an unending sigh. There's a trace of citrus in the air; it grows a little stronger then steadies to a gentle intensity. He will buy oranges on the way home. He wants to pull cool segments apart, feel the rush on his tongue. Lesley Markham nods the nod of the sudden sleeper. Annie sweats. The room is hot, much too hot.

He quickly sealed the scent of oranges back in the bottle and replaced it on the dressing table. He considered sitting down but there was only the bed. His fingers smelt sweet and sharp. The thought was sudden and imperative: I shouldn't be here. Pulling his jacket from the chair he hurried out and started down the stairs. Lesley appeared on the landing below. 'It's alright,' she said, 'I can manage.'

In her room they sat on the floor. He picked up the crumbs from his biscuits and put them in the bin. She put on a tape of a woman singing of hurt; it wasn't in English but it was unmistakable.

'Lucy gave it to me,' said Lesley. 'Egyptian, she said.' From a brightly painted tobacco tin she took some cigarette papers, a small pouch of herbal tobacco and a small brown lump wrapped in cling film. 'Do you indulge?'

'Not any more.' Cannabis lowers the sperm count, he thought automatically. His sacrifice for the cause.

'Shame.'

He wondered whether she should be getting stoned in her condition; 'in her condition' – the voice of his mother. At the same time he knew it wasn't relevant, he knew Lesley wouldn't have the child. He realized he wanted her to look different, to fulfil some stereotype he had internalized through his whole life: he wanted her to glow; she looked a little tired. He watched her roast the dope with a lighter and crumble it into the tobacco she'd laid in the cigarette paper. He longed to be doing it himself. She rolled it up and ran her tongue along the glue. He looked away. Then she was tucking in the roach and smoothing the paper down. She examined the joint critically.

'Hmm. Not bad.'

Lesley lit up and inhaled deeply. Dan found himself holding his breath, too.

'You're not really going to make me smoke this on my own, are you?' Lesley held out the joint to him and the moment grew as clear and cold and hard as crystal, and on and on rang the Egyptian woman's foreign, familiar pain.

12

USHA KNOCKED ON Helen's door again, shivering a little in her dressing gown. She had seen Dan leave the house and catch his lift but there hadn't yet been any sign of Helen; she must still be at home. The door opened a crack.

'Oh, hi,' said Helen and opened the door fully. She was swathed in a big white towel which she clutched together above her breasts, and wore a pale blue towel wrapped turban-like around her hair. 'I've just got out of the shower.'

'I can come back.'

'No, it's fine. Really. How's the job hunting going?'

Usha followed her into the living room. 'That's what I came to tell you. I've got one.'

'That's great. Tell me all about it.' Helen sat on the sofa and curled her legs underneath her. Usha sat in an armchair, taking the cushion with the cover she had admired into her lap. The embroidery felt like a kind of Braille under her fingers; the tips stroked over it again and again in an insistent, absent search.

'Well, don't get too excited,' said Usha. 'I start next week in the cash office up at Sainsbury's.'

'It'll be good experience,' said Helen. She picked up a bottle of moisturiser and poured a white slick into her palm. She rubbed her hands together and began smoothing it slowly into her arms.

The room is like a cave. It is dark and warm, the soft heat is a cushion all round them.

Moments passed.

'I can smell flowers,' said Usha. Helen's smile was slow. Her fingers drew firmly along her flesh.

'I'll make some tea when I've done this,' said Helen. 'You want some?'

'Please.'

'Tell you what –' Helen pulled the towel from her head. 'You put the kettle on and I'll go and comb my hair.'

Her hair stuck out in all directions; she looked like the doll of a child who hadn't got the hang of hairbrushes. Usha stifled a smile.

'What?' said Helen, blue eyes quizzical below the wilderness.

'Nothing.'

'Oh.' They looked at one another, smiling. 'Well,' said Helen eventually, 'you know where the kitchen is.'

When Helen returned the kettle was on, its white noise ragged among the smooth tiles and worktops. Usha was looking out of the window.

'You have a better view than me,' she said. 'I didn't know you could see the Royal Pavilion.'

Helen came to the window. 'We get a good view of the sunset, too. Sometimes the buildings look like they're on fire.'

Usha was aware of Helen standing behind her. I can feel the heat from her body, she thought; warm flower scent.

The roar from the kettle was numbing. Usha turned and Helen's eyes were on hers; their blue looked darker now, like a dusking sky. The moment stretched into a slowed-down time, then snapped as the kettle clicked off.

Helen looked away.

Usha exhaled, giving up the breath little by little, sure Helen could hear the hammering of her heart.

The everyday sound of teaspoons and cups soothed her pulse; the feeling of panic that made her want to laugh careered through her like a trapped beam of light. She sat at the table, tracing the marble pattern with her finger, knowing she would look at Helen but delaying it.

Helen brought the cups over and put them down. She looked just the same. The kitchen looked just the same. The clock ticked quietly.

'A couple of friends and I are going out tomorrow night,' said Helen, 'and I wondered if you'd like to come.'

'Where are you going?'

'I'm leaving it up to Maggie. The plan is to collect her and Lou from Maggie's place and go on to wherever.'
'I'd love to.'
'Good.'
She must have put the mascara on when she went to comb her hair, thought Usha: because of me; for me.
'I have an invitation for you, too,' said Usha. 'For Friday, for that meal I promised you and Dan.'
'Friday . . . I'll check with Dan but I'm sure it'll be okay.'
They smiled at one another.
'Well . . .' said Helen.
'Well.'
The telephone rang. Helen got up. 'I'll collect you tomorrow, about seven. Is that okay?'
'Yeah, fine. I'll see myself out.'
As she left she heard Helen pick up the phone and say hello. A pause, then, 'Oh, hello Moira,' in a voice compressed with sudden weariness.
Usha closed the door and returned to her flat. She wandered into the kitchen and looked out of the window towards the wall at the end of the small garden. The view was much better from upstairs. It felt like you could see for miles.

Her arms were beginning to ache. Holding the unfinished plait in her left hand she ran the right over what she had done so far. A loose strand tickled over her fingers. The plait went from being too tight to too loose.

'*Sit still.' Mum briskly braids Usha's hair with the same ruthless efficiency with which she will button her into her school coat. Jaz waits, brushing out his hair; long sweeps down the nocturnal black, his eyes narrowing and closing like a cat's. Mum will twist it into a snake and tether it out of sight, pin it beneath the cotton handkerchief patterned with cherries that Jaz has in his hand.*

He yawns and grins at Usha; his hair shines in a room stained with morning sun and speckled with the sound of the elastic winder snapping around and around Usha's plait.

As Usha sighed and lowered her tired arms Helen arrived.
'Ready?' said Helen.
'Nearly. I'm having hair trouble.' Usha untangled the last of the plait

and began to brush her hair. 'I can't get it right. Thinking upside-down and back to front isn't my strong point.'

'I'll do it for you.'

'It's gone seven.'

'It won't take a minute.'

Usha stood at the mirror and Helen divided her hair into three lengths and began the plait. Her fingers brushed against Usha's neck. Usha watched her in the mirror.

'You have lovely hair,' said Helen as she put the elastic winder around the plait. 'I often regret having mine cut.'

Usha smiled as their eyes met in the mirror. 'Yours looks nice. Soft.'

They stood looking at each other's reflection.

'Well,' said Helen. 'I guess we're ready now.'

'Thanks,' said Usha. 'I'll get my coat.'

The King and Queen was busy but they managed to find somewhere to sit. Maggie bought a round and Lou helped her carry the glasses to the table.

'I'd like to propose a toast,' said Maggie, 'but I can't be arsed. Cheers.'

'I'll drink to that,' said Lou. 'I'd better do it now while I have my one real drink.'

'It counts even if you haven't got alcohol, you know,' said Helen.

'Yeah, but the trouble is, when the toasts start getting silly it's hard to enter into the spirit of things if you're sober.'

'Oh, I don't know,' said Usha. 'Non-drinkers can have a good time as well. I even go to bed after midnight sometimes.'

Maggie laughed. 'You impulsive thing, you. I think I will propose a toast, after all. So – to toasts.'

'To toasts,' they chorused, and drank.

Lou smiled tightly at Usha. 'So, is it a religious thing? Not drinking, I mean.'

'Not for me. I just don't like it.'

'What, none of it? Wine, beer, spirits – they're very different, you know.'

'I know.'

'Have you tried them?'

'Some.'

'Aha!' said Lou. 'So there might be a drink you like but you haven't tried it because you don't try because you might not like it.'

'That doesn't seem unreasonable to me,' said Helen. 'I mean, if you didn't like, say, potatoes, you wouldn't keep trying them prepared in slightly different ways, would you?'

'Hmm.'

'It's not only the taste,' said Usha. 'It's the effect.'

'You mean the loudness, the unaccountable belief that one has become extremely amusing, the lack of brain function the following day if you've had a good night . . .'

'Yeah, those things.'

'I'm sorry, you've lost me,' Lou said. 'These are reasons *not* to drink? Oh God.' She drained her wineglass.

'The British are so uptight it's a useful way to shed a few inhibitions,' said Maggie. 'It seems to me the problem is arranging things so you don't lose too many. Or worse, too many too soon.'

'Drunk people say things they don't mean,' said Usha.

'And very drunk people say things they *do* mean,' said Helen. 'She's got a point, you know. Very drunk people don't even have the sense to say the things they mean to other very drunk people who wouldn't be able to remember it. They'll find someone like Usha, confide in her, and then puke on her shoes.'

'Wipe-clean footwear is obviously what's needed,' said Lou. 'Wear your wellies with pride, Usha, for you are one of the great undrunks.'

'Are you going to use Usha as a Steve substitute all night?' said Helen.

'I thought only for the first half hour or so until I burst into tears and bare my soul.'

'Time's up,' said Maggie looking at her watch.

'And I'm all out of tissues,' said Helen. 'So let's skip the tears and go straight for the soul.'

Lou sighed. 'I guess Helen has a point.' She shrugged. 'Sorry, Usha.'

'It's okay.'

'Well, no, it isn't,' said Maggie, 'but it's nice of you to say so. Ever since I've known her – and that's longer than I care to remember – she's had this habit of attacking things that are not the things she wants to attack at all. She's not picking on *you*. But you're easier.'

'Must we amateur-psychologize me quite so early in the evening?' said Lou. 'It's embarrassing.'

'Don't worry,' said Usha. 'I won't tell anyone.' She smiled tartly. 'At least no one you know.'

'Oh God. Someone get me a drink,' said Lou. 'Perrier, no ice – I don't want it getting diluted.'

'I'll go,' said Helen. 'Usha, will you give me a hand?'

While they waited at the bar Helen apologized again for Lou.

'It doesn't matter,' said Usha.

'I'm so used to Lou's ongoing disaster with Steve that it didn't occur to me that she might mind someone she didn't know hearing all about it. It's such an integral part of her, it's like imagining you can look at someone and not see their hair.'

'Talking of hair – Maggie's is amazing, isn't it. It's like . . . I don't know . . . like a halo or something.'

Helen laughed. 'Maggie with a halo. Now there's a thought.'

The barman brought them their drinks and change. 'Oh good, a couple of fifty pences,' said Helen, handing them to Usha. 'Choose us something on the juke box.'

They took the drinks back to the table and Usha made her way to the juke box. She began to read down the list of titles.

'Well, look who it is,' a man said. 'Hello? Usha Dhillon, come in please.'

She turned and saw a tall Asian man with close-cropped hair generously spiked with gel.

'Sorry, I can't quite . . .'

'We fought over the last samosa at –'

'Yeah, Veena's wedding.'

'I let you have it.'

'I should think so,' said Usha. 'I got there first.'

'Not as I remember. But it doesn't matter. Surinder's the name – I guess you've forgotten.'

'No, no – well, okay, I had. But hello again.'

'How's the course going?'

'Um, I'm taking some time out right now,' said Usha reluctantly. 'A few . . . things to sort out.'

Surinder moved closer to her to let someone pass behind him. He stayed there. A few droplets of sweat glittered on his upper lip.

'I'll be honest,' he said. 'I've heard a few things. There's a white boy, isn't there?'

'Was.'

'Last I knew, you were living together.'

'You seem to know a lot. Or think you do.'

'You know how it is,' said Surinder. 'You can't keep anything quiet around here.'

'Apparently not.'

'So, it didn't work out for you.'

'Yeah, well.'

'But a bit of experience isn't necessarily a bad thing.'

'Depends on the experience.'

'When I say *experience*, I mean, you know, as a woman.'

Usha looked at him. 'What?'

He giggled; a strangely high-pitched sound. 'I was thinking – you know, me and you, we could have some fun.'

'I –'

'You know what I'm saying. A girl like you –' She turned away. He grabbed her arm. 'You've got fussy all of a sudden.' For the briefest moment he pulled her against him; she felt the thrust of his hips, then he released her. He wiped the sweat from his upper lip.

'You know, I think it's good that our women are out there getting educated and that, but you're not doing them any favours. Parents will think their daughters are going to end up like you.'

'Better than having a son like you, I'd say.'

'So what about this music then?' said Helen, appearing at Usha's side.

Surinder looked at Usha. 'Hope to see you again soon.' He gave her a little wave, turned and disappeared into the crush at the bar.

'Friend of yours?' said Helen. 'Hey, are you okay?'

'Help me choose some music to cheer us all up.'

They stood side by side reading the list and talking about the titles; when Helen laughed Usha felt the cold space forced around her by Surinder begin to ebb away and she became aware again of the faint, whispering scent of flowers.

13

'I LIKED HER,' said Maggie. 'I did wonder if I'd have much to say to a twenty-something – I find it can sometimes be pretty hard going, you know – but she's really nice.'

'You're only forty, for God's sake,' Helen said.

'So I'm old enough to be her granny. How old is she anyway?'

'Twenty-two.'

'We talked star signs,' said Maggie. 'She's a Leo.'

'When's her birthday?'

'Exactly five months after mine – August fifteenth.'

Clammy hands. She signs a name. The corridors are hushed; the rooms stiller. The nurse is professionally kind, neutral. Yellow roses, looking just opened, stand in white porcelain: artificial; dry petals that rustle like husks. A woman in the TV room talking of bruises on her thighs the last time, at the other place; dark, as big as a fist. They handled me, she says, like a piece of meat. Helen sees the nacreous sheen on stringy red, hears the thump onto a cold, cold slab.

Her legs sweat against pink sheets; flooding afternoon sun turns the blind piss-colour, taut skin stretched over a drum full of light. Glossy magazines prodded with fat fingerprints; a pile of books no one will be there long enough to read. She counts the spines bright as building-blocks: five; she counts them again; still five. A newspaper neatly folded, smooth with unuse. She picks it up: a photograph of a tank, its killing arm broken in two; flat people in a cartoon she can't find room to think about; polite lettering gathers into a date: Saturday 15th August. Her fingers are dingy with dissolving letters; grey streaks now on the sheet, she rubs and rubs but her hands will not come clean.

'Are you alright?' said Maggie. 'You look a bit strange.'

74

'I'm fine.'

Maggie looked dubious. 'Hm.' She poked a pile of papers with a ruler and made a face. 'I suppose we should do some work.'

'Irritating, isn't it, the way it interrupts conversation.'

'Tell you what – I'll give you a new challenge.' Maggie picked up the bin. 'Now let me see. Ah, yes.' She took it to the side of the filing cabinet and put it down. 'More of an oblique angle. See how you get on with that – I can't help feeling you've been getting a little over-confident.'

'No problem. Watch this.' Helen screwed up a piece of scrap paper, aimed and threw. Jim came quickly through the door and unwittingly placed his head in the paper's path. The missile bounced off and rolled to a stop at Maggie's feet.

'Good God, where did that come from?' she said.

'Why is it that whenever I come in here there's something going on?' said Jim.

'It's an illusion,' said Helen. 'You've usually just missed it. I guess that's the cross you've been given to bear, Jim.'

'Your hands are all covered in Tippex,' he said.

'Do we have any thinner? That'll get it off.'

'Don't give her any more solvents, Jim,' Maggie said. 'She's been sniffing the marker pens again.'

'That's not fair. It was only once. Alright, so maybe twice. I can handle it.'

'And how do you explain the blue around your nostrils?' said Maggie.

'Someone passed it to me and I didn't want to look naive.'

'Jesus Christ,' said Jim. He handed Maggie a piece of paper. 'This afternoon's agenda. You are coming to this meeting, aren't you – I mean, your double act hasn't been booked elsewhere?'

'I'm sorry, you'll have to ask our agent,' said Maggie. 'But she's out buying drugs at the moment.'

'Three o'clock,' said Jim. 'And bring the figures for the last quarter with you.' He left, shaking his head.

Maggie picked up the ball of paper and handed it to Helen.

'Take a letter, Mrs Clifton. And try not to screw it up this time.'

On the way home Helen went to Hannington's to look for a radio. She looked at the rows of them and balked; too many, too much choice.

'Helen!' Moira was making her way towards her. 'What a surprise!'

'Moira.' She tried to sound moderately pleased.

'Doing a little shopping, are you?'

No, thought Helen, I've come to contact my home planet through the display satellite dish. 'That's right,' she said. 'We need a radio.'

'Lovely.'

Moira was wearing a white furry hat; Helen stared at it, trying to figure out if the fur was real.

Moira realized where Helen was looking. 'Is there something . . . ?' she said, gesturing vaguely at her hat.

'No, not at all. That's a very nice hat.'

Moira looked at her suspiciously. 'I've worn it before.'

'I suppose I hadn't paid attention properly. It looks . . . warm. Fluffy.' And you look like a giant cotton bud, she thought.

'Well, thank you.'

'Anyway, I'm sorry I can't stop. I have to go up to the third floor to . . . to get some towels.'

'You need towels?'

'Mm. Don't know how we get through so many.'

'But there are plenty in your airing cupboard.' A pause so tiny only Helen and Moira could have noticed it. Then, 'So Dan said.'

'Did he? Fancy that.' Helen pushed the rising urge to laugh back down and allowed herself a small smile. 'Well.'

'I'll let you get on.'

'Right – can't stand here chatting or the store will shut and I won't have those sheets – um, I mean, towels.' She beamed. 'Linen. Now, make sure you don't stay in here too long: we don't want your head overheating, do we? Bye then, must dash.' Helen made a break for it.

She went up to the second floor and wandered around. The underwear department was edged with black lacy bras and panties on special offer and she stopped to look. She bought some, thinking it would surprise Dan to see her wearing them, thinking she would do something nice for him for a change.

Usha opened the door.

'I know it isn't time,' said Helen, 'but Dan rang – there's a meeting on and he can't make it tonight. I thought I could stop you going to any trouble and we could –'

'I've bought the ingredients so we might as well cook them, yeah?'

'Well, if you don't mind . . .'
'Don't be daft,' said Usha.
'Right, well, I'll come back later then.'
'Come in now and chop some vegetables.'
'Okay, but I must pop back upstairs – I'll be back in a minute.'
'I'll leave the door on the latch.'

Helen ran back upstairs to fetch a bottle of wine but decided against taking one. She didn't want to be the only one drinking. She looked around, wanting to take something down to Usha.

She sat down in the armchair and took the cushion into her lap. She thought about going out to the corner shop to buy . . . some chocolates, perhaps. Then it came to her. The cushion: it had some of Usha in it, after all. She went to see if she had any wrapping paper, hoping that Usha hadn't been merely polite when she seemed to like it so much. She couldn't find any paper. She looked at the crumpled collection of plastic bags in the kitchen cupboard. They seemed only to make the cushion more second-hand.

The phone rang and Helen started violently. She let the machine answer.

'Oh hello, Daniel, this is Mum. Hello, Helen, this is Moira.' She always felt compelled to give a translation. She always sounded slightly offended, too, as though suspecting they were deliberately not picking up the phone.

Helen grabbed the cushion and her handbag, and fled.

She pushed open Usha's door. On every surface in the living room candles glowed: in saucers, bottles, some floating in bowls of water scattered with petals, some wedged into bright Plasticine shapes – stars and crescents and wavy lines; a spectacular devotional disarray; lulling, silky light, smooth as syrup.

'Like it?' said Usha, coming out of the kitchen.

Helen nodded. 'It's . . .' It seemed pointless to elaborate. 'Oh, I brought you this.' She handed Usha the cushion. 'I hope you don't mind that it's . . . well, you know, it isn't new or anything but I thought . . .'

'You can't want to give it away. You made it.'

'No, I do. It seemed . . . right that you should have it.'

'That's wicked – I loved it the first time I saw it.' She put her hand on Helen's arm. 'I'm really touched.' She put the cushion down on the sofa. Its colours seemed to shift in the fluid light. 'Come and meet my brother.'

All the edges in the kitchen seemed harsh. Helen blinked. 'It's bright in here,' she said.

'That'll be Jaz's aura,' said Usha. 'He never goes anywhere without it. Helen, this is my brother, Jaz; and Jaz, this is Helen from upstairs.'

'Hello,' said Jaz, and they shook hands. His handshake was firm, his charcoal-grey suit impeccable, his dark blue turban beautifully tied.

'So,' said Helen. 'What can I do?'

'Um.' Usha looked around.

'If this poor woman you've conned into coming here is going to get anything to eat,' said Jaz, 'you're going to have to look at the book.'

Usha delved under the bulging carrier bags on the counter and pulled out a cookery book. 'Page twenty-four,' she said, handing the book to Helen. 'That's the plan. And a sort of curry thing.'

'That's the Punjabi term, obviously,' Jaz said to Helen.

Helen looked at the book. 'You're making chapattis – I've never seen that done before.'

'Oh, Usha's *seen* it done loads of times, haven't you, Ush?'

'Okay, so I've never done it before. It isn't difficult, though, look at the recipe. I've got the flour here.' She picked up a bowl and held it out to Jaz, who took a step back. She laughed. 'Don't worry, your suit is safe.' She grinned at Helen. 'He's so vain.' Usha put down the bowl. She looked around. 'There was an apron here when I moved in.' She took it from the back of the door and put it on. 'Right. Flour.' She picked up the bowl and put it down again. 'But I need to make some room first. Okay, Helen, I have a job for you. Look through these carrier bags and see what vegetables you can find. We should have cauliflower, carrots, potatoes, muli – well, you know the kind of thing you're looking for. There are some chillies somewhere, too, in a little brown bag with some ginger.'

'You're such a bullshitter, Usha,' said Jaz, leaning against the door frame and folding his arms. 'Naming ingredients doesn't make you a cook.'

She poked at the flour and turned swiftly on Jaz, who managed to deflect her hand. 'Hah!' she exclaimed. 'Got you!' She turned to Helen. 'Mind you, I was aiming for the end of his nose and all I've managed is a bindi.'

'Sorry?'

'The decoration you sometimes see on Indian women's foreheads.' She turned to Jaz. 'It suits you. Perhaps you should wear one.'

'I am not even going to answer that. And I think you should clean this off me.'

'Oh do you now?'

'Well, you put it there.'

'He has a point,' said Helen.

'But that doesn't mean I have to do what he says. When we were kids he would always end up being in the right – I could never work that one out. Do you remember, Jaz, that time by the swings – hey, that reminds me . . . I was in the park today and there are still loads of daisies. Hold on a minute.' She went to the living room and came back carrying a daisy chain. 'I made you this,' she said to Jaz. 'Do you remember, you showed me how to make them?' She put the chain around his neck. He didn't seem to worry about his suit. Usha licked the end of her finger and rubbed the flour away. 'There.'

Helen stopped rustling the carrier bags. Usha and Jaz looked extraordinary together. Helen felt winded. Jaz put his hands on Usha's shoulders and with exquisite gentleness moved her away and kissed her on the forehead.

'Get back to the kitchen, woman, now you've found out where it is.'

Usha found her place in the cookery book again and began scrutinizing the instructions. Jaz's fingers lingered over the daisies' innocent eyes. An electronic sound chirruped from his suit. He reached inside and took out a mobile phone, a slim model that didn't spoil the line of his jacket.

'Hello?'

Usha measured water into a jug.

'So what have you done?' Jaz asked irritably into his phone. He paused. 'Mm. And then what?'

Usha looked at him. 'What a yuppie,' she said to Helen. 'And to think I knew him when he wore much smaller suits.'

'You know, Subash,' said Jaz, 'you're about as much use as –' He listened for a few moments. 'Yeah, yeah. Alright. I'll be there. Just don't do anything.' He snorted. 'You can manage that, you've had plenty of practice.'

'Subash works for Jaz,' said Usha. 'He's our cousin.' She lowered her voice. 'He's the world's most useless person but he's family – what can you do?'

'I'll be there in ten,' said Jaz and folded his phone away.

'What's he been up to now?' said Usha.

'We've got someone else's delivery because of him, and an advertised promo starting tomorrow on stock that's still at the Seven Dials depot.'

'But you'll be back, yeah?'

Jaz shook his head. 'I don't think so.'

'Oh Jaz,' Usha said impatiently. 'I've got all this stuff –'

'I've got to go. I'm sorry, alright?'

'No,' sniffed Usha, 'but I suppose the demands of commerce and your obscene profits must come first.'

'Good girl: you're getting the idea. Anyway, it's not like I'd planned to come for food. There isn't usually any here,' he said to Helen. 'You're an honoured guest.' He ruffled Usha's hair. 'See you, kid.'

Usha glared at him. 'I wish you wouldn't do that.' She raised her flour-dusted hands. 'Give me a hug, then.'

'No chance.' He gestured to his suit. 'This is cashmere.'

'Nice to meet you, Helen. Hope you survive Usha's cooking. And I'll see you soon,' he said turning to Usha, 'phone you tomorrow.' He hurried off.

Usha went back to the book and read the recipe. 'I'm rapidly going off this idea,' she said.

'I'll help,' said Helen. 'It shouldn't take too long.'

'I have an even better idea,' said Usha. She got up and went into the living room. Helen followed. Usha rummaged around in a pile of papers. 'Here it is,' she said. They sat on the sofa. 'The Golden Temple Takeaway,' Usha read. '"The best anywhere." I like it: it's to the point. "We deliver." Even better.' She grinned at Helen. 'What do you reckon?'

'Well, food *does* taste better out of foil containers . . .' mused Helen.

'I've always thought so.'

'You should have said. I needlessly spent all those hours slaving over a hot casserole when you came round –'

'Food tastes better out of foil containers at *my* place,' said Usha. 'This is a natural takeaway zone. Trust me.' She handed Helen the takeaway menu. 'You choose for both of us.'

'What a team.'

They looked at each other and suddenly Helen was touching Usha's hair. Analysis crushed down on her. She took her hand away.

'Oh God, I'm sorry. I ... I don't ...' She lowered her gaze and gave a small miserable laugh. 'It must be the candlelight.'

She looked up as she felt Usha's hand on her own. She touched Usha's cheek; smooth, warm. Their kiss filled the space between them and when they drew apart they were both trembling. They smiled shakily and filled the space again.

The curve of Usha through fabric, then free of it as they touched; mirrored, completely known, wholly unknown. Helen, appalled at her black lace, started some mad apology; Usha silenced her, took the impediments away.

The simplicity astonished Helen; they seemed to hear a murmuring whisper beyond them both and listened without effort; she lay with her foolish smile reproduced on Usha's soft, new face and though some candles guttered out, leaving their sweet, crisp smell, most burned bright and steady, gilding the air while she and Usha turned and turned down familiar, untrodden paths.

14

Dan pushed his cold hands deep into his pockets. The bulbous dome of the theatre seemed to loom over the little park. The building's fire exit opened and for a moment he could hear the melancholy tones of instruments being readied for performance. The door closed. A match flared and briefly he saw the face of the man in evening dress as he lit a cigarette. Dan looked again at the black gates clawing at the space between the park and the street. His heart lurched. He watched the figure; darker than shadow the shape moved through the black pools between the lampposts. Each fierce white light briefly lit Lesley's paled face and funereal hair. As she approached he saw the red slash of her mouth and the stylized bruising of her eyeshadow.

'God, I'm cold,' she said. Her witchy appearance faltered close up; the tip of her nose was a definite pink. She sniffed. 'But I didn't want to come to your office – I mean, I know you don't want people to see –'

'I never said that. And see what, exactly? Look, Lesley, you know I'm concerned about your situation. That's why I'm here. So, what did you want to talk about?'

'Can we walk? It'll help me warm up.'

He saw how thin her coat was. She must be freezing. He was surprised at the curl of pleasure he felt at her discomfort. 'Let's do that,' he said.

They set off towards the confection that was the beautifully lit Royal Pavilion rising in eastern splendour into the damp English air.

'The fact is,' said Lesley, 'I'm not pregnant.'

'No baby.'

'No baby.'

'That's good news – a big relief.'

'I suppose it is,' she said. 'But I . . . never mind. It's much better this way.'

'There's plenty of time, Lesley. You have years and years ahead of you for having kids, if that's what you decide you want.'

'That's part of it – the fact that deciding wasn't involved. I'm not expressing this very well. I'm not even sure what it is I'm trying to say.' She sighed. 'I couldn't have gone ahead with it; but I'm sure that I couldn't have got rid of it, either.'

'You're bloody lucky you haven't had to make the choice.'

'You sound like my dad,' she snapped.

'It's a dirty job but someone's got to –'

'Okay, okay. But, even though I was horrified, I was proud, too, in a weird way.' She smiled. 'I could make a life.'

They walked on, thinking of her uncreated child. Silence held them together as they walked. Dan worked his hands up into the opposite sleeves of his coat; like small, cold paws on his forearms.

'Well, ' said Lesley eventually. 'Can I interest you in a coffee? I've got the car.'

Little fish going round and round. Other people from the house coming home; footsteps in the hall outside her door; voices only words away from being in her room, with her, with him.

'I should get home.'

'Will you ever . . .' She shrugged. 'I'll give you a lift, then.' She put up her hand. 'Don't worry, I'll drop you round the corner.'

'Could we stop on the way? I need to pick up some marking from another lecturer's flat.'

'Where would you like me to hide?'

Dan took her naked hand in his. 'He's away. He left yesterday evening for a couple of weeks.'

They turned their backs on the Royal Pavilion's clean white lines and began to walk towards the gate.

Dan looked at his watch: eleven forty-five. He watched the right-hand indicator on Lesley's car blinking at the junction, then she turned and was gone. He walked around the corner and approached the flat. Usha's window was lit but the glow was soft, as though just a lamp were on. He let himself in the main door. Should he knock at Usha's flat? He paused by the door; he couldn't hear anything, no voices, no music. He went upstairs.

Helen was sitting on the sofa, reading a book. The TV was on, the sound turned down.

'You're home late,' she said. 'Is everything okay?'

'I had to get those essays from Peter's afterwards.'

'Oh right. How did the meeting go?'

'Oh, you know.'

'You must be tired.'

'It's been a heavy day.' He turned to look at her; he felt he was forcing his body to act. 'So how was the meal?'

Helen closed her book. 'Nice. I met Usha's brother. He's quite … striking.'

'Good looks must run in the family.'

'Do you fancy her then?' said Helen. She had high colour in her cheeks; she'd probably drunk plenty of wine.

'I didn't say that.'

'But do you?' She wasn't looking for a fight; she seemed genuinely curious.

'I don't know. I don't really know her.'

'She's a nice girl. Woman.'

'I hadn't thought about it. Mildly, I suppose.' He loosened his tie. 'Why? Do you go for the brother?'

'Jaz.'

'Right, I remember Usha saying now.'

'He's too good-looking. There's something about that that makes me uncomfortable.'

'Interesting.'

'Inferiority complex, I suspect. Maybe it's some deeply instilled feeling that a man shouldn't be prettier than a woman. All very sexist and socially programmed, I suppose.' She used the remote control to turn off the TV. 'How's Peter?'

'Okay. Panicking about what to take. We had a discussion about how many pairs of underpants he should pack, then there was a sock crisis, but he calmed down when I reminded him that it is possible to buy socks in America.'

She looked at him curiously. 'Why is your hair wet?'

'It isn't.'

'Yes, it is. At the ends, by your collar.'

'Oh those. Yes. I had a shower at Peter's. You know, I thought by the time I get home it'll be late and I thought I might as well do it there. His suitcase was all dusty and I got kind of grubby.'

'I would have had Peter down as the type to be ready days in advance,' said Helen.

'I think time caught up with him. But he'll be fine – he's got three alarms set for the morning.'

'That's more like it.' Helen stood up. 'Talking of showers, I'll have one before bed.'

'You look nice.' She was wearing a silky black shirt and a long green skirt. 'Have I seen that shirt before?'

'Only twenty-three times. Approximately.'

'Well, it looks nice.' He touched the glassy fabric; Lesley's faded black cotton had felt rough. He dropped his hand.

'Thanks.'

Her cheeks were still pink; her eyes shone. 'My wife is a beautiful woman,' he said, awash with sudden sentiment.

She smiled. 'Your wife is also a smelly woman,' she said. 'I'm off for that shower.'

'It's bed for me, too,' Dan said. 'I'll turn the lights off in here.'

She left and reappeared again almost immediately. 'Oh,' she said, 'I nearly forgot. Mick rang for you while I was at Usha's; there's a message on the machine.' His whole body jerked. 'How did he manage to get out of that meeting?' said Helen. 'There must have been some swift manoeuvring there.'

'I . . .'

'He's a slippery bugger: he got that sabbatical, too, when no one was supposed to. You should try the sneaky approach, Dan, that's obviously the way to get what you want.'

'Obviously.' The word struggled out. Helen didn't seem to notice.

Dan splashed his face with cold water to try to clear the morning sluggishness but he still looked bleary from lack of sleep. He turned sideways and looked at himself in the big bathroom mirror. He pulled his stomach in. He pushed his hands together and examined his biceps and pectorals. He concentrated on holding his stomach in while he mixed up his shaving foam, trying to convince himself that it was his posture that was at fault. He ran a sinkful of hot water and applied the foam. He swished his razor in the water and noticed that his stomach had dribbled back into place. He looked in the mirror, at his whippy Santa beard, and met his own eyes. Ho, ho, ho, he mouthed.

He felt something on the floor under his foot: it was a fabric label. He picked it up: '100% Cotton Gusset. Size 12.'

Helen came into the bathroom. 'Have you seen my bracelet?' she said. 'Ah.' She picked it up from the shelf.

'Have you bought some new underwear?'

She gave him a sharp look. 'What?'

'I found this.' He handed her the label.

'Oh, right. Yes. New knickers, some of the old ones were knackered.'

'Knackered knickers. Has a nice ring to it.' He pulled his stomach in again, watching her in the mirror.

'Mm.' She went to the linen basket and took out a carrier bag.

'What's in the bag?'

'The knackered knickers.'

'How come they're in there? In a bag, I mean?'

'I ... put them in there last night. There didn't seem any point in washing old ones I wasn't going to keep.' She banged down the lid of the basket and the smell of worn clothes all crowded together was shoved at him. 'What's with the interrogation?' she demanded. 'I buy my underwear for my benefit, not yours.'

'That's a bit of a non sequitur, isn't it? I was curious, that's all.'

She looked sheepish. 'Sorry. I didn't sleep very well. I'll get the breakfast going.' She smiled at his reflection and left.

He began to shave, drawing clean pink roads through the snow. Helen came back into the bathroom. 'At least *I* use the bloody basket,' she said, holding up yesterday's guilty underpants. She dropped them into the basket and left shaking her head.

He watched the blood ooze from the cut's straight line. He dabbed at it with the towel; the mark gradually reappeared, the blood thickening into a soft, horizontal scab. His belly was hanging again.

He finished shaving, using the razor gingerly, all too aware of the raw edge stalking over treacherous, slippery skin.

'He lives near the department. It doesn't involve much work – it's only a couple of cats and some plants.' Dan reached for the marmalade: then

left the jar where it was and used Helen's low-fat spread on his toast. 'I can go at lunch time, or stop by after work.'
'You've been missing the ride home with Greg recently, anyway.'
'Mm. It's all this departmental assessment stuff. I have a huge pile of things on my desk to get through.'
Helen gestured to the table. 'Aren't you going to eat your other slice of toast?'
'Not today.'
'Are you feeling okay?'
'I'm fine,' said Dan. 'I thought maybe I'd try to cut back a bit.' He patted his stomach. 'I'm getting a bit too round for my liking.'
'You look the same as ever to me.'
'I want to avoid middle-age spread, that's all.'
'You look fine. And you're hardly middle-aged.'
'I don't want to wait till I get there to worry about my health.'
She looked at him. 'What's the matter, Dan?'
'Nothing. Just because I show a little concern about myself doesn't mean –'
Helen raised her hands. 'Alright, alright. I'll get some salad stuff in.' She made a note on her shopping list. 'But don't go nibbling at Peter's place.'
Dan had a wild urge to laugh. 'I can't see me getting into Whiskas somehow.' He got up from the table. 'I thought I'd go up there today. I can leave out enough food for the weekend. I'll go in to the department, too, I think. I can make a start on those assignments.'
'Don't forget your dad's coming round tonight to pick up that wine kit you never used. About seven, he said.'
'Oh, I'll be back long before then. What are you doing today?'
'Well . . .' Helen looked at her list. 'I've got to go to the shops. Usha might come with me; I said I'd call in on my way past.'
'I think I'll make a move now,' said Dan. 'The sooner I go, the sooner I get back.'
As he came down the stairs Usha's door opened.
'Oh,' she said. 'I thought you were . . .' She held her scarlet dressing gown closed at her throat.
'I'm sorry about last night,' he said. 'I had this work thing and –'
'No problem,' she said.
'I missed meeting your brother.'

'Oh well. Another time.'

'Well,' he said. 'Must be off. Why don't you go up? Helen says you're off shopping together later.'

'Yes.'

'Right. See you, then.'

'Bye.'

He walked to the front door, sure she was watching him, but when he turned at the door she was on her way up the stairs. The silky dressing gown moved like ripples spreading over viscous red. She paused, as though about to look back. He went out quickly.

As he walked to the bus-stop, the cold air made the cut on his cheek sting. He touched his face, expecting a trace of thick, sticky blood on his fingers, but there was nothing.

His face went on stinging.

15

'What do we do now?'
'Do?' Usha laughs.
'I'm serious,' says Helen.
They are sitting on opposite sides of the kitchen table. Helen, tidied away inside her clothes, fidgets with a piece of cold toast. Her eyes are so blue Usha feels the colour like a breath.
'Everything feels weird,' says Usha. 'But it's a good weird. Isn't it?'
'What about Dan?'
'What about me?'
'Perhaps we should...' Helen glances at her and then begins to scrutinize the label on the marmalade jar.
'Forget it ever happened?'
Helen doesn't reply, simply looks at her.
'I don't want to forget,' says Usha. 'I want to do it again.'
A tiny sound escapes from Helen.
'I...' Helen gets up, begins to gather plates and cups from the table. 'We can't...'
Usha stands, moves to her. 'Show me,' she says to Helen. 'Show me you don't want this.' She kisses Helen, feels response flowering from her mouth. They're both shaking. Usha draws open her dressing gown.

'So, how was the world of money counting today?' asked Helen, wiping clean the little bald heads of the mushrooms.
'There's been a rush on coupons from packets of cheese. Chrissie had to go and work on the tills: the smell made her feel sick.'
'It must have been really bad,' said Helen.

'No, it was okay. Being pregnant seems to have made her extra-sensitive to some things, that's all.'

'You never told me she was pregnant.'

'Didn't I? Oh well.' Usha poured herself a glass of orange juice and sat at the table.

Helen filled the kettle and plugged it in. 'Does she get morning sickness?'

'Not any more. She looks healthy – but she might always have looked like that for all I know.'

Helen set a saucepan down heavily on the cooker. 'Her first, is it?'

'No idea.'

'Aren't you interested?'

'Mildly,' said Usha. She looked at Helen. 'What's the matter?'

'Nothing. Nothing's the matter.' Helen banged a cupboard shut and poured some oil into the saucepan.

'Nothing,' repeated Usha.

'That's right.'

Usha looked at Helen's back. The whisper from the oil began to creep into the silence. Helen moved the pan off the heat and turned to face her. 'It's just that I . . .' She touched Usha's cheek and took a few paces away from her. 'I'd like to have a child. I can't.' Her arms hugged at her own body. 'Now you know.'

'You . . .' Usha didn't know how to narrow the sentence down and let it drift.

'I had an infection, years ago.' Helen smiled crookedly. 'You see before you a faulty woman.'

'These days can't they –'

'They can, often. It's a long, long story, Usha. It's not impossible but about as likely as . . . me spontaneously combusting. That's how Dan put it.'

Usha felt there was nothing adequate she could do in the face of Helen's sudden, revealed want. There was something enormous and daunting about it and it swamped her. Little fat Chrissie; and this woman burning with a bright, stifled fire.

Helen put the saucepan back on the ring and finished chopping the onions. Usha watched her work. When she walked past, Usha reached out and touched her lightly, and was suddenly angry that she had seen Dan do the same thing. Helen leant over; Usha felt the touch of her hair, that open kiss. Helen drew back and as she did so her blouse gapped; she wasn't wearing a bra. Her nipples nudged at the rich blue silk. Usha cupped the gentle weight of her breast. The timer on the cooker buzzed and Helen went and pottered with pans and ingredients. Usha looked at the childless woman and couldn't see anything missing.

Jaz sank into the chair. 'I've got a terrible headache.'
'What happened? You scared me when you said you were ringing from the hospital.'
'It's a long story.'
'I've got plenty of time.'
He took a deep breath. 'First of all, there were these two guys. In balaclavas.'
'Oh God – where?'
'In the car park at the back of the shop. Subash and I had just locked up. Suddenly two blokes appeared carrying bits of old plank. And one says, "You're getting on the boss's nerves. You're too cocky."'
'Who's the boss?'
'Beats me.'
'Come on, Jaz.'
'I have a suspicion.'
'You should report him to the police. You should –'
'Get real, Usha – I'll deal with this myself.'
'By ending up in Brighton General.'
'Let me finish.'
'But –'
'Just listen. The other guy says, "We're here to teach you how to be a better businessman." I get shoved and he yanks my turban off. All of a sudden Subash clutches at his chest, chokes out, "Oh, my heart," and falls on the floor. He's lying there and it's obvious there's nothing wrong with him. We all just look at him. Then the first guy looks at me and I can see he's trying not to laugh. He sort of waves his stick but it's all a bit half-hearted. Then I recognized him.'
'You're kidding!'
'"What's all this about, Ricky?" I said. "Oh bloody hell," he says and drops his bit of wood. He takes off his balaclava and says it's his little boy's birthday soon and there's been no work for months and he couldn't

pass up the chance of a few extra quid. "I wouldn't have hurt you," he says, "I was only aiming to scare you."'

'That's alright then, is it?'

'Ricky's a good bloke.'

'Good blokes attack people in deserted car parks, do they?'

'He wouldn't have done anything. So, anyway, the other bloke legs it. Ricky picks up my turban and brushes it off and hands it back to me. I decide to take him to the shop and let him choose something for the kid.'

'What's wrong with you? He –'

'Shush. He'll be useful to me now, that's why. So we go off back across the car park and Subash calls out, "Hey, what about me?" "Sorry, man," I said, "I thought you were dead. I was going to get a bin liner."' Jaz grinned. 'Only Subash could try to make out he's a martyr because he's got oil on that disgusting jacket of his.'

'So how –'

'I'm nearly done. We all went back to the shop. Ricky chooses a pair of jeans and I have to go to the stockroom to get the right size. I go to pull them off the shelf when suddenly I get hit on the head – by an iron, of all things. An iron falling from the shelf where Subash had put it because he "thought it might come in useful".' Jaz gave Usha a weary look. 'He found it in a skip a couple of mornings ago and thought maybe it could be fixed, so he did what any sensible person would have done – brought it inside and put it on a high shelf in the worst-lit part of the stockroom.' He began to unwind his turban. 'Ricky took me up to the hospital. Eight stitches.' An off-centre tonsure, surprisingly pale, and, crawling from the damage, stitches like insect legs.

'Oh Jaz. Your hair.'

'My head, you mean.'

'No wonder you've got a headache.'

'Subash seemed to think he was vindicated because it was a steam iron.' Jaz sighed. 'No, I don't understand it either.' He finished his tea. 'I should make a move.' He picked up the turban and began to retie it.

'What's going on, Jaz?'

'I'm doing very well. That means someone else is losing business along the way.'

'Here, let me do that.' Usha tied the turban for him. The dark blue

silk was dry as paper. 'Where did you get this cleaned? They overdid the starch a bit.'
'A friend. She's learning.'
'Who has Jaz been seeing?' says Mum. 'I know you know. Tell me.'
'No one. I don't know.' Usha keeps her eyes fixed on her mother's; to look away would be to admit to the lie. Her mother's mouth is fixed in a grim line that binds her face in anger.

The girl is Italian; she rests her head on Jaz's shoulder, has all the wide-eyed appeal of a baby animal. He says something to her and she laughs; her little puppy tongue licks at her lips, pink against her small sharp teeth. He holds her hand; her hand that is small and plump, like a paw.

Later he laughs about her, says she keeps her mouth firmly closed when she kisses. 'Most of the time,' he says, 'but she's learning.'

'You should stick with the local dry cleaners,' said Usha. 'They're more reliable.'

'But not as pretty.' Jaz picked up his coat. 'I'm off home to bed.'

'Have some more tea before you go.'

'Well . . .'

They sat in silence while he drank. Usha sat on the floor, resting against the warmth of his leg, waiting for the touch of his hand on her hair to tell her it was time for him to leave.

16

'I HAVE TO go.' Helen sat up and swung her legs over the edge of the bed.

Usha curled her long body around Helen, her head resting on Helen's thigh, her hair tangling across the sheet. Helen could hear the ticking of the watch on the bedside table. Usha wriggled close; she nuzzled Helen's belly. 'You smell nice.' She looked up. 'Don't go.'

'Dan will be home soon.'

Usha sat up. 'I want you to stay.'

Helen said nothing. Usha's mouth at her breast; her hands, not demanding, but sure, passing their certainty to Helen. Usha was always so sure. Helen let the absence of doubt wash over her, loosed the hunger.

The letter flap in the main hall banged. Helen jumped and guided Usha's head away. 'I must go.'

Usha lay back and drew the sheet over herself. Helen dressed, aware of being watched.

'Will I see you later?' said Usha. The sheet was tight over the curve of her breasts.

'It's difficult.' Helen fastened her belt. 'You know it isn't that I don't want to.'

'What's the time now?'

Helen picked up her watch. 'Half-seven.' She wriggled her hand through the metal bracelet.

'Your watch is on upside down,' said Usha. 'When will he get home?'

Helen took off her watch and put it back on. 'Maybe not until half-nine, but I have to –'

'Do you have sex with him?'

There is something fierce about him, but it's held back. He feels different; his body moves differently. Or is it that he's strange to her now because he isn't Usha? Definitely anger; he's being a bit rough. It excites her, this managed punishment. He keeps his eyes closed. She closes hers, strains against him as he holds her down.

Helen sat on the bed. 'Usha . . .'

'Is it better?'

'What do you expect me to say?'

Usha fidgeted with the sheet. 'That you'll come back. That I matter.'

'Oh God. Of course you do.' She stroked Usha's shoulder. Usha shook her off.

'Don't pacify me – answer me. Will you? Will you come back?'

'I . . . Yes. Nine o'clock?'

'We'll go out,' said Usha decisively. 'It's time we saw each other somewhere other than here.' She leant forward; her kiss was simple and demanding and Helen let her take her fill. Usha, always so sure.

As Usha was putting on her coat Helen heard Dan opening the main door. His footsteps paused outside Usha's door. Helen could feel him standing as still as she was. There was a pause, then a quiet knock. Usha put her arm out as if to restrain Helen and raised a finger to her lips. They all stood there; the silence was like a dense fog that crammed the ears.

Usha brushed her hair as they listened to Dan's footsteps continuing along the hall and up the stairs. The door of the flat closed.

Helen exhaled. 'That wasn't very nice.'

'Did you want to talk to him?'

'Well, no –'

'Then don't complain.' Usha fastened her coat. 'Let's go. I feel like I can't breathe here.'

They closed the door to the flat very quietly and tip-toed down the hall. Helen went out the main door first. Usha crossed the threshold and, looking straight at Helen, slammed the big door.

'Christ!' hissed Helen. She looked up to the first floor windows even though she knew the front door couldn't be seen from them. 'What did you do that for?'

'Don't know,' shrugged Usha. 'But I'm not sorry. Anyway, he doesn't know that it isn't me coming in.' She motioned to Helen. 'He won't be able to see us if we go out through here.' She led her through a gap in the hedge into the garden of the house next door. Smiling, she picked a leaf out of Helen's hair. 'Don't look so serious.'

'You're irresponsible.'

'You say the nicest things. Oh come on, it wasn't a major crime.'

'No, but –'

Usha grinned. 'So let's get on with our evening out.'

Helen felt her irritation fading. Usha's face was alight with mischief and it was hard to resist her. Helen kissed her quickly; Usha's lips were always warm.

'I'm sorry,' said Helen.

'You can kiss me whenever you like.'

'No, that's not what I meant.'

'I know it isn't,' sighed Usha. 'My poor serious Helen.'

They quietly made their way out into the bright street. As they walked Usha linked her arm in Helen's.

No one can tell, Helen thought, we're a couple of women friends, that's all. She felt ashamed of her shame; she didn't want to deny Usha, but that was better than anyone knowing. She tried to relax her arm but it continued to feel like a prosthesis; her real arm was wrapped tight around her body, holding everything in.

Usha suggested they go to the new café in Sydney Street. They walked down to Grand Parade. Victoria Gardens stretched out to the right, sandwiched between two main roads. The flowerbeds had been dug over and the damp earth lay sullen, its cosmetics stripped away.

'The tulips they grow here are beautiful,' said Usha. 'Red and yellow all squashed together, right up to the edge of the beds. You should draw it.'

'Seems a shame to have it stuck in the middle of the road like that. You can spot the tourists – they're so determined to have the Brighton experience they'll sit right in the middle of a load of bus fumes and take photographs of each other.'

'The flowers don't seem to mind it.'

'Maybe the Council puts artificial ones in so we won't know,' said Helen. 'Perhaps we've stumbled on a conspiracy.'

They crossed the road and turned left up Church Street. Helen was beginning to get used to the rhythm entailed in walking arm in arm. Although their arms were clumsy in thick coats she was aware of Usha's warm skin not far from her own. Suddenly Usha snatched her arm away. She looked like she wanted to run. The woman approaching them was in her thirties. She wore a padded coat like a deflated duvet; emerging from the bottom were brilliant green loose trousers gathered at the ankle and gold shoes that click-clacked busily towards them.

'Usha!'

'Hi, Auntie.'

'You're a bad girl, not to have been in touch.'

'I'm sorry, but you know how things are . . . This is my neighbour, Helen. Helen, this is my Aunt Rani.'

Rani's eyes were curious but friendly. 'I don't get to meet many of Usha's friends. I sometimes think she's ashamed of me.'

'She's my favourite aunt and she knows it,' said Usha to Helen.

'So, how are you getting on?' said Rani. Helen could feel Rani's concern like a weight. 'You know you can come and see me any time.'

'Things are fine,' said Usha. There was a pause. 'You?'

Rani nodded. 'Everything is good. I saw Veena this morning. She's looking well.' She leaned towards Usha. 'Maybe she's begun a baby, huh? It's about time she and Kirpal started –'

'We must go, Auntie – we're late.'

'You will come and see me, won't you?' said Rani, putting her hand on Usha's arm. 'You – we – have some things to sort out.'

Usha was already beginning to move away. She walked backwards for a few steps. 'Take care.'

Rani waved and Helen trotted after Usha. The crackle of Rani's footsteps faded away. Usha slowed down. They walked along side by side, not touching.

Her muscles are aching; sweat stretches a long gritty line down her back. She struggles with the mattress's obdurate lurches, falls with it into the hall. She props it against the wall and as she goes back into her room hears the heavy sigh of it folding to the floor. The room is completely empty. Indentations in the carpet are the ghosts of furniture; pale geometry marks the posters' absence. Bob has helped her move things into Dan's room, into the hall, into the already cramped living room. Dan will be back from his trip in ten days. Bob thinks she's planning a surprise. But this clearing is as imperative as vomiting; she works without knowing why, aware only of the enigma of its necessity.

Lying on the floor she stares up at the light. When she closes her eyes she can see weird shapes pulsing in her personal darkness. The carpet is prickling at her through her shirt. A heart beats somewhere above her as Bob practises on muffled drums. Her bruised vagina cringes away from her legs. The heart stops. She waits for it to restart. Silence crawls all over her.

She waits.

'What on earth possessed you to offer to look after his cats?' said Helen.

'His flat is close to the department,' said Dan. 'It was no trouble.'

'Usha said maybe you were using it to have a torrid affair.' The words sliced somewhere deep in her chest; she thought Dan must see her revealed through the wound.

Dan opened his mouth, closed it and opened it again. 'Where the hell would I find the time?'

'It was only a joke.'

'You know I've been working to clear the backlog. And that stupid assessment stuff, for God's sake.'

'I know. Come on, Dan, where's your sense of humour?'

'I guess I'm tired.' He looked sheepish. 'Sorry.'

'Affairs take a lot of energy – I don't think you can spare it.' She smiled, wanting to hug away his tiredness; Usha's body was in the way. She patted his arm. 'I'll get you some coffee.'

He caught her around the waist as she stood up and slipped his hand up her skirt. She felt the erratic ticking as he snagged her tights. She pushed his hand away. 'You'll ruin them.'

'I'll buy you some more.' He squeezed her breast, too hard.

'For Christ's sake, Dan, that hurt.' She pulled away.

'I misjudged it. Sorry.'

His expression was hard to read. She cupped a hand to her breast as she went to the kitchen and the feel of Usha flickered through her. Dan's actions often seemed coarse now. Usha's firmness of intent was a grace, an agreement.

Helen prepared the coffee, aware that the comparisons had begun.

The whisper of their skin, the meshing and freeing of fingers, the breath like sea shifting, currents calling at the edge, at the middle. Curve of a belly, curve of a breast, Usha's mocha skin; it smells distantly of cinnamon, a faint keen edge as though she has recently come in out of the wind, a blurry trace of something almost eclipsed; Helen breathes absolute need, absolute pleasure; diffuse, benevolent fire, woven deep.

'I think about you all the time.'
'Even when you're having sex with your husband?'
Helen blushed. And nodded. They giggled conspiratorially.
'You know,' said Usha, 'I'm glad you don't have children. This – us – probably wouldn't have happened at all.'
'Why?'
'You wouldn't have let it. The threat would have been too much.'
Helen sighed. 'I have felt threatened. So much confusion about my desire. About you.'
Usha smiled. 'And it's all so simple.'
'Well, there's simple, and then there's not quite as complicated as you thought at first.'
'Have it your way. But it's even less complicated than that, honest.'
'Okay,' said Helen. 'I look forward to realizing it.'
'You said the infertility thing is a long story.' Usha plumped up a pillow and sat back. 'I'm listening.'
'You know about the infection: it affected my Fallopian tubes. They're pretty damaged.'
'There's nothing they can do?'
'No. My ovaries produce eggs quite happily but transporting them around is a bit of a problem.'
'So if your ovaries are okay . . .'
'I know what you're thinking,' said Helen. 'What about the test-tube baby type of thing?'
'And?'
'This is where it gets difficult to explain. I could put myself up for that but . . .' Helen took a deep breath and exhaled slowly. 'For all I say, I guess I don't want a child badly enough. That's what Moira said.'
Fat folder bulging with instructions on how to make a grandchild. Moira trying to shove her into a space that doesn't fit, happy to eviscerate baby-shaped flesh from her.
'You told me Moira also said that putting swear words in dictionaries advocates their use.' Usha raised her eyebrows. 'Does Moira have anything sensible to say about anything?'

Helen laughed. 'Not that I know of.'

'So, go on.'

'Yes, I could have surgery on my tubes. Ten per cent chance of success. And every month wondering if this is the month it will have worked. Or direct implantation of an egg that's been fertilized outside: chance of success – minimal. And the strain . . .'

'But these things *would* increase your chances, wouldn't they?'

'God, it's difficult to explain. I've been investigated, poked, prodded, I've had my tubes X-rayed, I've had a laparoscopy – they shove a tube through your belly button that they can see through – I've had speculums winding me open and closed, and rubber-gloved hands grubbing around while stupid doctors see only a malfunctioning organ with an incidental, inconvenient person attached; and the nurses with their neat little uniforms that make you feel that having your knickers off is sheer bad manners – they all try to hold facile conversations with me about fucking *holidays*. Oh God, oh God, I can't let it happen any more, I can't *invite* it, I can't.' She was shaking; clutching a pillow to her she buried her face in it for a moment, then raised her head. 'To go through more . . . to have eggs implanted . . .' She looked at Usha, almost pleading. 'It would be functional rape.' She shook her head. 'No.' She held the pillow tighter. 'No.'

'It's okay,' said Usha, taking the pillow from her. She held her and rocked her gently. 'No more.' Helen could hear her steady, confident heartbeat.

Usha laid her back on the bed and in the warm comfort of her mouth Helen let it all go. When she came, her face was wet with tears but she smiled and smiled, and Usha's beam returned her light.

17

*Y*OU ARE HERE. A black arrow bleeding into purple fuzziness behind the scratched plastic. The sunlight made his eyes hurt.

'They closed it down,' said Lesley.

'Looks like they closed the whole town,' said Dan. An unimpressed cat watched them from a window. The street looked as still and flat as a photograph.

Lesley stepped back and looked up at the curly writing over the window blindfolded with posters. 'The Misses Larousse Exhibition of the Grotesque,' she read out. 'There was a two-headed cat,' she added wistfully.

'Stuffed, presumably.'

'Of course.' She shot him a look. 'How do you expect it to live?'

How did it manage to grow up? he wanted to ask. 'Let's get a drink somewhere,' he said. Two hours in the car heading for Lesley's surprise. An exhibition of the dead. The weird dead. He cheered up. At least it was closed.

They walked down the main street. The atmosphere was glutinous; Dan felt the effort of putting one foot in front of the other; sounds seemed to take too long to reach them. Even the breeze lifting Lesley's hair did so slowly, letting it fall with apparent relief.

'Strange place,' he said.

'Mm. Great, isn't it?'

'Shame about the museum.'

'No call for it these days, I suppose. People are too complacent.' Lesley nibbled at a hangnail. 'They're not interested in mystery any more.'

'Maybe the exhibits were a bit . . . gross?'

'They made you think,' she said. The hangnail had begun to bleed. She wiped it absentmindedly on her black skirt.

'What about this place?' suggested Dan. Leaded windows bulged like eyes. A sign tempted them to 'HAVE A HOT UNCH'. The little plastic 'L' clung to the lower rim of the sign. Lesley tapped the case and the letter joined several others at the bottom of the frame.

'Random events,' she said. 'I'd like to know what the other letters down there are. It might spell something.'

'Are you expecting a message?'

'Don't be snide, Dan. Rationality isn't everything.'

'What if it spelt "lopk"? What would that mean?'

'You're being stupid now.'

'I'm not. If spelling something is significant, why shouldn't *not* spelling something be significant as well? And "lopk" might be something in another language, you never know – the message might be to scour all the dictionaries you can find.'

She rolled her eyes and turned into the pub doorway.

'It's a reasonable question,' he said. 'How do you decide what's meaningful?'

'How do you?' she replied without looking around.

'Doesn't she look awful,' said Lesley, looking over at the barmaid. 'All that make-up.'

'You can talk.' Her lips had left a kiss on the glass.

'Mine is a statement,' said Lesley.

'You mean you're young and she isn't.' Deep lines ran their crazy paving around the woman's eyes but her cheeks looked soft and youthful. The scars from sucking countless cigarettes dented the skin above her lips.

'It's a question of aesthetics,' she said defensively. 'So, do you fancy her?'

Dan tried to imagine admitting to the puzzling desire that had prickled through him, however briefly, when the woman had spoken, her voice cosy, like she was reading a bedtime story. 'Hardly,' he said.

'Well then.' Lesley repeatedly tapped one of her rings against her glass. 'Our day trip hasn't really worked out, has it?'

'I'm sorry. I haven't been much fun.'

'Not as much as usual,' she conceded. She fondled his knees under the table. 'You can practise later.' She grinned.

I should stop this, he thought.
He thought about the soft white flesh of Lesley's inner thighs instead.
'Drink up,' she said. 'There's another place I want to take you.'

Dan followed Lesley through the iron gates. The wrought metal strained into spikes at the top; the old blood of rust made his hand orange. The sunlight cut sharp, pale edges, even into the dead rustle of the grass. Sodden leaves were squashy under their feet and the open smell of mould rose up as they walked. Trees meshed branches above them, netting out the overblown clouds.

'Often in the summer you can't see the sky,' Lesley said.

Rhododendron, heavy with dark, greedy leaves, criss-crossed over itself in ostentatious success, mumbling away into shadow.

'It was an ornamental garden once,' she said. 'There's a big house . . .' She waved her hand. '. . . somewhere.'

'Does anyone live in it?'

She shook her head. 'It's something civic now. This bit's too far away for them to be bothered with.' She stood and looked around. 'There's the little Chinese birch. It's just past there.' The trunk was hung with shreds of satin skin. She took hold of one as she passed and it tore away as neatly as a plaster.

The figures were set on a large square base. Dan's eyes were on the same level as Jesus's crotch. A woman slumped at His feet, reaching up to the Son of God, fingers taut with pleading. He stood, impassive, gazing over her head, a child stretched over his arms, its throat exposed.

'After years and years of trying, the couple had a child,' said Lesley, running her hand over the softened jag where the tip of the woman's nose had been. 'They planted the garden to celebrate. On her fifth birthday the little girl fell in the pond and drowned. They had this memorial made.'

'Oh God.' It could as easily have been a depiction of withholding as of taking away.

'They drained the pond but on the anniversary the mother tried to drown herself in the stream that had fed it. A gamekeeper found her and dragged her out but her brain was affected. So the wife was turned into a child.'

'What happened to them?' He didn't want to know. Knowledge was smothering him.

'The husband sang her nursery rhymes and continued to exploit the proletariat.' She tried to look up Jesus's gown. 'Or something like that.'

A clot of rage struggled in his throat.

'It's only a story,' she said. 'Overprivileged people get all the attention. Infant mortality was worse with the poor.' She shrugged. 'Sure it's sad. But the only reason they didn't buy a baby was because they thought they were superior. They couldn't breed, but –'

'Christ!'

'What?'

'Was it true? Was any of it true?' He knew he was holding her arm too tightly; he squeezed harder.

'You're hurting me!'

'Answer me.'

'Yes,' she said quickly, prising at his fingers. He released her. Rubbing her arm she glared at him. 'What is it with you?'

'Why did you bring me here?'

'The trees. The statue. It's beautiful.'

'I want to go back to the car.' His voice was quavering, his throat tight.

'Then we'll go.' There was puzzled pity in her look. He couldn't bear it.

In the car he heard the weary necessity of his tears but muffled somehow, like overhearing someone through a wall. He didn't feel better afterwards. Lesley patted him uncertainly then tried to hold him, but the contact of their bodies felt polite; forced apart by the gear lever, by him.

Maybe she was angry with him. He was tired, too tired to pay enough attention. She put his coffee down.

'Thanks.'

Helen gave him one of her tight smiles and went and sat next to Usha on the sofa.

Helen and Usha. Usha and Helen. Each like the negative of the other.

'So, Usha, how's the great world of commerce?'

'Raking it in. But you know, I'd never realized how much money smells.'

'Filthy lucre,' he said. In the silence first Helen then Usha blinked.

He felt like a particularly boring exhibit. He picked up his mug by the edge; it was hot and in his hurry to get hold of the handle he spilled a little coffee onto his trousers. 'Oh bugger.' He patted the patch: hot and damp as breath for an instant on his leg then just slightly darker brown fabric. He looked up, sensing an exchange between the women, but they were looking at him. Helen leant on the arm of the sofa; a fraction of a second later Usha leant towards her own. Their symmetry suddenly irritated him.

'You've been working late then,' said Usha.

'Too much to do in too short a time,' he said. 'The usual thing.' He sipped his coffee. Too hot. Heat fingered out through his chest.

'Still, no cats to feed now,' she said.

'No. No cats.'

'Helen mentioned it.'

'Uh huh.'

Helen was looking at Usha; that assessing, pleased look she had when she had finished a piece of work. They must have been talking. What had she told her?

'I worked in a supermarket once,' he said. 'Filling shelves. It was all women on the checkouts in those days.'

'And now there are equally crap opportunities for both sexes,' said Helen. 'Choice, you see. If the Conservatives have done one thing for this country . . .'

'It'd be a bloody miracle,' he chorused with her. 'Old joke,' he said to Usha. She suddenly got to her feet.

'I'll be going,' she said abruptly. 'I have work in the morning.'

He closed his eyes and tilted his head back against the soft murmur of their voices out in the hall. He thought about being in bed with Helen, the way her head tucked in so neatly under his chin when she cuddled up to him. Lesley was angles, apologies. But she snuffled as she dozed, like Wally had when he was a puppy.

'What are you grinning at?' said Helen as she came back into the room.

'A stray thought.' He opened his eyes. 'Is Usha alright?'

'Fine. Why?'

'She seemed a bit . . . subdued, I suppose.'

'I think the money-counting's getting her down a bit. Piles of colour-coded paper and no windows.'

'Poor kid. Maybe she could find something else. Or even go on the tills – that would be better, wouldn't it?'

'Mm. If it was me I'd rather avoid the great British public.'

'And their screaming kids.'

The slightest pause as they watched the child word take flight.

'You look terrible,' she said.

'Why, thank you, wife.'

'Exhausted, I mean.' She yawned. 'I'm pretty bushed myself.' She took his mug. 'Bedtime. After you in the bathroom.' She picked up her and Usha's cups and headed for the kitchen. Her hair was tied back into a little pony tail; pale down fuzzed her neck.

'Helen . . .'

She turned. Her fingers stretched to support the cups. 'Mm?'

He wondered what he thought he could say. 'Nothing. Doesn't matter.'

She turned away again. He heard her singing while she rinsed the cups but it was too quiet for him to identify the tune.

He went to brush his teeth.

The lad is bony, angular with spite. A pus-ripe spot mountains on his forehead.

'Nice football,' he says.

Danny turns it in his hands, feels the trickle of the piece of something that's been in there since he got the ball. His stomach is heavy, thumping sluggishly with his pulse. Sun spills over his head like hot water.

'Present from your mummy, was it?' The boy sniggers, then the other three. Danny is minute; a speck in the recreation ground. The boy takes a step towards him. Danny steps back. Another step. Another step back. Happy malice in the boy's face.

'Give us it.'

Danny imagines running. He had a dream where he could fly. It was so easy. He was crushed when he woke. All lies.

The boy grabs for the ball. They're rolling on the grass. Loud breaths. Danny sees the feet of the companions; a row of shoes, a row of legs. Silent. Watching. Curled round the ball he kicks out. Something soft, a gasp, no more motion. He stands. The lad's face is the colour of pearly phlegm. Danny can taste dust on his lips. The ball is solid space under his arm. They all look down at the pain. Something sharp and cold pierces Danny from the inside. He kicks the boy's arm, hard, enjoying the bruise he won't see, then runs and runs, full of an energy he doesn't want, that he doesn't know how to escape.

'Budge over.' Helen got into bed, smelling minty. Her hair was kinked where the winder had been.

'Your hair's dented,' he said, stroking it. Lesley's hair reminded him of dried flowers. Helen's felt liquid in comparison, its smooth blondeness very much alive.

The corridor is gloomy. He sees Bob ahead, talking to a girl. She walks away, her long blonde hair like a light, something fluid about the unhurried sway of her hips.

'Who was that?' he says, casually.

'It'll recover,' she said.

He felt shut away from her. Was she just the same? Was it him?

She snuggled down under the duvet. He reached for her, suddenly anxious to feel her skin, her breasts. He stroked her hip and round into her pubic hair.

'I'm tired,' she said. Gentle and final.

'I'd like . . .' He wanted her to comfort him. '. . . I want to hold you, that's all.' He must use her to comfort himself.

A while later he could tell by her breathing that she was asleep. He lay fitted around her, waiting for sleep, listening to the whisper of Usha's music creeping up through the floor.

18

Usha got up and went to the window. The snow was falling more thickly now, great gouts of white pressing down on the ground. Stray flakes clung silently to the window and dissolved. 'I want you for myself,' she said. Her breath cobwebbed at the glass and was gone. 'I hate it. You and him. It drives me mad.'

'We haven't . . . for quite a while now. It doesn't feel right.'

'But you go to bed together, get up together, have breakfast and dinner together. You know what I'm talking about.'

Helen nodded.

'Come be with me,' said Usha. Suddenly simplicity and absolute certainty: the power flooding through her made her smile. 'I can give you something he never could.'

'A discount at Sainsbury's?'

'I can grow us a child.'

'Jesus.'

'Or if it's a girl, Meera might be nice.'

Two bright spots of red had appeared on Helen's cheeks, crude as rouge on a china doll.

'Don't joke about it. It's cruel.' Helen's voice had shrunk to a whisper.

'I'm serious.'

'This isn't something you do like . . . like buying a present.'

'This is for us. It's perfect, isn't it?'

'And I suppose Sainsbury's have a semen counter now?'

'Who needs it? You have a dispenser right in your own home.'

Helen laughed bitterly. 'Excuse me, Dan, would you mind giving me some sperm so I can leave you. Yeah, right.'

But Usha could see the light firing her eyes. She stroked Helen's cheek. 'I mean it,' she said, falling into blue. She held Helen's hand against her belly. 'Just imagine,' she said.

The heavy snow made the world beyond the window a restless blank. The main front door opened and closed: Dan coming home. Helen didn't move but continued looking at Usha, refusing to believe her and refusing not to.

'Did I tell you Mum's been having headaches?' said Jaz, as he was leaving.

'She's seen the doctor?' asked Usha. 'And I don't mean Dad.'

'Dad examined her but says there doesn't seem to be anything wrong. He prescribed her –'

'Some painkillers. I'm right, aren't I?'

Jaz nodded. 'She's been complaining of aching all over as well. I think she just needs some exercise – she mopes around the house when she's not at work.'

'And obviously your medical diagnoses are in great demand, what with you having a degree in Business Studies. The new face of the NHS.'

'I think you're spending too much time with that Helen. You even sound like her.'

'Helen's great. She makes more sense than you do.' Usha tried to imagine explaining the space inside her that was Helen, the absolute necessity of holding her. And she loves me, she thought excitedly, wanting to tell him. He sat there: handsome, familiar, completely oblivious. She felt irritated with him for not noticing she was changed.

The room is like a cave. It is dark and warm, the soft heat is a cushion all around them. Thick blue curtains reach down to the floor; one slit, as thin as paper, draws a bright line in the velvet.

'At least she's older and wiser than you,' he said. 'Maybe that'll be a good influence.'

'Maybe.'

Jaz glanced at his watch. 'I'm late.' He ruffled her hair. 'See you, Trouble.'

'I wish you –'

'Wouldn't do that. I know.' He grinned. 'Life, eh?'

He ruffled her hair again and dodged out of the way of her retaliation.

When he was gone she curled up with the cushion, waiting her turn, aware of Helen's other life being played out above her.

Usha answered the door.

'Hi,' said Helen. 'I'm on my way out. I have to pick up some stuff for dinner.'

'Come in for a minute.'

Usha kissed her. Helen's mouth was soft and sweet as fruit.

'New lipstick,' said Usha. She kissed her again. 'Tasty.'

'My God,' said Helen. 'I've just realized you're wearing an apron.'

'You make it sound like a perversion.'

'I just haven't seen you in one before.'

'You have. The night . . . I cooked.'

They exchanged a smile.

'Well, the frills are very becoming,' said Helen.

'I'm sure they looked even better on Ivan.'

'You may be right. Anyway, Maggie rang and said how about a get-together Friday night?'

'Will Lou be there?'

'Don't know,' said Helen. 'If you'd rather not –'

'I don't think I should let her get me down. And I liked Maggie, it'd be good to see her again.'

'Right,' said Helen. 'I must get to Safeway.' She opened the front door. 'Why *are* you wearing that apron?'

'A friend of mine from uni is coming by sometime soon – she's very into order. She used to write down all the calories she ate until she read that this could mean she was heading for an eating disorder. Now she keeps a daily running total in her head.'

'Much less noticeable.'

'Poor Cara. Food is her enemy *and* her best friend. A bit like you and Dan.' Usha paused. 'I shouldn't –'

Helen shrugged.

'So, Cara and possibly Tracy – she's doing French – will come. Maybe tomorrow, or maybe next weekend.'

'I have to go to lunch at Moira's tomorrow.'

'You said.'

Usha watched Helen leave then wrestled the vacuum cleaner out of the cupboard and hoovered up part of the carpet's speckly pattern. When she was done she tied her hair back, put on some rubber gloves and went to the kitchen to fetch a duster. As she set off back into the living room the doorbell rang.

It was a balding man in his sixties. He looked her up and down.

'I'm looking for Mr Liebovich.' Usha opened her mouth to answer. The man continued. 'You work for him, hmm?'

'I –'

'How did he persuade you to come in at the weekends? You people are hard workers, I'll give you that. I was saying so to our Mr Iqbal on the corner only the other day. And you ladies are such pretty things, like brightly coloured birds, you are.' The man stopped. 'Now where was I? Oh yes, I've a message for the Cliftons upstairs. I'm Mr Clifton senior.' His eyes narrowed. 'You do speak English?'

Usha had a vivid image of snapping a rubber glove into that well-fed face.

She nodded.

'Tell you what, I'll write it down.' He fished a pad out of his back pocket and wrote a note. 'So if you could pop this through their door – save these old legs a trip up the stairs.' He folded the page with excruciating precision and held it out. He and Usha looked at it. He jiggled it slightly as though trying to tempt a timid animal with a tidbit. They looked at it some more then Usha cracked and took the note.

'Thank you, my dear.' He turned and made for the front door, then paused. 'Oops!' he exclaimed and came back. 'Nearly forgot.' He pressed a fifty-pence piece into Usha's free rubber-gloved hand. 'Not at all,' he said and bumbled back down the hall and out of the front door.

Usha stood in her doorway, gazing at the coin.

'No textbook today?'

Surjeet sat down beside Usha.

'It's hard to concentrate in here,' said Usha.

Surjeet looked around the canteen. 'No hallowed halls of learning here, just real life.' She leant forward and peeked at the cover of Usha's magazine. '*True Confessions*, hmm? I'm more of a *Hello!* person myself.'

'I found it on the table –'

'Of course you did. Nothing wrong with a bit of relaxation.'

A fight broke out in the lunch queue. A long ribbon of tomato ketchup wriggled through the air and landed ripely on the overall of a young man near the back.

'Aaah!' he yelled. Clutching his chest, he fell to the ground. 'I am killed!' he cried.

'Those lads,' tutted Surjeet. 'Not enough work to do, that's their problem. They want to try the tills for a change – *I* don't have the energy for that sort of thing.'

They watched two men drag the lad in the tomatoed overall along by his feet while he gave a hearty rendition of the funeral march. Coming through the door was the assistant deputy under-manager of Morning Goods and Fancy Confectionery: he put his pen into his breast pocket and strode purposefully, and with some satisfaction, towards the mêlée.

Surjeet began to get up. 'Oh, I nearly forgot. Me and some of the girls are having a night out, and someone suggested that you might like to come.'

'When?'

'Friday, we thought.'

'Sorry, I can't. I've got something on.'

'Oh dear what a shame another time maybe,' said Surjeet without punctuation.

'Yeah, another time.'

Surjeet left without looking back.

She holds out her arms and admires the brocade curling around her cuffs, rough as string against the pink satin. The same gold decorates her collar, scratching at her neck. She eases it away from her skin, feels the claws against her fingers.

'Stop fidgeting, Usha,' says her mother, whose own salwar-kameez is black shot through with rainbow threads. She looks like fireworks.

Dad uses a pencil to scratch under his turban. Mum snatches it away and straightens his tie again. He carries the tray loaded with cups to the living room; Usha and her mother follow.

An Indian woman with greying hair sits swathed in pale blue. She speaks; to Usha it is a soft metallic rain, spotted with meaning. Something about the cups and ladies. Mum replies in the same alien harmonies.

Dad puts the tray down on the table. 'We do things a little differently here,' he says. 'It is our choice.'

The lady speaks again and looks at Usha. 'Usha,' she says: another nugget of meaning. She gestures her to come forward. She fingers Usha's kameez, speaking half-familiar sounds that are the stuff of stories, of songs.

'Greet your grandmother,' says Mum. 'She's come all the way from India.'

Usha embraces the woman's knees, speaks the Punjabi she has been taught for the occasion, feels the stranger's hand on her head. Feels, too, the immediate transfer of interest as the door opens.

'Ah!' rings the metal-edged voice. 'Jasbir!'

Everyone turns to look at him.

The brocade scrapes at Usha's throat.

'Is that dress new?' asked Helen as she came in.

'No. I was sorting some stuff out and rediscovered it.' Usha looked down at herself. 'I'm not sure about it – I like the colours but it makes me look pregnant.'

They looked at each other.

'Not that there's –'

'No,' said Helen.

'I meant what I said.'

'You can't know that this feeling will last.'

'No one ever can,' said Usha.

'You're young...'

'Oh please. Where do you get off telling me my decisions are inferior because of my age? What's the magic threshold – twenty-two point four years? Twenty-eight and three-quarters, providing I also own my own yoghurt-making machine?'

'Don't be silly.'

'Is it any wonder? Don't punish me because you're afraid of what I'm offering.'

'Of course I'm afraid! And so should you be.'

'Your problem is you confuse the unknown with your fear of it. Where's hope? Where's sheer excitement?'

'You go too fast,' said Helen. 'I feel like I'm always trying to catch up.'

'I may get there first but that means I've had time to look around.'

Helen nodded. 'I know.' A small hopeful smile. 'I'm trying.'

'Only sometimes.' Usha slipped her arm around Helen's waist and planted a gentle kiss on Helen's ear. 'That reminds me, I haven't put my earrings on yet.' She fetched them from the bedroom and put them on. 'Well, how do I look?' she asked.

'Those greens and reds are great on you. Like those amazing rainforest birds.'

Usha pushed away her irritation; Helen couldn't help it if her father-in-law had already spoiled the words.

'Do you do Christmas, Usha?' Maggie grinned. 'I hope that's not an annoying question.'

'Do you mean me personally or Sikhs?'

'I meant you. It would seem a bit weird for Sikhs to do the baby Jesus thing.'

Usha and Helen exchanged a glance. 'Well,' said Usha, 'my father's always been into doing English stuff so it seems natural to have a tree and presents and all that kind of thing. And we celebrate Sikh festivals, too.' She grinned. 'He likes to have a good time.'

'So there are advantages to this dual-culture stuff,' said Maggie. 'How do I apply?'

'Try living in Punjab,' said Helen.

'Does it snow there?' asked Maggie.

'I have no idea,' Usha said.

All the different smells are like voices trying to get her attention, mingling with the shouts of the people-crammed market. Her hand slips from her mother's and she feels the shove of a wave of people lapping at her back. Too many colours. Too many sounds. She opens her mouth to try to drown them out with her own voice. Jaz is suddenly there, her hand is cupped in his. She lets the breath she has gathered go. 'What are they saying?' she asks. 'Why can't I understand what they're saying?'

'I was taken there once when I was little,' said Usha. 'It was hot.'

The waiter gave them menus and disappeared behind the line of plastic palms that separated the two serving areas. Usha idly watched him through the palm leaves. He approached the corner table and took out his pad. Surjeet looked up and straight at Usha. She nudged Geeta. The gazes of half-a-dozen Asian women dominoed in her direction. She gave them a little wave. Geeta waved back and Surjeet nudged her again, hard. The scrutiny made Usha feel trapped.

'I'm off to the loo,' she said. She escaped down the narrow passageway into a pinkly tiled Ladies' reflected back in a pink-tinted mirror. Little pink flowers were printed in curlicues on the cubicle doors.

When she came out of the cubicle Surjeet was looking in the mirror. 'Doesn't do much for your skin tone, this mirror, does it?' she said.

'You're not pink enough to start with, that's the problem,' Usha replied.

'You don't have that trouble, do you?'

Usha stood beside her and looked at their reflections. 'We look pretty much the same to me.'

Surjeet arched her eyebrows. 'You know what they say about appearances.'

'That you shouldn't believe what you see. Or, should that be what you think you see.'

'Hmm.' Surjeet adjusted the drape of her chunni. 'Another one of your friends has arrived. Shouldn't you be getting back?' She picked up her handbag. 'Unless you want to listen to me have a wee.'

'I'll give it a miss, thanks,' said Usha.

'See you Monday, then.'

Dismissed, Usha opened the door.

'Oh, I meant to tell you,' echoed Surjeet's voice.

Usha turned.

Surjeet peeped around the cubicle door. 'I nearly forgot,' she said. 'Surinder says hello.' She closed the door and locked herself in behind the clusters of painted petals. She began to hum.

The rustle of fabric drove Usha out into the corridor. There was nothing else for her to do but go back to the table.

19

'You were late back last night,' Helen said.
'Peter's got a new computer.'
'You hate computers.'
'Well, Peter doesn't,' said Dan. 'As a matter of fact, it was quite interesting – the word-processing package could be useful.'
'My God, you'll be saying you want a car next.'
Dan looked at the marmalade jar then took a bite of his plain toast. 'Funny you should say that. Evie's selling her Metro and I had this sudden longing for a car.'
'I don't know why she ever bothered with one. She only lives in Brighton.'
'Hove, actually.' He sipped his coffee. 'We could afford it.'
'But we've talked about this – remember the environment? The grubby green bits between here and the office?'
'I know. Still . . . It can be a real pain having to rely on other people to give you lifts.'
'Get a bus. Get a taxi.'
Dan made a face. 'It's not the same.'
'It'd be all very well for you. I can't drive.'
'I'd take you places.'
'So *I'd* still have to rely on someone else to give me a lift. You don't mean *we* should get a car – *you* should.'
'You could take lessons.'
'I don't want to,' said Helen. 'I don't want a car.'
'You don't want me to have one is what you're saying.'
'No. Yes. Is it?'

'Sounds like it to me. And there *is* something miserable about being so determinedly green.'

'Are you working up to a "humourless environmentalist" joke?'

'No,' Dan said. 'But our little gesture doesn't make any difference to anything. That's all it is – a gesture.'

'If everyone tried –'

'But they're not going to, are they!' He pushed his plate away. 'What's the point in our worrying about things if hardly any other bugger does?'

'The principle remains –'

'Fuck principles.'

'You'll be considering a career change to politics, then, now you've got the slogan sorted out.'

'When are you going to grow up?' said Dan. 'Righteous posturing is pointless.'

'Grow up?' said Helen, her voice rising. 'You want a car? Fine. But don't insist it's a part of maturing that I haven't managed.'

Dan shook his head. 'You are so straight in some ways.'

'Hold on. First you tell me that I'm in a tiny minority, then that I'm part of the establishment.'

'I mean you're rigid,' said Dan. 'Once you've made your mind up you won't change it even in the face of bloody good reasons why you should.'

'But it's you who's deciding which reasons are the good ones. Doesn't that make you a teeny bit partisan?'

'Christ almighty. All this over one harmless remark.'

'One?'

Dan stood. 'A few, then. One of these days I might even get to say something without you correcting me.'

'Maybe if you stopped to think first there wouldn't be so much to find fault with.'

'How tedious for you. I'll give you some peace, shall I? This afternoon I'll pay a perfect stranger to take me for a nice drive through the rolling Sussex countryside. Green enough for you?'

'Not really, since –'

'For pity's sake!' His face loomed at hers. 'No answer was required. What do you need – subtitles?' His forefinger was suddenly large in her field of vision. 'Don't answer that!'

He banged out of the flat. Helen sat at the table for a few minutes to give her time to get the sense that he was really gone. Then she went to get changed. She needed to see Usha.

Usha's door was slightly ajar. Music Helen didn't recognize squirmed out through the gap.

She pushed the door open. 'Hello?' The living room was empty; the music was coming from the bedroom. Helen knocked softly. No reply. She felt a sudden stab of fear; TV movie images crowded in from their deep hiding places. Slowly and quietly she turned the door-handle. The music rushed over her.

A young woman with a froth of blonde hair stood in white lace bra and panties, holding a small tangle of green velvet. Usha, wearing a big T-shirt that came down to her knees, was behind the girl, intent on the bra's catch. As Helen caught sight of her she undid the bra. At that moment Usha and the girl saw Helen; the girl clutched her bra to her breasts and crossed one leg protectively over the other. She looked like she desperately wanted to go to the toilet.

'What's going on?' demanded Helen. Her voice sounded reedy to her, like it was made of split plastic.

'It's okay, Cara,' said Usha, handing her the brilliant cascade of her dressing gown from the back of the door.

'Okay?' said Helen, unable to control the wretched rise in her voice. 'I find you fumbling around in someone's underwear and you say it's *okay*?'

Usha turned off the tape player. 'She couldn't get it undone –'

'So you were giving her a hand. How very thoughtful,' Helen hissed.

'I think –' said Cara,

'Don't speak,' ordered Helen.

'Cara is a friend from university,' said Usha carefully. 'She's trying on some clothes that I'm getting rid of.'

Helen saw the clothes piled on the bed, recognized the emerald velvet as a halter-neck top, saw Cara's nervous face watching the madwoman. She wanted to howl. A noise behind her made her turn. A funfair mirror version of Usha, a short, plump Asian woman wearing the green and red dress. Helen felt the corner drawing tighter around her like a noose.

'Who the hell are you?' she demanded.

The little round face widened its eyes. 'I'm Tracy.' The voice was ripe with Scouse.

'Tracy?' repeated Helen idiotically.

'You can call me something more foreign if it makes it easier for you.'

Appalled, Helen stuttered, 'No, no ... I ... that is ... I would like to die now, please.' Her heart ignored her and continued its embarrassed grip on her chest.

'There's a coincidence,' said Usha, 'because I could kill you.'

'Now, come along, girls,' said Tracy, bustling around Helen into the room. 'No fighting in front of the guests.' She turned to Usha. 'Well? Aren't you going to introduce us?'

Helen had the sensation that she was hurtling down something deep; she felt clenched, certain that she must soon hit the bottom. It kept not happening; the imminence tormented her, its malice sure and cold in the cage of stares.

'I'd better go,' she said. Usha's anger rippled out, shoving, shoving.

Tracy tutted. 'Do I have to do everything myself? Right. Let's start this whole thing over again from the beginning. You must be Helen from upstairs. I'm Tracy, and this is Cara.'

Cara smiled weakly. She looked at Usha. 'You know,' she said, 'farce works best when you've got a vicar as well.'

Usha threw her a furious look, then paused. A smile tugged at her. 'It is a bit like that, isn't it.'

'Maybe I am the vicar,' said Helen.

'I think I've missed some of the plot,' said Tracy. 'Why don't we turn over and see what's on the other side?'

'I really think I should –' began Helen.

'Forget it,' said Tracy. 'You've got another chance. I'd take it if I were you.'

'Stay,' said Usha.

She stayed, feeling tolerated, feeling frightened.

'You don't trust me,' said Usha.
'It isn't that.'
'Why don't you trust me?'
'I do, I do,' said Helen.
'But I've made you think that I might not be faithful?'

'No, of course not,' Helen sighed.

'You were so ready to believe –'

'I'm not proud of it,' said Helen. 'And it says a whole lot about me, not about you. Cynicism and vulnerability is not an attractive mix.'

'It is when it isn't aimed at me.' Usha snuggled up beside her on the sofa.

'Oh God, it's good to feel you there.' Helen hugged her. 'It felt like I'd never be alone with you again. And I was scared.'

'Of me?'

Helen nodded. 'That you would punish me by leaving me, basically.'

'Why would –'

'Logic doesn't have much to do with it.'

They sat in silence for a while.

'I want to show you how much you mean to me,' said Helen.

'You do,' said Usha. 'I know it's difficult but –'

'I mean *do* something. Something definitive.'

'The times we're together – you can't get much more definitive than that.'

Helen stroked Usha's breast through the ruddy cheek of the bunny printed on her T-shirt. 'If you're going to do that, you might as well do it properly,' Usha said, pulling the T-shirt up and redirecting Helen's hand onto her skin.

The murmur of Usha's breathing mingled with her own, and the warm silk of skin was sleek under her hands. A thousand miles distant the building admitted her husband but she turned away from him, turned to her lover's rich seams, exploring the dark and the light, holding all the world in her hands.

'I don't want to tell her – not yet.'

Duncan looked at her. 'Not like you to keep something from Maggie. But the tattooist's confidence is like the doctor's – your secret is safe with me.'

Helen looked around at the designs crowding the walls. 'Which are the most popular?'

'It depends on the type of person. Men often like women.' He laughed. 'Tattoos of, I mean. Animals are popular: dragons and unicorns, hearts with scrollwork – that's the sort you see with a name on it. Flowers, birds, swords, skulls: you name it. I tattooed a penis on someone's bum once. I never did figure that one out but she was happy.'

'I want a bird.'

'Well, there's the eagle . . .' He paused. 'Not really you, is it?'

'No, I know the kind. Lots of colours.'

'Ah, something exotic.'

Helen was troubled by that. 'Maybe not, then. But that's what I've seen in my mind's eye.' She looked at the pictures. 'I don't see here what I see here,' she said, tapping her temple.

'Hmm.' Duncan looked meditatively at the designs. He picked up a pen. 'How about . . .' He drew for a few moments and turned the paper around so Helen could see. '. . . something like this?' It was very like a magpie, the wing feathers outstretched like fingers, the tail fanned out. 'And what we do,' he continued, taking up a red pen, 'is add colours . . .' He shaded with green, yellow, blue. 'A marvellous bird. Something you've never seen before – but maybe just because you never imagined it.'

'That's it!' She hugged him. 'Exactly right.'

'You can think it over first, you know. We don't have to do this today.'

'I want it now, Duncan. I have thought about it.'

'It'll be with you for life.'

'Yes.'

'Though there are ways to get rid –'

'No.'

He raised his hands. 'Okay. Next question: where?'

'I want to be able to see it, so I thought here, on the upper arm.'

'It's true you'd be able to see it. But have you thought about having the choice of not showing it?'

'I don't want to hide it,' Helen said.

'Maybe not now,' said Duncan. 'But later you might –'

'I know you're trying to be helpful. But I know what I want.'

'Come and sit down, then.'

She took her shirt off.

'All prepared, I see,' said Duncan, indicating her sleeveless top.

'Impulse planning.'

She felt the cool shock of air rush over the lick of alcohol on her skin. Duncan took a disposable razor and removed invisible hair, then picked up a black ballpoint pen. 'As you can see, I use only the finest precision instruments,' he said. He began to draw the design onto her arm.

'I never had you down for wanting a tat,' he said. 'What are you marking?'

'Having you mark, you mean.' The rush was beginning.

'Mm. It's big, isn't it, this thing?'

Suddenly bashful, Helen felt the heat of her blush.

'Anyone I know?'

She shook her head.

'Sure?'

She didn't answer.

He paused and tilted his head, surveying his work. 'You know, Hazel would never have a tattoo. Said it wasn't ladylike. She did plenty of things that weren't ladylike – thank God – but she was always presenting me with these little mysteries that I could never quite fathom.' He put the pen down and began to fill little pots with colours that looked like a child's paintbox. 'It was like she was a house of rooms, where some doors were open and some shut.' He picked up the tattoo gun and inspected the end. 'Some doors would open if you pushed gently enough on them. Others were shut tight, no give at all. I don't think even she could open those.' He pressed the trigger experimentally and the gun whined. 'Sometimes you can put all your energy into trying to batter your way in, then when you finally sit down for a rest you notice an open door right behind you. Only you were making so much noise you didn't hear it.' He took hold of her hand and rested it across his thigh. 'Here we go.'

The drag of pain followed the outline as he traced it occasionally dabbing blood away. The gun's silence was filled with the smarting of her puzzled arm.

She cycles full-pelt to the turning area. Loose gravel gathered in the curve's eye sprays out as the back wheel slips away into the air. She hits the ground, arms outstretched. Her hands drive along the grizzled tarmac in an extended graze that continues to burn as she stops, face next to gravel that looks as big as pebbles this close.

'Okay,' said Duncan. 'Red first, I think.'

The note of the gun was deeper. The pain was a fact now, entirely bearable, not unpleasurable in its necessity. The other colours were painted into her; she grew sleepy as he ministered to her. Presently he sat back.

'Well,' he said. He smiled and pressed a little more blood from her arm. 'That's it.' He pointed to the mirror on the wall. 'Take a look.'

A brilliant bird hovered on her skin. She touched it; the colours were raised, like the thickened threads of embroidery. 'It's beautiful.' She was surprised that her voice sounded unsteady. She felt the urge of tears tangling with the smile she couldn't seem to stop. 'It really is.' She touched it again. 'Thank you, Duncan. Thank you so much.'

'Some people do find it a very cathartic experience,' he said. 'I have regulars who say that the need for another tat builds up gradually until they absolutely must release it.'

'I don't think I'll be needing another one,' Helen said, stroking the pink-hazed skin around the bird. 'This is it. It's exactly right.'

'It'll need some care at first. Come and sit down.' He used sticky tape to secure a folded tissue over the tattoo. 'Leave this on for a few hours, then wash the area – very gently – using a mild soap. You don't need to cover it after that, but bathe it with plain water three times a day. Finally – and this is important – don't pick or scratch at the scabs! Let them come off naturally.'

'How long will it take to heal?'

'It varies,' said Duncan, 'but a few weeks to be completely healed. The skin has to renew itself. But basically, even when it itches, don't interfere with it – you'll damage it.'

'I had chicken pox when I was twenty-six,' said Helen. 'I know about not scratching.' She put her shirt on. 'I can't believe I've done it.'

'It's a significant act.'

'I guess that's it. A manifest decision.'

Duncan began to pour away the ink from the little wells.

'Can I do anything?' asked Helen.

'It's alright. I did most of the clearing up after I shut the shop.'

'But you will let me buy you a drink?'

'Of course.' He turned off the lights and handed Helen her handbag. Outside, the air was damp and cold. She pulled on her gloves and fastened her coat, aware, behind her shivering, of the warm core where the magical bird beat its wings.

'I don't know,' said Dan. 'I don't need anything.'

'Christmas presents aren't about things you need,' said Helen. 'They're about things you want.'

'Surprise me.'

'Big help you are.' Helen consulted her list. 'Oh God, I haven't got anything for your parents.'

'What about that book on the Gulf War my dad was talking about?'

'That wasn't a war, it was a conflict that could only –'

'It was only a suggestion,' said Dan.

'It's bad enough we're going there for lunch without having to get them a present as well.' Helen sucked the end of her pen for a moment. 'I'll go and wander around the Lanes. I'm bound to find something no one else wanted to buy because it was so horrible.' She looked at Dan. He was gazing at a blank bit of wall. 'That was a joke,' she said.

'Sorry, I'm feeling a bit distracted.' He ran a hand through his hair, his fingers lingering fractionally at the thinning part. 'What do *you* want?'

'Surprise me.'

'You're right. That's no help at all. I'll go and have a bath – maybe that'll help me think.' He got up, then turned suddenly to Helen. 'Let's have a good Christmas,' he said. 'A really good one.' Unhappiness seeped from his voice. 'Let's make things better.'

'We can try, can't we.' She didn't want to feel anything, didn't want to be made to focus.

He bent down to kiss her, putting his hands on her upper arms. She flinched.

'What?' he said angrily.

'Nothing.'

'Your arm's padded.' His anger dissolved away to confusion. 'Bloody hell, is it a bandage? Are you hurt?'

'I'm fine.'

'What has Maggie got you into now? Has she –'

'She's done nothing,' said Helen. 'She doesn't even know.'

'Know what?'

She eased her sleeve down and lowered the tissue.

'God,' said Dan. 'Is that real?'

'Of course it's real.'

'Duncan?'

'It's what he does for a living.'

'Yes. It's colourful. More, it's . . . surprising.' He sat down. 'Why?'

'Why not?'

'There's always more reason for taking an action than for not taking it,' Dan said.

'I just wanted to.'

'Isn't it kind of permanent for a spur of the moment thing?'

'Who said it was spur of the moment?'

'I don't know. I assumed...'

'I planned it. I was sober. Here it is.' She wanted more from him. 'What do you think?'

'It's... done. I... What do you want me to say?'

'I want you to tell me what you think.' Stop being so miserly, she thought, it's easy enough for you to give me what I want.

'I think I like it,' he said. 'It's difficult – I didn't know you were going to do it so it's hard to take in.' He grinned. 'You're still surprising me after all this time.'

'And you haven't seen the one on my bum yet.'

He was taken in just for a moment. 'Yeah, yeah. What does Maggie think of your bird?'

'She doesn't know yet.'

'Oh.'

'I thought I'd wait until it had healed.'

He watched her cover the bird up. 'Well, well,' he said. He looked pleased; she was irritated, knowing he was taking credit for himself, as though being married to her meant that he'd done something unexpected, too. He leant over and kissed her; she felt the exploratory touch of his tongue.

'It's kind of sexy, actually,' he said, smoothing her hair.

'Dan...'

He sat back. 'You're right. What a ridiculous idea. What can I have been thinking of?' He stood up again. 'Don't tell me – you're saving it as a Christmas present. Now that really would be a surprise.'

She looked at him. She had no answer.

'I'm off for that bath.'

When he'd gone she reached under the dressing and touched the rinded bird in its fixed flight over the soft, damaged skin of her arm.

20

'But we're going to my parents on Christmas Day,' said Dan. 'Only for lunch,' Helen said.

'So we get the morning to ourselves then.'

'I've already invited her. She doesn't have anywhere to go.'

'What about that brother of hers?'

'He's away.'

'Anyway,' Dan said. 'I wasn't aware that Christmas is a Sikh festival.' He noticed her fingers brushing over her sleeve, tending the invisible colours.

'Like you're a Christian,' she snapped. 'That's why you celebrate Christmas, I suppose.'

'No, avarice is my religion as you well know. What's your excuse?'

'She's English – why shouldn't she do English things like Christmas?' she asked calmly.

He felt cheated. He wanted conflict. 'She isn't English!'

'English is her first language,' said Helen, striking off items on her fingers. 'She was born here. She grew up here, went to school here, has made all her decisions, all her mistakes here.' She threw up her hands. 'What else does it take?'

'What does she think?'

'If she was here I'm sure she'd think you were being a bit of a wanker, too.'

'Very droll. I *meant*, does she think of herself as English?'

Helen looked a little surprised. 'I don't know, actually. But this isn't about Usha at all. I'm not going to play, Dan. You said yourself we should try to have a good Christmas.'

'And that includes inviting strangers for Christmas, does it?'

'She's hardly a stranger.'

'Not to you, perhaps.'

'What's that supposed to mean?' she said. He could see that staying calm was an effort. That would have to suffice.

'It seems like you're down there every five minutes. And that's only when I'm here. Presumably you're at it when I'm not as well.' Her expression was unfathomable but it was at least a reaction. 'Isn't she a bit young?' he continued. 'Or is it that you enjoy being more experienced, you know, able to sort out her problems, give advice.' She just looked at him. 'Like a mother, you might say.'

'That was low,' she said, flushing. Triumph and shame cleaved through him. 'Will you stop now?' she said, her eyes bright. He nodded. They looked at one another over the distance.

'I can tell her not to come,' said Helen. 'In fact, it would probably be better if she didn't.'

'It's no great hardship.' He forced a smile that seemed to drag at the muscles of his face. 'Maybe we need someone there to make sure we keep the gloves on.' He saw Helen looking at his hand; it was tapping an irregular, abstracted rhythm on his thigh. It stopped when both of them noticed.

'I've got a twitch,' he said. There was a pause, he saw the smile tugging at Helen's mouth, then the release hit them both. They laughed, and kept on laughing; tears blurred Helen away and the ache in his stomach muscles was like bruising from small, insistent fists.

Usha's blouse was a lustrous dark grey that made Dan think of guns.

'Merry Christmas,' she said.

'The same to you,' he replied, haunted for a moment by the echoes of the playground.

'With knobs on,' said Usha with a grin.

'They still say that, do they?' Dan said.

'When I was in the infants they did. But a lot can change in fifteen years.'

'It can indeed.' He looked to Helen but she was plumping up the cushions on the sofa and he couldn't see her face.

'This is for you,' said Usha, holding out a parcel gaudy with little fat Santas and sprigs of holly.

'You shouldn't have,' said Dan. 'But since you have, thank you. I think the gallant thing to do is to let Helen open it.'

'It's for you.'

'Oh. Right.'

It was a box of some kind of sweets. The pastel pink and pale green squatted in the box, pressing stickily against the tissue paper. Dark brown flecked against the green like grit in a snowball.

'They're traditional Indian sweets,' said Usha. 'The green ones are pistachio.'

'And the pink?' said Helen.

Usha laughed. 'Red food colouring is involved.'

Cochineal comes from squashed up beetle bits, thought Dan, imagining a deep red juice clotted with –.

'I'm on a diet,' he blurted out.

'One won't do any harm,' said Helen.

'I'll have one later with some coffee,' Dan said, closing the box. 'Thank you.'

'Something to drink, Usha?' Helen asked Usha. 'I made some lemonade.'

'Sounds good.'

'Dan?'

'Nothing for me, thanks.'

As Helen got up from the sofa the phone rang. 'I'll get it,' she said.

Dan sat facing Usha and wondered what to say.

'Wrong number,' said Helen as she came back in from the hall and headed for the kitchen.

'It must have been a nightmare at the supermarket in the run-up to Christmas,' said Dan.

'Worse for the people on the shop floor,' said Usha. 'Some people had two, even three, trolleys, packed to the brim. The whole thing's enough to put you off food altogether.'

'That would help my diet.'

'Get a job in a supermarket, then.' Usha's voice was flat. She was looking at him like . . . Her face cleared as Helen returned and he didn't know what he'd seen.

'Dan's bought a car,' said Helen handing Usha her lemonade.

'What sort?' Usha asked Dan, running her finger around the rim of the glass.

'A Metro.'

'A red one,' added Helen, sitting down next to Usha. 'With a gold stripe down the side,' she added with mock admiration.

'I didn't get it because of the stripe.'

'So why did you get it?' Usha looked at him steadily over the glass as she sipped her lemonade. Her intonation had been Helen's. Helen sat beside her with a blank expression rounded off at the bottom by a polite arrangement of lips approximating a smile.

'The usual reasons, I suppose,' he said. 'You know, freedom of the open road, that Easy Rider feeling when you're at the lights with another Metro.'

'And if you were on that open road, free, where would you go?' asked Usha.

Somewhere dark and quiet, he thought, and far, far away. 'I don't know,' he said. 'I'd have to think about it.'

'If you were being spontaneous,' Usha said.

'I'm not sure I'm any good at spontaneity.'

'Helen, is Dan good at being spontaneous?'

'Oh yes, if he keeps to the list of instructions I've provided beforehand.'

'Thank you, Helen. I know I can always rely on you.' Usha was smiling; lovely face, edged with ... contempt. Contempt for him. It was like brilliant light, keen as a laser, coming straight from her centre. Anger churned in his belly. 'You find that amusing, do you?' he said, leaning forward towards Usha. He felt he was at the edge of something.

The small boat bobbed on the restless water. Waves reached over and smacked at its sides. The light was peculiar, a grey that leaked dirty yellow and seemed to push back against the rising wind.

'No,' he said. 'I'm not going.'

The boat struggled as though it had arms that were bound.

'It's only a shower,' Mike said.

Dan looked down into the boat. Old water moved excitedly in the bottom. The thunder shoved closer.

'No,' Dan said. 'No.'

Usha's look beckoned him. 'It might not have been funny but maybe it was true.'

He didn't understand: he was being buffeted by the energy streaming off Usha but its suddenness bewildered him. Helen's look blended apprehension and a pity he didn't at first recognize as for him.

'I think this —' began Helen. The phone rang. 'I have to get that. I'm expecting a call from my mother.'

Usha's scathing amber eyes scrutinized him. He wanted her to leave. More, he wanted Helen to help him; what the hell was the matter with this bloody girl?

'Wrong number again,' said Helen. 'Same person. Some foreign woman.' She began to recount an old anecdote about the time she had stood in for a friend on a switchboard. As she spoke her hand wandered to her hidden bird; wordlessly Usha gently touched it away and carried on drinking her lemonade. The action was so quiet that Dan didn't realize at first that he'd seen it. Then he found himself replaying it. And again. Something distant shifted. He looked at them side by side on the sofa. Helen and Usha. Usha and Helen.

Usha was looking at him again. An understanding passed between them that should have been visible, should have had shape and substance it was so complete. Helen's story ground to a halt. Dan was convinced he could hear the tinsel rustling in the warm air swimming from the radiator.

'What?' said Helen.

'Dan has us sussed,' said Usha. 'Don't you, Dan.'

Helen was as still as a sculpture, hand frozen in mid-gesture, fingers stretched into wing-tips. Dan was aware of the air feeling padded, of sound and movement muffled, while he saw the arch of Usha's eyebrows and the edges of her mouth with crystalline clarity. Helen tried a laugh that aborted miserably. She folded her hands into her lap, bowing a face seared with a livid blush. Dan felt he ought to say something but all he could think of was Lesley and how he had no right to the anger that held him by the throat.

'What now?' said Usha. She exuded an elation fringed with fear: she watched Dan warily. He thought of the breasts beneath her blouse, the frill of her inner lips glossy with desire for Helen, of the looks passing between the two women as they excluded him. Usha uncrossed her legs and the sussuration of the tights beneath her skirt gored a dazed desire into his gut.

'Helen and I need to talk.' Dan said. Helen turned dumb eyes on him and then on Usha, the pain of her division making her movements awkward.

'What does Helen think?' said Usha. 'Maybe she thinks you're all talked out. Maybe she's found someone who *listens*.' She took Helen's hand. He thought of Helen's blondeness against smooth brown flesh.

'Don't do this, Usha,' said Helen.

'Well –'

'It isn't helping anything.' She looked at Dan. 'This is hideous.'

He didn't want her bloody understanding, he didn't want anything from her, he didn't want her and Usha sitting opposite him. They were breathing his air, suffocating him. He was a ridiculous man.

'Enough,' he said. 'Why don't you both go. I don't have anything to say.' He stood up. Helen flinched slightly but Usha looked up at him, refusing to be intimidated.

'Come on,' said Helen to Usha. 'Dan's right. Let's go.'

'Look on the bright side,' Usha said to her, 'at least you won't have to spend time with that awful woman.'

He felt unexpectedly protective towards his mother. Whilst it was true she was awful, that Helen had told Usha transformed the observation into an unwarranted insult. 'Where do you get off judging people you don't even know?' said Dan.

Usha stood up, pulling Helen to her feet. 'I trust Helen's judgement.'

'She married me, don't forget.'

'But would she marry you now?'

Dan turned on Helen. 'You're unnaturally quiet. Normally you pronounce on everything whether anyone's interested or not.' It was as if an inky liquid were beginning to trickle into his vision. 'Come on,' he insisted. 'Say something.' He was dimly aware that his voice was getting louder. He stepped towards Helen. Then Usha was there between them, her face disgorging her full contempt.

'Leave her alone,' she said. 'Just let us be.' She and Helen began to walk to the front door.

He felt a huge expanse of space open up around him. 'Fuck you,' he said, his voice seeming to pipe in the big air. He thought about saying it again but didn't feel he could raise his tiny voice above a whisper; anyway, there was no one there to hear.

The phone. He turned his attention away; it would only be her mother.

He could answer it. He could tell Pat what a wonderful Christmas he was having.

Sheer malice.
Perfect.
He picked it up and waited for Pat to speak.
A long silence. He thought he could hear breathing. Then, "Allo?' An uncertain, foreign, female voice.

'Look, you stupid bitch. How many sodding times do you have to dial a number to realize it's the wrong bloody one?'

'And a merry fucking Christmas to you, too,' said Lesley.

'Oh Christ.'

'And him. It *is* his birthday.'

'What do you want?' he said.

'Where's your wife?'

'She had to go out.'

'Any chance of seeing you later?' He had nothing to stop him yet he didn't want to go. 'Christmas Day at home is so deadly,' Lesley continued. 'I need to get out for a while.'

Why not? She was soft and warm and didn't know enough to damage him.

'I'll meet you outside the Dome,' he said.

'I can pick you up nearer home. I still have Dave's car. His leg isn't better yet.'

'I bought a car.'

'Brilliant! I'd love to have one. One of the lecturers was selling a Metro at the end of term but Dave said it was a real disaster. What sort have you got?'

'It's a surprise.'

They arranged to meet at about seven. Dan decided he would go to his parents' house for lunch. Despite the disarray of his life, he was hungry. It was a comfort to find that something so normal could still happen to him.

'I'm sorry I'm late,' he said when his father opened the door. 'Damn car wouldn't start.'

He had sat there, turning the key, listening to the deranged engine noises emanating from beneath the bonnet. Yards away, concealed by the hedge, the two women listened to him fail. When, suddenly and inexplicably, the car had started he had wheelspun away from the kerb in his effort to keep it going. Metro Man burns rubber.

'Where's Helen?' Jack asked.

'She . . . had a crisis.'

'A crisis?' Jack closed the door and sealed them in.

'Her friend.' Dan waited for his brain to help. 'Her friend's father had a heart attack this morning. She's gone to be with her.'

'Oh dear. Is he . . . ?'

Dan found himself thinking of his own father's heart, its juicy beating, how one day it would stop, how one day he would try to breathe and nothing would happen. Why don't you ever touch me? he thought, looking at his father's hands fidgeting in another Christmas cardigan.

'No, he's not,' said Dan. 'But it is quite serious. Maggie's very upset.'

He felt the voodoo of lying begin its search for Duncan.

'Oh dear,' said Jack. 'Oh dear, oh dear.' He paused at the living room door and lowered his voice. 'But I wasn't looking forward to the girls being together, I must confess. It's all a bit awkward, isn't it. Not that I mean to say anything against Helen, oh no, far from it, a lovely girl, spirited, you might say –'

Not 'girl', 'woman', Dan could hear Helen correcting. She probably wouldn't say it but he would be able to hear her thinking it.

'I know what you mean.'

'Daniel?' His mother opened the living room door. 'Daniel!' He was always struck by how surprised she sounded to see him, when she knew full well he was coming. She hugged him; he felt the press of her breasts against him and the huff of her breath near his ear. He wanted to push her away. He stepped back and bent and kissed her fragrant cheek. She peered around him as if into a necessary cage.

'Helen won't be able to come,' he said and repeated his lie.

'What a shame,' said Moira. 'What a terrible thing to happen on Christmas Day.'

'A terrible thing to happen on any day,' said Dan.

'Especially Christmas, though.' Moira tutted and shook her head. 'Christmas is a happy time.' She went back through to the kitchen, humming as she went.

And I can't even drink, Dan thought.

'No, I can't, Mum,' he said, pushing his plate away. 'I'm completely stuffed.' A plodding voracity had pushed him beyond appetite to forcing food into an aching throat until he could bear no more.

She put the dish of potatoes down on the table. 'If you're sure.' She beamed at him. 'It's good to see you eating a proper meal. When you were a teenager you ate like you hadn't had a decent meal in days – and it was only a few hours since.'

'I'm not a teenager now. I have to watch what I eat.'

'Oh rubbish. You know I don't want to criticize Helen but I don't hold with this going vegetarian nonsense. Men need meat.'

'Maybe a bit less meat won't do any harm, eh?'

'But none at all, Daniel! I don't know where she gets these ideas from.'

He thought of Usha eating at their table. Not then: but when; how long? 'It's a combination of things,' he replied. 'There's the environmental side, for a start. And when you–'

'It's fashion, if you ask me. When people start keeling over from lack of proper nourishment, they'll soon forget about this nonsense, you mark my words.'

'It's hardly a fad, Mum. There are whole nations who don't eat meat. Take India – what about all those Hindus?'

'And look how skinny they are! That proves my point, doesn't it. Famines, too.'

His meal was heavy in him. Chewed food, compressed; imagine the sound in the mouth, the sluice of spit, the implacable grind of teeth. Bile corroded the back of his throat.

'Famines?' he said incredulously. Weariness coated him suddenly; he wanted only silence. 'You're probably right,' he said, willing her and the clatter of plates away. Helen's problem was that she could never let things go. Though hadn't she, now? She'd looked at him from behind Usha, a stranger's glance. Then she'd left without a turn, her face, her eyes lost to him. And the sweep of Usha's long hair blanking him out.

'There's a lovely Christmas pud for afters,' Moira said, picking up the plates. 'And nice thick custard.'

Had there been room his stomach would have heaved.

'Those Argies had it coming,' came his father's voice from the depths of the armchair where he'd settled himself with his new book. 'It says here that –'

Dan's chair screeched over the polished floorboards as he pushed it back. 'Toilet,' he mumbled, and fled.

The wallpaper was a rash of tiny flowers that seemed to move when he looked at them. He sat on the edge of the bath and embraced his punished stomach. He closed his eyes, and loosed a long breath as hot, furtive tears began to spill from the darkness.

He could hear nothing except the beating of his heart. The dream was gone, leaving only the dread. The blue light from the clock showed him his fist clenched on Helen's pillow. He brought his hand to his face; he could smell Lesley on his fingers. He spread his limbs out into the cold, empty stretches of sheet. The fear still clutched at him, ungraspable ghosts throwing shadows. He got out of bed and put on his dressing gown. A floorboard creaked under his feet. He thought of the flat downstairs; Helen's warm body; Usha's gaze penetrating him, pouring disdain into the breach.

He sat on the sofa in the dark until he could see the hidden room, feeling he was becoming invisible in the process. When the cold began to bother him he went to fetch the duvet. On the way back the light on the answering machine caught his attention, an unblinking red to announce there was nothing to say. He sat on the chair and switched on the lamp; pain swooped down into his eyes. Squinting, he found the number in the address book and followed Helen's neat instructions.

He listened to the phone ringing: backing the gaps between the tones, minute, incomprehensible voices somehow frantic over the distance.

Duncan answered. 'Hello?' Sleepy; puzzled. 'Hello?' Alive. Dan hung up.

He turned off the lamp. Wrapping the duvet close about him, he rested his head back against the cold wall and looked for a long time at nothing at all.

21

Usha lay looking up at the cracks in the ceiling; five jagged rivers, the only features on an unfinished map.

Helen came back from the bathroom and sat on the edge of the bed, stroking Usha's thigh. 'Well,' she said.

'Well.'

'Here we are.'

'You could show some enthusiasm,' said Usha.

'I wish getting to this point had been less messy, that's all,' Helen said, rubbing her face. 'It's exhausting, all this emotional trauma.' Her hands seemed to smear a dull red over her cheeks. She looked down at Usha. 'I feel things are out of control now.'

'You worry too much.'

'I'm serious, Usha.'

'Uncertainty does this to you. You didn't like it when we got together because you hadn't planned it out first – but you've got used to it.'

'I love you.'

'You didn't plan to leave Dan either – you'll get used to that, too.'

'Well, I haven't exactly left, have I? I mean, leaving the flat this morning doesn't mean that I . . .' She looked down at her hands.

'I could shake you sometimes!' exclaimed Usha. 'Just go for it, for once in your life.'

'Dan and I have a history. I –'

'You and Dan *are* history. *This* is your future. You don't need him.'

'He *is* the sperm bank,' Helen said sarcastically. She shook her head. 'Why should he do anything to help us?'

'History,' said Usha triumphantly.

'He wouldn't just disappear.'

'But it would be *our* child.'

'You're unbelievable! Use him, then dump him?' Helen's eyes were wide, her colour high. Usha wanted to touch her.

'You're always telling me what a fundamentally nice guy he is. Once he realized that you and he are finished, he'd leave us to it.'

'This is unreal.'

'No! It's being realistic. Saying out loud what's underneath all this doesn't make me a monster.'

'It's grotesque.'

'Then there won't be any child.'

'So be it.' Helen's face was closed.

'You don't mean that. You may be willing to deprive yourself but you'd deprive me as well?'

'That isn't fair.'

'No, it isn't.' Usha had the sense of losing her hold. She renewed her grip. 'I thought you wanted to be with me.'

Helen sighed. 'You know I do.'

'I want us to have a baby.'

'You don't know what you're saying.'

'Aah!' Usha leapt off the bed and wrapped on the cold splash of her dressing gown. 'Don't tell me what I know! You can't stand it, can you? I can do what you can't and you can't deal with it. You want to stop me because then you won't feel bad about yourself.'

'Who's telling who what they think now?'

'The difference is I'm right. *We both want the same thing.* Why must you complicate it?'

'Because it *is* complicated.'

'Then we sort it out,' said Usha.

'We have to agree on the complications first.'

'Maybe it isn't them we're disagreeing about, but how important they are.' Usha raised her hands. 'And don't tell me again about how I don't understand. If an understanding is different it doesn't mean it's lacking.'

Helen looked very small somehow. Usha put her arms around her. Helen's hair smelt faintly of sugared almonds.

'The way you rush at things scares me,' said Helen.

'You call it rushing, I call it embracing the choice I've made. Like now.'

'Maybe what we're thinking of simply isn't meant to be.'

'Sikhs aren't into fatalism. Nanak's outlook – he's the founder – is "with your own hands carve out your destiny". He's right: if you really want something you can make it happen.'

'Sikhism schmikism. It's you. You're arrogant and you're stubborn.'

'Whatever. Same result.' She didn't feel that comfortable talking to Helen about any aspect of religion. Helen thought it was all programming and manipulation. Usha felt a connection to something, though; not a set of rules and regulations, but a Something; a quiet intelligence; not benign, not malignant, but there, like sky or temperature.

In the quiet building she held Helen's hand and waited for her to reach the necessary conclusions.

'I have a couple of days off,' Usha said, as she scrubbed Helen's back to a startled pink. 'We could go away somewhere.'

'Everywhere will be booked up,' said Helen. 'Or closed.'

'Mm. I'd like to get away from here for a while.' A small blue scab bobbed on the water. 'Part of a wing's come off.' The revealed skin was smooth and a slightly paler blue. Usha gently rinsed Helen's arm, feeling the bumpy surface under her fingers.

Alex's scar twists angrily through his precious skin. She can see the javelin arcing towards him as he runs across the field. An Alex she'll never know, about to be pierced; the handful of boys struck silent by inevitability; the fierce green of his eyes as he heads back to the changing room to the stopwatch ticking on the bench. Felled, he wonders who's been hurt as the blood shines on the teacher's hands.

'It could have been worse,' Alex told her. 'At least it didn't hit anything vital.'

He ran to that intersection of flesh and metal.

All they could do was watch him run, watch him drag the point of pain away from their vulnerable bodies.

Helen curled up on the sofa wrapped in the vast soft towel that Jaz had given Usha.

'I should get dressed, I suppose,' she said. She and Usha observed her not doing anything. 'I don't want to put the same things back on. They're in-law clothes.'

'Borrow some of mine.'

'It seems silly when I have cupboards full of stuff upstairs.'
Usha felt the weight of the flat above pressing on her ceiling. 'Not really,' she said. 'I don't want you to go up either.'
'He isn't there.'
'No.'
They listened. The ceiling crept a little lower.
'Come on,' said Usha, pulling Helen to her feet. 'Let's go and find you something of mine.'
The clothes in the wardrobe were so crowded together they seemed to be holding their breath. Usha wrestled with a hanger and the wardrobe gave it up reluctantly. She held a black skirt with a dark red floral design worked deep into the fabric. 'And my black jumper. You look good in black. It's the blonde hair and alabaster skin that does it.'
'Alabaster?'
Usha grinned. 'I read it in a book. Or was it *Hello!?*' She shrugged. 'It's a good word. You don't get to use it very often.'
Helen pointed at a pale blue sleeve that had squeezed out of the crush. 'What's that?' She held the skirt while Usha pulled the garment out.
'It's a salwar kameez,' Usha said. 'A long tunic – the kameez – and matching leggings, basically.'
'It's an amazing colour. Like the washed-out blue you get high in a summer sky. But the satin makes it look cool, like ice. Do you ever wear it?'
'Not these days. It's a special occasion outfit, really.'
'It looks . . .' Helen abruptly shut up.
'What?'
'Doesn't matter.'
'Come on. What?'
'It's embarrassing. Let it go, eh?'
Usha cocked her head and waited.
Helen capitulated. 'I was about to say, "It looks ethnic".'
'Well, it is. You worry too much,' Usha said. 'It isn't the *noticing* that's a problem, it's how you act on it. If you act on it.' She held the kameez against Helen. 'Just because you're discriminating doesn't mean it's discrimination. Why don't you try it on? It's a good colour for you. Picks up on your eyes.' The pain of that blue tip-toed around Usha as she looked deep for a few seconds.
When Helen had the salwar kameez on they looked at her in the mirror.

'The material is beautiful.' Helen smoothed her hands down the fabric. 'It's like liquid.'

'I forgot something.' Usha rummaged in a drawer. 'Here we are.' She pulled out the pale blue chunni decorated with silver glass beads.

'*You're a good daughter,*' says Mum, pulling unnecessarily at Usha's clothes, straightening the already straight chunni. '*So clever. I knew you would get good grades. That Veena, she's a good girl, but not clever like you.*'

Jaz says, '*You look like a wife.*' He's smiling. She doesn't know what he means.

'You put the scarf on like this.' Usha draped the ends back over Helen's shoulders and arranged the loose fabric at the front. 'There.' They looked at the effect.

'I feel very elegant,' said Helen. 'But kind of alien, too.'

'Or you can wear it like a winter scarf, putting one end back over your shoulder. The length of the chunni means you can use it to cover your head as well.' She arranged it over Helen's hair. 'You do that when you go into the gurdwara, as a sign of respect.' She grinned. 'It's also useful for keeping your ears warm.' She looked at Helen's bare feet. 'I have some silver sandals but I haven't got a clue where they are. Never mind. Let's have a look at you.'

Helen did a twirl. She looked ... bleached. Usha burst out laughing.

'What?' said Helen, perplexed. 'It doesn't look that bad.'

'No, no,' said Usha, catching her breath. 'It isn't that.'

'Tell me what's so funny then.'

'There's only one word for it,' said Usha. 'You look exotic.'

Helen looked at her reflection. She nodded. 'I like it, though. It's comfortable.' Usha pushed the chunni back off Helen's hair. 'This is a nice scarf, too,' said Helen, holding up the end and peering through its translucence. 'Like a veil.'

Usha took hold of both lengths of the scarf and drew Helen to her. Their kiss was voluptuous, almost sleepy. Keeping hold of the material Usha pulled Helen one slow step at a time towards the bed. When she could feel the mattress against the back of her legs she released the chunni and pushed it off Helen's shoulders. She was a pliant statue; Usha could feel the roundness of her breasts under the chill, slippery fabric, the hardening of her nipples.

The doorbell rang. Dan's image jammed its way in between them and they separated.

'Let's ignore it,' said Usha. They looked at each other, waiting. Anxiety was clouding Helen's face again. Usha's heart was pounding. 'What does he want?' she hissed. 'Why doesn't he leave us alone?' The bell rang again; a long, impatient blast, followed by the rattle of the letter flap. 'Bloody bastard!' said Usha.

'Hey, Trouble!' came a muffled voice. 'Open the door!'

'It's Jaz,' said Usha, relief breaking over her. 'Trust him to arrive when he isn't supposed to.' She went to answer the door, realizing that she would have to explain Helen's presence, knowing at the same time that she wouldn't tell her brother the truth. Not yet.

'What are you doing here?'

'Thanks very much,' said Jaz. 'It's nice to see you, too. Do I get to come in or what?' He wore a white shirt of soft, expensive material. She wanted to stroke it.

'You said you were spending the day at thingie's house,' said Usha closing the door behind him.

'Julie.'

'Has she stopped putting too much starch on your turban?'

'Her brother works at a dry cleaner so I get them done there now.'

'Oh dear,' said Usha. 'Sounds like she got fed up with cosseting you pretty quickly. She's got some sense, then. What did she do, kick you out?'

'Burglar alarm went off at the shop. I had to go and deal with it.' Jaz sat down. 'So as I was about I came to see my little sister. I *thought* you might be pleased to see me.'

'Was the shop okay?'

'Yeah. False alarm.'

'Maybe it was that troublemaker again.'

Jaz shook his head. 'I don't think so. That's being sorted out.'

'How?'

'The commercial world is nothing for you to worry your pretty little head about.'

'Jaz . . .'

'Things will be agreed amicably. I know what I'm doing.'

'As you're so fond of saying.'

'Who's in the bedroom?'

'What?'

'Don't play for time, Ush. There's someone in there. Tell me it's not Alex.'

'It isn't. After everything that happened? Of course it isn't.'

'Yeah, right.' He walked swiftly to the door.

'No, don't, Jaz, I'll –'

He opened it. Helen in frosted blue; surprised mouth; hands clasped together in their characteristic struggle. She took a breath to speak.

'Sorry,' said Jaz said and closed the door. 'Whoops.' He sat down. 'What's she doing here? And in that get-up?'

'She and her husband have – She's . . . staying here.' Usha stood up. 'For God's sake, Jaz, you can't go barging into places like that.'

'So I was a bit hasty,' he conceded. 'But he's the kind of bloke who'll keep on turning up.'

'Not here.'

'Okay.'

'I don't suppose it would occur to you to apologize,' Usha said.

Jaz spread his hands. 'I did!'

'To me, I mean.'

'It was a mistake. I said so.'

'You called me a liar and then violated my privacy.'

'"Violated your privacy": is that one of your legal terms?' He looked amused.

'This isn't funny!'

'Okay.' He composed his face. She could see the smile in his eyes and wanted to hurt him. So often he didn't see her. She sat heavily on the sofa; the small, entertaining sister.

'Tell you what,' he said, '*I'll* put the kettle on.' When he came back he sat next to her and patted her leg. 'So,' he said, 'why *is* your distressed neighbour wearing your Sunday best?'

'It's complicated,' she said.

'You thought a bit of dressing up would take her mind off her problems?'

'Something like that.'

'It looked quite good,' said Jaz. 'She looks like an advert for minty ice-cream.'

'I'll tell her you said so.'

'How long has she been here?'

'Only today. There was a . . . they had a row. He's gone out.'

'Stressful time, Christmas.' The kettle clicked off. 'Kettle's boiled,' he said presently.

'I'll go and get Helen,' said Usha. She turned to Jaz and smiled sweetly. 'You can make us all a nice drink.'

Their eyes met as the engine coughed and coughed but didn't start. Then silence.

'Poor Dan,' said Helen – but no trip to the window this time to gaze at the back of the hedge: Usha felt a brisk swipe of satisfaction. They waited; it would be a slam of the car door or another attempt. The engine began its hunt again.

Usha sipped her tea. 'Persistent, isn't he?'

'You have to give him that,' said Helen looking towards the window. Mist thickened the air, smearing it with damp.

The car started and the engine roared impotently as Dan pressed the accelerator to the floor. They heard the car move off, with the clutch slipping and the engine howling, but without wheelspin. Helen nodded to herself. Usha felt again the spikes of resentment at Helen's support for Dan. I'm being childish, she thought, throwing her book to one side, I can't even let him start his car.

'Right,' said Helen. 'Time to get some knickers.'

'He's probably booby-trapped the flat.'

'He's mechanically incompetent, so I shouldn't think so.'

'Booby-trapped it badly, then.'

'Ease off, Usha.'

How she hated that elder sister tone. 'You're bloody bossy sometimes,' she said.

'And you're bloody bitchy sometimes. And how many times do I have to tell you not to bloody swear.'

There was a sock on the floor outside the bedroom door. 'Some things don't change,' Helen said. 'God knows where the other one is.'

One pillow lay neat and undented; the other was at the foot of the bed with the missing sock lying on top entwined with a pair of underpants.

Helen opened a drawer. 'Bloody hell,' she said. She opened the next one down. 'Look,' she said. 'They're empty.' She laughed a little uncertainly. 'What's he done with my underwear?'

'It doesn't matter. We can –'

'It *does* matter.' Anger painted shadows into Helen's face, making her look suddenly older. 'What's this?' She picked out a sheet of paper from the third drawer. '"Dear Helen",' she read, "I know you'll come for some things when I'm not here. I put all your underwear in a bin liner to take to the dump because I know how much that would piss you off. I have lost my nerve. I'm not very good at this kind of thing. You can put them away, though. Dan. P.S. I am drunk."

'Well, he was nearly spontaneous.' Usha tried to moderate the sourness twisting her voice. She smiled to reassure Helen that she was making the effort.

'I hope he wasn't drunk just now when he went out,' Helen said. 'He could kill himself.' She looked at Usha.

'Come off it, Helen. I don't want that either.' I don't want tragedy, she thought: I just want to win.

'He wouldn't drive in that state.'

'*He* didn't think his wife would turn out to be a lesbian. Maybe you didn't know each other as well as you thought you did.'

'Using the past tense makes it sound like one of us is dead.'

Usha shrugged. She looked around the room. The space that Helen had shared so intimately was oppressive. The cover of the book on one bedside table was nearly the same shade of red as the one on the other side.

Helen began to screw up Dan's note. 'Let's have a look,' said Usha, holding out her hand. Helen hesitated: it was only tiny, the slightest change in her posture. She crushed the note into a ball.

'As threatening letters go, it wasn't much, was it?'

'I wanted to read it.'

'Finding that bin liner is what I want.' She took aim at the rubbish basket by the dressing table. 'Watch,' she said. 'I'm good at this. At the office Maggie and I –' Usha took sudden hold of Helen's wrist and snatched the paper from her hand. Helen said nothing as she smoothed out the paper.

'. . . You can put them away, though. I love you. Dan.'

Usha looked at her.

'What would have been the point of telling you?' Helen said. 'It doesn't mean anything. He was pissed.'

'I suppose it makes life easier if you can miss out the bits you find inconvenient.'

'Look –'

'No, *you* look. If it didn't mean anything, why hide it?'

'Because I knew it would mean something to you.'

'What upsets me is you deciding for me,' said Usha.

'Talking of love when you're pissed is of no consequence. You're as likely to propose to the lamppost that's propping you up, or at least try to get it to come home to meet your parents.'

'So things said in extreme states of mind aren't to be believed?'

'Probably not. In my exp–'

'"Oh, Usha, my Usha,"' moaned Usha, tilting her head back, her voice starting the urgent rise to climax. '"I love you, I love –"'

Helen's lips were set in a thin line and her eyes hurled pure blue dislike. She wheeled abruptly and hurried out. Usha screwed up the note and threw it at the bin. It glanced off the edge and landed in one of Dan's slippers.

A moment later she heard the rustle of plastic from the bathroom as Helen found the bin liner. She went to lend a hand, determined to be seen to be gracious despite their disagreement; it was Helen who was in the wrong, after all.

22

'SHE'S PATHOLOGICALLY CURIOUS,' said Helen. 'What a thing to ask – "What's it like doing it with a woman?" What did you say?' Usha lay curled on the sofa with her head on Helen's thigh.

'It isn't an answerable question.'

'Anyone would think you'd been doing it with a giraffe or something.'

'Come on, you know Maggie. She only says what other people are often thinking.'

'Other less rude people.'

'You call it rude, I call it forthright.'

Usha sat up. 'I'm sorry. For some reason Maggie makes me grumpy. This old friend that knows you so well. I bet there isn't anything you wouldn't tell her.'

'Why are you fretting?' Helen patted her thigh. 'Lie down again. My leg's cold.' Usha curled against her; Helen rested her hand on the curve of Usha's hip. 'We fit together well.'

Usha sighed. 'I suppose I want something of my very own. Something of you.'

'You know you're special. My tattoo –'

'That's amazing.' Usha turned her head and kissed Helen's stomach through the silk shirt. 'But it's not what I mean.' She settled down again. 'Tell me a memory you've never told anyone else. Something awful, maybe. I heard about one guy who put a moth in the microwave.'

'Well, I can honestly say that has never even crossed my mind.'

They watched the silent images flashing across the television screen.

A lioness buried her face in the rich red belly of the fallen zebra, eyes narrowed in pleasure. The next moment cubs frolicked around her as she lay in the sun cleaning their small faces, her tongue buffeting them, making them blink.

'Maybe we could get a cat,' said Usha. 'I wonder how much tinned zebra is.'

Helen looks at the small wooden box; Daddy shows her how the glass front goes up and down.

'There he is,' he says.

She looks at the small white mouse. Its whiskers tremble as it looks out of the glass wall. She and Daddy must look huge; monstrous eyes swivelling in the sky.

'It's lovely to have something to care for,' says Mum and makes little kissy noises: pushed together like that her lips look shrivelled.

'Isn't he sweet?' Daddy says. Helen feels vacant. The mouse isn't disgusting or anything; it just is.

Once the mouse bit her and she was pleased: it didn't want to be there either. It took years to die, to rid her of the responsibility. It lay like a toy, its tiny feet stiffened into claws, its eyes blank, bloody beads.

'It's a natural part of life,' said Daddy, cuddling her. He couldn't know she was crying because all she felt was relieved.

'The summer of our second year at university I stayed in England and Dan went travelling. I remember, the weather here was sticky. You only had to think about moving and you broke out in a sweat.' Helen was aware of her palms getting damp. Nausea hauled at her stomach. 'I missed a period. I did the sensible thing – though I wanted to ignore it, to trust that everything was fine.' She watched the sun setting over the Serengeti. 'It wasn't.'

'So –' Usha made to sit up.

'Stay there. Please? I didn't know if Dan and I would stay together. I had my degree to finish. I knew what had to be done.' She took a deep breath and exhaled slowly. 'I had a good doctor. He gave me a referral.'

Usha was still. 'A *good* doctor?' she said dully. 'He helped you kill your baby.'

Helen felt her chest was beginning to split open. A wail was trapped way back in her throat, tangled in barbed wire; she could taste the metal. 'A co-operative doctor,' she said quietly. 'And it wasn't a baby.' Her voice leaked away to a whisper.

Usha rolled over and looked up at her. 'What was it then?'

'More accurately, a collection of cells with the potential to be a baby.'

Usha pushed Helen's hand aside and sat up. 'Twisting the language doesn't alter the truth. But if it makes you feel better –'

'Hah! Well, yes, of course, anyone can see that I'm really happy about the whole thing. Oh, I'm just fine,' Helen said bitterly.

'It's denial, isn't it: "collection of cells".'

'Don't you think I haven't thought about it? Haven't read accounts of fetal development? Tried to measure the exact nature of what I did?'

'It doesn't change the outcome.'

'My God. You are so simplistic.'

'You didn't have to kill it.' Usha's jaw was determined. 'You could have had it, given it up for adoption.'

'I wasn't strong enough. It was a long time ago – I was young.'

'The same age as me.'

'Different person, different time, different decision.'

'I don't agree with abortion.'

'I don't think I do, either,' said Helen. 'But it is a question of choice. It has to be. If it's any consolation, oh righteous one, it's the fucking reason I can't have a child now. Do you feel better now? Do you?'

Usha looked down at her hands. She shook her head.

'You asked me to tell you something I'd never told anyone: well, you have that now.'

'You must have told Dan.'

'No.'

'Maggie.'

'No. No one. Ever.'

'I'm so sorry,' said Usha. 'It's difficult. Theory meets reality, you know? I think that abortion is wrong, always wrong – then you . . .'

'Maybe it is always wrong. Then I have done wrong. And been punished.' She felt tears heating her eyes as Usha took her hands. 'Whichever way you look at it, it looks like justice.'

Usha held her but all she wanted to do was hide herself away. The familiar weight hadn't been lifted; it was only heavier and more odious.

The lid sat on top of the washing that was clambering out of the linen basket. A shirt sleeve stretched down the side like a root. Helen looked at her watch. It was half-past two. She hadn't heard Dan coming into the building before about half-four. She dragged the linen basket into the kitchen. She worked part-time, so she looked after the washing. She hadn't changed that; she didn't want to. It was easier not to think about why.

She sat at the kitchen table while the washing machine gurgled and swooshed. Like a laundrette for one, she thought. The flat seemed alien; she was a silent visitor, a burglar who crept into kitchens looking for comfort. She looked around. No dishes on the drainer. The tea-towel hung neat and uncreased. She looked in the pedal bin: the piquant spike of sweet-and-sour sauce from the uppermost takeaway box made her mouth water suddenly. She sat down again, feeling like a detective poking around in the exposed trivia of the murdered. The washing machine finished its succulent chugging and clicked into one of its thinking modes. The flat was silent.

She picked up the free newspaper and, with absolutely no interest, studied the furniture advert on the first page in minute detail. Somewhere in amongst the stripped pine and the universal-fit floral suite covers she was thinking. She closed the paper and got out a notebook. She tore off a page. She stared at it: all words seemed inadequate, loaded. Keep it simple. 'Tomorrow, 6pm. Please?' She inserted 'Dear Dan' at the top and '(Here)' at the bottom. She propped it on the table then moved it to the counter. She stood in the doorway and looked into the kitchen, then put the note back on the table. She sat down and, resting her head on her arms, she watched their clothes go round and round.

The white crushed velvet top made her breasts look coated in snow. Helen tugged at the hemline of the close-fitting lilac skirt. She scrutinized herself in the mirror propped on the armchair. My arms look like worms, she thought. She raised them, turning them so they caught the light. Or shiny snakes, maybe: she felt better. She tugged at the skirt again, unhappy with her fat knees.

Dan moves in her, his unfamiliarly brown hands resting on her knees. Their eyes meet. He smiles; sound in his throat like a purr.

Helen pushed the memory away, guilty at the warmth blossoming in her.

'Okay,' came Usha's muffled voice through the bedroom door. 'I'm ready.' She opened the door.

For a moment Helen saw Jaz, then he was gone and it was Usha in the expensive dark blue suit, a yellow shirt the colour of richest daffodils and a silk tie lambent as night clouds. Her hair was gathered into a chignon and between eyes sultry with kohl and soft sweeps of bronze and deep, intimate pink, she wore a blue and gold bindi. Gold and shattered light glittered in the curve of her nostril.

'Bloody hell,' said Helen.

'You're dead articulate, you are.' The regal young woman put her hands in her pockets and admired herself in Helen's mirror. A heavy scent like summer dusk followed her lazily. A dark, fuchsine lipstick moistened her mouth. Her face was a beautiful man's, a beautiful woman's. Her thick eyebrows drew together into a frown. 'I forgot my bracelet.'

Helen felt her own colours were retarded; she was an after-image that one would try to blink away, the ghost of a ghost. Usha smiled at her, almost sly. Helen felt a kick of desire that was close to anger. She wanted Usha naked, vulnerable. She wanted to inflict pain. Her voice squeezed past her. 'You ...' Have too much power. '... look incredible.' She touched the slender earrings that dropped from Usha's ears like slivers of dark water. 'I haven't seen these before.'

'They're new. I couldn't resist them.' Usha was smiling again.

'You *know* how good you look.'

'It's you who's telling me.' Usha's arm was firm around her waist. Their breasts were touching. 'You don't look bad yourself, as it happens.' She kissed Helen's throat. Heat diffused through Helen like something overturned. She fumbled at Usha's belt but the cold clasp shoved back at her fingers. She found the zip, hurried it down. Warm silk. Her hand moulded to Usha's shape. Usha closed her eyes: the colours were dark as flesh.

She felt Usha's hand on her wrist; gentle pressure to make Helen wait. The anger blistered again. She wanted her fingers made wet.

Usha sidestepped neatly and Helen's hand was empty. Usha did up her fly; the zip sounded electrical, efficient. Something warlike still clogged Helen's veins. Usha looked at her and understood nothing. 'I'll get my bracelet,' she said, watching her own reflection in the mirror as she left.

They could hear the music as they approached the club. The bass pushed the air seductively at them.

'Well.' Usha turned to Helen. 'Let's go and see what a lesbian looks like.' The light from the street had stripped all her colours away but Helen could still see them. She picked a thread from Usha's shoulder and smoothed back the tendril of hair that had eased itself from her bun. Usha held the door open and Helen walked into the vibrant gloom.

A fleshy woman in her forties just about wearing a small red dress gave Usha an appreciative look. 'Welcome to The Little Dutchgirl,' she said. 'Have a good night.' She winked at Usha. 'Happy New Year!'

'Hasn't she got a full-length mirror?' hissed Helen as they went through a second set of doors.

'She looked fine to me,' shouted Usha as the music finally got hold of them. 'Kind of free.'

It was impossible to talk. Usha mimed drinking and they went to the bar. The beat was physical; Helen felt its blows on her breastbone, its pressure at her throat.

Women danced on the crowded floor. Glistering fabrics shifted like maddened water. A slim woman in a tiny sequinned boob tube boogied out of the crush and up to the bar. A nipple strained out over the top of the material. She rolled her eyes and shoved the breast back in.

'God, don't tits get on your nerves sometimes!' she bellowed at Helen. 'Like bloody bags of jelly!' Her gaze slid over to Usha and stayed there. She moved, but not quite enough, as Usha returned with the drinks. Concentrating on the glasses, Usha had to brush against her as she squeezed past; amused, the woman gave her a leisurely once-over, a red-nailed hand resting casually on Usha's sleeve. She leant forward and spoke in Usha's ear.

Helen looked quizzically at Usha as she handed her a glass. Usha put her lips against Helen's ear. 'Lemonade,' she said.

Helen shook her head. 'That woman – what did she say?'

Usha laughed. The kiss of her breath on Helen's ear again: 'Nice suit. And then she put her hand on my bum.'

'Would you have told me if I hadn't asked?'

Usha cocked her head again. 'What?'

'I said, would you have –' A collective whoop of approval rose from the floor as the next number started.

Usha shook her head. 'What?'

> 'Last time she jumped out the window,
> well, she only turned and smiled...'

sang David Byrne while Helen watched people watching Usha. A woman wearing a black leather bra and a minute leather skirt tried to pull Usha onto the dance floor. 'Later,' mouthed Usha, smoothing her jacket sleeve. Helen sipped her lemonade. Alcohol warmed her tongue, described her throat.

'And vodka,' came Usha's close voice. 'I thought you'd like a drink.'

The rhythm of sex bound the dancers, and the bodies and voices celebrated.

> 'Come on, come on, I go up and down.
> I like this curious feeling. I know,
> I see. It's like make believe.
> Cover your ears so you can
> hear what I'm saying...'

Later, in the queue for the toilets, Helen met the boob tube again.

'I wouldn't leave her alone if I were you,' said the woman. She prodded her drooping curls then waved her hand dismissively. 'Hair. Who needs it.'

'She can look after herself.'

'It's not her I was thinking of.' Lipstick was expertly applied around the words. 'You two are new at this.' She pressed her lips together. 'It's a bit of a cattle market out there. I sometimes think we're worse than the bloody men.'

'But we have more taste,' called out someone behind them.

'And more stamina,' came a voice from one of the cubicles.

'And bigger bloody ears,' said boob tube, snapping the lid back on the lipstick. 'On you go, love,' she said gesturing Helen to a free cubicle. 'I was just being friendly,' she said to no one in particular.

'I wouldn't mind her phone number, either,' said the woman in the cubicle next door again. 'A nice brown binty would set me up lovely for the New Year. And I don't think that counts as racist,' she said, suddenly appearing over the partition: close-cropped hair like a thin woolly mat fuzzed the black woman's head. 'Do you?'

Helen smiled and shook her head. The black woman disappeared and she could piss in peace.

Midnight. The clamour of women. Usha's shirt damp where Helen's hands rest under the jacket. She tastes of salt, of the magenta shining on her lips. Their bodies are pressed together, sharing the collective pulse of the music that has rushed back in after the last chime. Women smile wildly around them. Helen doesn't want to think of any time beyond this but Dan is there; Dan is always there: Usha dances with them both, seeing only what she wants to see, looking only for the reflection she has made.

Helen stared into the dark. Usha's even breathing brushed at its edges but at the centre its silence was complete, curled into the impenetrable blackness. She thought about a life tucked into some damp fold inside Usha; half Dan; half Usha. She was intrigued yet revulsion plugged her mouth. It could not happen, this personification of her own redundancy. Dan would say no, she knew that, but in asking him she was exonerated; and Usha would not have to invent her way out of her foolishness. And ultimately? I will have neither of them, she thought, and that is exactly what I deserve.

As the sky began to lighten she fell asleep and into the dream of large, accusing eyes whose colour she could never recall.

23

Mike and Caroline's house was quiet. The two boys were out at the cinema with Caroline, and Mike was gardening. Dan was watching the concluding episode of a mini-series that he hadn't seen the rest of. Lettie slept curled up in an armchair. She was a miniature version of her mother, dark and often serious, but with a smile that made Dan want to steal her. On screen a woman was looking out of the window, watching a man on the street below walking away. Violins stirred. She buried her face in the bouquet he had brought her.

Lettie mumbled something, then her mouth opened in a wide yawn and she stretched her small chubby arms. 'You're crying,' she said. Her eyes were nearly navy.

Dan realized she was right: his face was wet. He wiped the tears away. 'No, not crying: leaking.'

Lettie sat up. 'Did that lady make you cry?' she said looking over at the television.

'No.'

Lettie looked stern.

'Well, maybe a little bit.'

Lettie nodded wisely. '*She's* crying now so you're not to be horrible to her.' Obviously Caroline's words but Lettie made them her own. She climbed up on the sofa and sat next to him. 'Of course, things on television aren't real,' she said.

'That's right.'

'I can see a bogey in your nose,' she said disarmingly. She thrilled him with a smile. 'You must use a tissue.' She fetched one from the box. She knelt next to him and clamped the tissue firmly on his nose. 'Blow,' she commanded.

'I'll do it,' he said, taking it from her. She stood on the seat next to him, one hand absentmindedly fidgeting in his hair, the other folding his ear down and up, down and up. She handled him casually, her immediacy perceiving him only as a large and genial toy. The sudden awareness that time would bring her the same knowledge and barriers as his own made him ache. He grabbed one of her ankles and tipped her over onto the sofa cushions where she lay giggling, her small naked feet working against his leg like a harmless cat's.

'Let's go and find Daddy,' he said.

'Yes,' she said, scrambling up. 'He can fly me.' She loved to be swung in the air by Mike; her trust was perfect, her enjoyment total. Dan wished she would ask him but it was only Mike who could give her all she wanted. He helped her into her socks and shoes and coat and from the back door watched her run down the garden to her father's waiting arms.

The front door to Lesley's house was ajar. The doorbell now consisted of two wires sellotaped to the door jamb with *Fry, scumbag* written above it. Dan knocked on the glass. Eventually the door opened and Alex put his head round. 'Oh, it's you,' he said. He looked relieved.

'I'm looking for Lesley.'

'She's not here.'

'We were supposed to meet in town a couple of hours ago.'

'Well, she's not here. Just me.' He turned and went back into the living room.

Dan decided to interpret this as an invitation to follow. 'How are things?' he asked, picking his way through the shared-house floor debris.

'Bit of a heavy night. You know what New Year's Eve is like.'

Mike and Caroline thinking of Dan thinking of Helen; no one says anything. The minute hand begins to slice away at the final half hour.

'I had a quiet one myself,' said Dan.

'God, my head hurts,' Alex said.

'Well, that's what happens,' said Dan philosophically. 'It's a shame you can't have the effects you want without the other stuff.'

'You couldn't go changing the bevvie, that wouldn't be right. Better painkillers, that's what we need.' He rubbed his face vigorously. 'I know what.' He headed for the kitchen. 'You want a lager?' he called out.

'I should . . . oh, what the hell.'

Alex came back holding a couple of cans and handed one to Dan. 'Plenty more where that came from,' he said. 'It was my turn to do the shopping.'

They hissed their cans open.

'So, where are we up to?' asked Dan gesturing to *Mary Poppins* playing in silence on the television.

'Dunno,' said Alex. 'Never seen it.'

'Oh. I thought you'd been watching it.'

'No.' Alex burped gently. He looked at Dan appraisingly. 'Do you reckon you're one of those New Men, then?' he said as though they'd been discussing it.

New? He'd never felt so used-up; he was dead flowers in stale water. 'I don't think so,' he said.

'I reckon you are,' Alex said.

'Maybe I am, then.'

'In touch with your feelings, that stuff.' Alex shook his head. 'Have you noticed that it's only some feelings women want you to be in touch with?' He shook his head again. 'I bet you're good at that.'

Dan did laugh this time. 'Just as well you haven't put real money on it.'

'Okay, here's one. I like women; I like looking at women. That's normal, right?'

Dan nodded.

'I can look at real women, the ones there in front of me.' Alex put his can on the floor and leant forward. 'What I don't understand is, what's wrong with looking at a woman when she isn't there?'

'An invisible woman.'

'Don't be stupid – I mean *images*. No woman actually there to be offended by you looking at them. Pictures, videos – I don't get what the problem is.'

'Well,' said Dan. 'Power relation–'

'I'll tell you something about power,' Alex said warmly. 'I was shit-scared that you were one of the girls when the door went. You know why? Because I was watching a video that they wouldn't approve of. A "dirty" video, whatever that means. They would give me so much grief, you wouldn't believe it, try and make me feel ashamed because I'm a normal human male. This is *sex*, for God's sake. You can't get much more natural than that.'

'I haven't really seen –'

'Neither have they! They don't even know what it is they're objecting to! These women aren't being forced to do anything – they're obviously having a whale of a time.'

Dan looked at the puzzlement on Alex's face. He had the unbidden, uncomfortable feeling that his own opinions were received conviction. Alex kept it simple: maybe it was.

'Anyway,' said Alex, picking up his lager and sitting back, 'I was right about you. You're on their side.'

'Maybe.' Dan digested some fizz. 'If you insist on sides.'

'You've never seen a skin flick, have you?'

'Nope.'

'How come?'

'Lack of opportunity, I suppose,' Dan said.

'But you're interested?'

'Yes, in principle. New experiences are always interesting.'

'*Disgusting,' his mother says, moving with impressive speed to the television set. She changes channel. Now a man is talking about Bible sales worldwide. He looks like he should choke, his tie is so fiercely knotted.*

That kiss in the film had definitely involved tongues. Dan is relieved, though, at his mother's action. A kind of paralysis had descended on him when sex and parent tried to occupy the same space.

'Disgusting,' Mum says. She goes to put the kettle on and leaves as a drawing of Eve before the Fall is displayed. Eve has no nipples. Nipples must be disgusting, Dan decides. Or is it breasts with nipples that are disgusting? His cock is interested in this debate. He tries to think about something else; his mother will be back soon.

'Right then,' said Alex decisively. He pulled a video box out from under his armchair. 'Purely for educational purposes.' He put the cassette in the player.

'What's the storyline?' asked Dan.

Alex burst out laughing. 'You can tell you're new to this. Plot isn't that important – look on it as postmodernism.' He put his fingertips together and looked at Dan over imaginary spectacles. 'Since the filmmaker knows that you know that you're watching a film he doesn't patronize you by trying to fool you that it's reality,' he lectured. 'Any structure you perceive is imposed by you.' He grinned. 'Something like that.' He paused. 'Or am I thinking of deconstruction?' He shrugged and drank some lager.

'So what is the flimsy excuse for a lot of rumpy-pumpy?'

'All you need to know is that we're at the point where they're well into rumpy and will soon move into the pumpy stage. Here we go.' He started the video.

The picture flickered crazily for a second or two then settled down.

The large pink breast on screen definitely had a nipple. The camera pulled back. Approaching the breast was a dark-skinned woman with long hair plaited into a single braid that lay down her back like black rope. Her dark hands fondled the breasts, small and earnest against the pale skin. She rubbed the nipples between her fingers, then bent her head and sucked greedily. The already abundant moaning and panting increased. The other woman reached down and cupped the dark woman's breasts, then stretching further, began to rub between her legs.

Dan looked at the depiction of what he had refused to think about. Usha raised her head and she and Helen exchanged a hungry, obscene kiss. He felt breathless, his chest compressed by something from the inside. 'You're a good girl,' moaned Helen. 'So good, so good.' His tongue had dried up. It lay in the huge cavern of his mouth where the teeth began to crumble. Blood was pumping through to his cock. Helen lay back and Usha began to work her way down her body. Usha wore an anklet of tiny bells and through the rasp of breathing it tinkled, a sweet, light sound following her feeding movements. He wanted to fuck his excited anger away, take the two women, have Usha hold Helen down, make her accept him again and again.

'Here,' said Alex from behind the glass that seemed to encase everything beyond Dan and the women. He threw Dan the video box. 'The story's on the back.'

Heat and Lust!! announced the cover above a photograph of the two women. Bowing her head, the topless Indian woman performed a namaste, standing before the white woman who was spilling out of a frilly bodice; their picture was superimposed against a painting of the Taj Mahal. Dan turned the box over. 'The height of the British Raj finds Colonel Blighty and his good lady wife in the sticky Indian heat. When the Colonel is called away on Empire business, the delectable young servant girl Mina is there to service Lady Blighty's every need and she performs her duties with admirable enthusiasm! Though she had thought her employer cold and passionless, when the Colonel returns unexpectedly, Mina finds out what her mistress sees in him . . .'

Dan was suddenly nauseous. The mistress pulled her servant's head urgently downwards; her expression ambiguous between pleasure and pain she clutched at the sleek black head, her demands guttural, incoherent, but unmistakable. Disgust spread through him like a hostile fluid hotter than his blood.

'Turn it off,' he said. His voice didn't sound like his own. Alex looked at him with curiosity. Dan hated his silly young face, his blindness. The desperation on the video rose. Dan headed for the video player.

'Hey!' said Alex. He stood in front of Dan.

'Turn it off.'

'What's your problem?'

'Please. Turn it off.' Dan's body urged him to shove the boy out of the way.

'Did you like it too much?' said Alex. His smile was spiteful, and knowing – when he knew nothing, nothing at all about anything. Their faces were too close. The woman's voice wasn't far off a howl now. The occasional carillon from the anklet was just audible.

Dan ducked around him and hit the 'Stop' button.

'Who do you think –'

In the pause Dan could hear his own ragged breathing. Then the sound of the front door closing.

'Fuck,' said Alex. The tape seemed to take forever to eject; there was a fussing around inside the machine and the tape appeared only when the machine was satisfied that the mysterious process was complete.

'Sit,' commanded Alex and shoved the tape under his chair. He used the remote control to turn the volume up on the television.

Lesley came into the room. 'Hi. I saw your car outside,' she said to Dan. 'Sorry about –'

For a joke, Dan's body made him laugh: he sounded like an ailing hyena. 'No problem.'

Lesley looked at him. 'That's alright then. Has Alex been keeping you amused?'

'Oh, yes. We've been watching . . . a bit of telly.'

'*Mary Poppins*,' said Lesley. 'One of my favourites. It's completely crap.' She sat down on the sofa next to Dan. 'So, where are we up to?'

A childhood's enforced viewing of appropriate films seemed like a benediction now to Dan: he must have seen it half a dozen times. 'Alex has been having a bit of trouble following it,' he said, 'but it's really very simple.'

'Should suit you very well, Alex,' said Lesley. 'Listen to the man: you might learn something.'

Alex made a face at her. He crushed his empty can and tossed it into the fireplace where it rang against the others as if it had been given a hefty kick.

What room is appropriate for receiving one's wife? he mused. He sat in the kitchen but all the hard edges drove him into the living room. He kicked off his slippers and sat on the sofa, working hard at looking relaxed. The doorbell rang and his heart leapt about like a puppy.

'Why didn't you use your key?' he said. She was pale; she had that anxious look he had seen in consultants' offices.

'I wasn't sure what to do. It seemed simpler not to.'

'Come in, then, now you're here.'

She perched on one of the armchairs. 'So, how are you?'

'Not fine.'

'Me neither.' They looked at one another for a long time.

'What's going to happen?' said Dan. 'Not seeing you has been ... weird.'

'It's like being a teenager – you know, you split up with someone and then never see them again.'

'Have we split up?'

She looked down at her hands and didn't reply.

'It feels more like we've been interrupted ...' he said. 'I can't imagine ... Bloody hell, Helen, don't leave me.' He realized in that moment that he hadn't taken her relationship with Usha seriously; he felt like he was shrinking. There was nothing to grip onto, nothing to stop everything swelling around him until he disappeared completely. 'You can't throw all we've been through away,' he panicked. 'We just need time to sort things out. Why don't –'

'Usha says she will bear a child for me,' Helen said. He stared at her. 'I'm sorry,' she said. 'There was no graceful way of saying it.'

'That's unbelievable. I mean, of course, if you say it **then** ... Is it her you want or just the baby?' he babbled. 'Not "just" – that's wrong. I mean, we – you and me – we *could* adopt, couldn't we? I know you've always said you didn't want to but why don't we reconsider ...' He cast around wildly. 'Why does that have to be everything? What about me?' His speech slowed as he reached his conclusion, the sense that surfaced and stayed. 'What about me?'

'Oh, Dan.'

'Stay with me. I know things have been difficult but –' She was only a few feet away across the carpet she had chosen but he seemed to have no way of getting to her. 'Are you a lesbian now?' he blurted.

'What sort of a question is that?'

'A simple one. I need clarification, for God's sake.'

'I don't know that I'm one thing or another. Usha and I . . .' She clasped her hands uncertainly. 'It feels right.'

'So you're telling me that we never did, is that it? Or have you been trying to make up your mind for the last thirteen years?'

'It isn't like that.'

'What is it like, exactly?'

'I care for you so much . . .'

He snorted. 'Yeah, right.'

'No!' she exclaimed. 'I do. It's like I'm not in control, Dan. I have to do this thing. Can you understand that?'

'I wish I could. You do realize what you're thinking of taking on?'

She nodded miserably. 'I can't say no.'

'Then I'm redundant.' He was numb.

Helen cleared her throat. 'No, I . . .' He could see she was trying to get words to come out but the way they needed to be joined together meant she couldn't.

The knowledge burst into him. 'Sperm,' he said.

'I, uh . . .' She blinked a couple of times. 'Yes.'

'You want me to have sex with Usha?' His incredulity made his voice squeaky.

She shook her head. 'It needs to be collected,' she said in a gruff whisper. 'In a container.' She forced herself to look at him. 'It must be fresh.'

'And you put it . . .'

Her eyes were full of tears. She nodded. A tear ran crazily down her cheek and crashed into her mouth. Her tongue came and tidied it away.

'Let me get this straight,' he said. 'You want me to wank – into an appropriate receptacle – and then give it straight to you.' He watched his fingers tapping rapidly on the arm of the sofa. 'Is there anything in particular you'd like me to think about while I'm doing it? I mean, we wouldn't want the product to be adversely affected by me thinking about something really disgusting like sex with my wife, would we?'

'That's up to you.'

'You make it sound very tempting, I must say.'

She stood up. 'I said I would ask and I have. Now let's forget it was ever mentioned.'

'Where else are you going to get it from?'

'Nowhere.'

'Oh, come on. I'm sure there are loads of chaps who'd jump at the chance to –'

'I wanted – *we* wanted . . .'

'Which "we" is that, Helen – the old one or the new one?'

She seemed lighter now; her old fire flickered. She looked about to go. He didn't want her to leave; even arguing was better than picturing her elsewhere when he was alone.

'I think I should . . .' She turned to the door.

He felt a burst of unexpected pride, of power. He was necessary. To bring life into being he was necessary. Suddenly that seemed enough. 'I'll do it,' he said.

'What?'

He felt absurdly happy; it was such a simple thing. 'You heard me. I'll do it.'

A new expression rearranged her features. 'Don't muck about, Dan. You obviously don't want –'

He reached forward and closed her mouth. Her skin was cool. 'I can do this for you. I will. On one – no, two – conditions.'

Suspicion pushed past the fear. 'And they are?'

'I get to name the result, if there is a result.'

'As long as it isn't anything stupid.'

'Oh ye of little faith.'

'What else?'

'I get to hold you. Now. For as long as I want.'

She felt familiar, and strange. She must have been aware of his erection but she didn't move away. Her hair smelt different but the scent of her neck was the same.

'I should have told you that once I got my arms around you I wasn't ever going to let go,' he said.

'You'll have to eventually,' she said into his chest. 'Your legs will give out.'

His legs felt strong; he was as rooted as a tree. He let her go, sooner than he wanted, afraid of beginning to sense that she didn't want to be there any longer.

He spent the evening wandering restlessly around the flat, thinking about himself, about Helen, about the possibility that was suddenly real: he skimmed over Usha; she was too difficult. No matter what happened he wanted to do what he could for Helen; he couldn't shake off the feeling, though, that today he had somehow managed to disappoint.

24

THE DAY WAS piercingly bright. Helen stood in the bay of the window where sunlight poured in through a fizz of dust. The sun in her hair made it gleam and Usha was reminded of the gold threads woven through Rani's best salwar kameez. She felt the familiar guilt at not going to see her aunt and the sting that pricked at her whenever she thought of her mother. She could have stood up to Dad, Usha thought; she had let Usha go. Usha's anger had leaked away, gradually, replaced by a hurt she didn't want to admit to, a hurt she disguised as the old anger whenever Jaz mentioned their parents. It was getting harder, though; she had waited so long for Jaz to make it better.

'It's beautiful out there,' said Helen.
'Let's go for a walk.'
'Are you alright?'
'I'm fine. I just want some air.'

'I love this stuff,' said Helen, touching the pink fluff of the candy floss. 'It's almost like it's not there.'
They walked onto the pier and stopped to look at the sea. Light glanced off the water and ricocheted around the closely packed waves.
'It hurts to look at it,' said Usha.
The wind tugged violently at Helen's candy floss. 'I'm going to lose this if I'm not careful,' she said. 'Let's sit down.' They sat in the shelter and Usha held her gloved hands over her cold ears. 'You won't be able to hear me if you do that,' said Helen as she tore off a piece of pink cloud.
'Pardon?'

Helen grinned and fed Usha some candy floss. 'I don't know,' said Usha, '*some* people get fed grapes – and what do I get?'

'Sweet nothing. Have some more.'

They finished the candy floss and watched the passers-by. A Japanese woman walked past carrying an inflatable alligator that was nearly as big as she was. She stopped near them and her husband took a photograph, then they swapped over; the woman took the camera and as she handed him the alligator the wind scooped it up and launched it over the tinseled sea. Talking excitedly they watched the silhouette dancing wildly during its descent onto the water. It landed and began to bob away towards France.

'Now that's not something you see every day,' said Helen.

'No,' said Usha, 'usually it's chip wrappers.' She stood up to get a better look and tripped over a pushchair. 'Oh! Sorry.' As she looked at the woman something seemed to shift and she watched pieces locking together. 'Dalip?'

The soft brown eyes searched and found. 'Usha!'

The room is like a cave. It is dark and warm, the soft heat is a cushion all around them. Thick blue curtains reach down to the floor; one slit, as thin as paper, draws a bright line in the velvet.

'I need to wear a bra,' Dalip says, smoothing the moony glow of her T-shirt over her small breasts. 'I've gone up a size in the last three months. I'm bigger than Veena now.' She opens a drawer and holds up two pale tangles. 'These are the new ones.'

The cotton is cool from the shadows.

'So's this.' Dalip pulls up her top. Butterflies decorate her breasts.

In the gloom she and Usha exchange a look. Outside, Dalip's brother is kicking a ball against the wall. It sounds like the house has a heartbeat.

Usha cups Dalip's breast, soft beneath the butterflies. The feelings flaring through her are hard to follow; but she doesn't want to take her hand away, and Dalip doesn't want her to, and these are certainties that go on existing in the room that is as warm as fur.

'What are you doing here?' Usha asked her. 'I thought you went to Leicester after you got married.'

'Yeah, I'm down visiting family.'

'How's Kamal?'

'He's doing great,' said Dalip. 'He runs a couple of clubs. How about Jaz?'

'He's fine. He's got as far as opening the next shop.'
'Not married yet?'
'Well, I've had . . .'
Dalip laughed. 'I know *you're* not married – I meant Jaz.'
Usha was irritated by her smugness. 'If you know I'm not then I expect you know Jaz isn't.'
Dalip was unperturbed. 'Still sowing his wild thingies, I expect.' She looked at Helen. 'Do you know Jaz? Ooh, I had a real crush on him when I was younger.' The child in the pushchair gurgled and waved mittened hands. 'This is what I've been doing for the past couple of years,' said Dalip. 'This is Jarvis Charan Singh, otherwise known as Jacey.' He looked solemn when he heard his name and looked up at Usha: for an instant she saw his mother looking at her in that starless room.

Then the significance of his existence hit her. She felt lightheaded; her belly tried to imagine the placid water in which he had floated, to see the space inside her that could stretch and fill with life. He was so real. She fought the panic that rose in her.

'He's beautiful,' Helen said. Usha saw her looking at the boy, analysing his features, trying to see what she might expect in half of Usha's child. Usha felt exposed, judged.

'He is,' said Dalip. 'And hopefully it's a sister in here.' She patted her stomach. 'I'm due July seventh.'

'Congratulations,' said Usha. She was overcome with distaste. Dalip isn't having a child, she thought, she's breeding. It's all so . . . biological.

'It's lovely having Jacey,' Dalip said, 'but I could have done without being pregnant. If only you could have them without all that hard work – I'd have a dozen like a shot.'

Usha looked at Helen but she kept her eyes on Jacey.
'You have children, do you?' Dalip asked Helen.
She shook her head.
'Towards the end with Jacey,' said Dalip, 'I hated everything, hated being fat and uncomfortable.' She bent down and adjusted Jacey's woolly hat. She laughed. 'I got over it, didn't I, sweetie? Hmm?' Jacey smiled at her without comprehension, loving the shape of her voice. Dalip stood up. 'I was lucky. The weight dropped right off after he was born.'

'You've always been skinny, though, haven't you,' Usha said.

The top stair creaks; it sounds like a whimper. Usha snatches her hand back and Dalip covers herself.

'There you are,' says Dalip's mother. Her earrings clink when she moves her head; they are gold filigree, like little gates. 'Have you done your homework?'

Dalip nods.

'Then come and help me downstairs.'

When the homework that Dalip has copied from Usha comes back from the teacher she gets a 'D': Usha has an 'A'.

Dalip doesn't invite her back to the house again.

'I've got a very fast metabolism,' Dalip said mildly.

Usha felt questions in her look. 'Well, it was nice to see you,' she said, looking at a point somewhere past Dalip's left ear.

'And you.'

Dalip began to set off. 'Oh, Usha,' she said, stopping a short distance away. 'Mind you invite me to the wedding.' She waved and turned away quickly.

'I never liked her,' Usha said.

'Maybe you're too alike.'

'That is a joke, isn't it.'

'There was something about her . . . I don't know what it was –'

'You don't know her,' said Usha shortly.

'True. Jacey was sweet, though.' She could feel Helen looking at her but kept her eyes on the sea.

They walked home in silence. Dan's car was parked outside like a patient pet. Helen only glanced at it but she did look.

A light rain made sharp by the wind scraped at Usha's cheek. She squatted at the side of the bike trying to get the padlock undone. Helen had told her to jiggle the key. She'd jiggled and wrenched and jiggled again, but the cold metal kept her out.

'Having a bit of trouble, are we?' said a male voice that seemed to have a smooth layer on it, like cream. Usha looked round. Surinder smiled.

'I'm fine,' she said.

'Doesn't look like it.'

Usha stood up. He was holding a small white polythene bag. Something slid around inside it, something fleshy and dark against the thin barrier.

'Funny,' he said. 'I didn't have you down as the cycling type. Come to think of it, you've got the legs for it.'

'Yeah, I find them so much easier than the flippers I had before.'

'Still clever, then,' smirked Surinder. 'You know, Ush, sarcasm isn't an attractive feature in a woman.'

'Is that right?' The rain was getting heavier.

'There you go again.' Surinder tutted. 'Such a shame.'

'Never mind, eh,' said Usha. She wondered which way Surinder was going. She could leave the bike and walk the rest of the way home.

'I can't help feeling you don't like me,' he said.

'Does it make any difference?'

'It does to me. Remember last time we met? I meant what I said, you know. You're quite a woman. And call it coincidence, but I'm quite a guy. We could have a lot of . . . fun.'

'You should record yourself and play it back when you need a good laugh.'

Surinder shook his head. 'You do need to be taught a lesson.'

She took her handbag out of the basket. 'Well, I'd stay and listen to your advice but I can't think of anything worse, frankly.' She shoved the key into her pocket. 'Except taking it.'

'Men can smell a girl like you a mile away.' His eyes were dark, blank.

A small brown dog sniffed at Surinder's leg then attempted to mount it. Surinder looked down. 'Oh God.' He shook his leg vigorously but the dog held on tight.

'Oi! Charger! Come here!' An overweight man made a great show of hurrying over. He shoved the dog with his foot. 'Leave him alone!' Charger attempted a rematch. 'I'm sorry, mate,' the old man said to Surinder. 'He's a bit frustrated. I've got something from the vet but it's the devil's own job getting those pills down. He gave me some drops for the dog as well.' He burst into a laugh that sounded like it would be his last. Charger considered the allure of Surinder's trousers but seemed distracted by his owner's cough.

'No, really,' spluttered the old man. 'Please accept my apologies.' He put out his hand.

'Just get the dog out of here,' said Surinder. 'Before I do it for you.'

The fat man and the fat little dog waddled off together.

'I suppose you think that was funny,' Surinder said.

'I haven't said a word.'

'I know what you're thinking.'

'Ah. How do you do that then?' Usha folded her arms.

'I'll see you again,' he said. He looked at her coldly. 'You think about what I've said, yeah?'

She gave him time to get away. She fished the key out of her pocket and fitted it into the lock. It turned sweetly and the staple swung free.

Water hissed under the tyres. Up ahead the big roundabout was crowded with traffic. She headed for the footbridge. The air above the road was pressed down by the rain and the sour traffic fumes found taste in her mouth. Keeping her head down against the sting of rain she pushed the bicycle across the bridge; her hands, as they grew colder in the sodden gloves, felt too big to hold the handlebars. She longed for the dry warmth of bed and the comfort of the sleeping Helen. Usha often woke first, and enjoyed being witness to Helen's unconscious existence: when she was asleep she grew untidy. The first puzzled blinks of blue beneath dishevelled hair brought her arms out to find Usha: like a child, Usha felt, arms raised in the hope that a passing grown-up will decide to lift them to steady, omnipotent heights.

She stepped in a puddle and the water found its sure way between her toes. Her eyelashes were sodden and dripped the strange dry wetness into her eyes. The path was beginning the slow hill down to the end of the footbridge. She started to get on the bike and nearly crashed into someone.

'Oh, sorry,' she said. 'I was –' She looked up and into Surinder's eyes, hard and dry under his umbrella.

'You should look where you're going.'

'My eyes are full of rain.'

'That's quite poetic.' He scrutinized her without grace, like he was observing her through a two-way mirror. 'Your face is a mess. Kohl everywhere.' Usha attempted to push the bike around him but he stepped in front of her. 'Don't be in such a hurry.'

'What do you *want*, Surinder? I'm cold, I'm soaked and I'm all out of conversation.'

'You behave like you're too good for me. Hah!' His smiled switched on and off like a flashgun. 'Girls like you –'

'You've got a bit of a thing for "girls like me", haven't you? What would your mum think of you sniffing around the sort of girl we've all been warned about?'

'There are whores and wives, you know that. Your behaviour –'

'Is none of your business!'

'Tell that to your family. They *know* it's my business; it's everyone's.'

'And you've spoken to them, have you?' She tried to manoeuvre the bike around him, but again he stepped in her path.

His face smoothed in satisfaction. 'As a matter of fact –'

'Will you please get out of the way?'

Surinder took his umbrella down. Rain spattered dark into his suit. The small plastic bag he carried looked covered in sweat. 'A polite request from Usha,' he said. 'That's better. You're getting the hang of it now.'

For a strange instant, she thought he was falling but he pulled her head towards him and she felt the crudeness of his tongue in her mouth. She tried to pull away but his grip was too strong for her to free herself completely. 'Get off!' she spat. She shoved at his face with damp woolly fingers, making contact with the tender swell of an eye.

He clutched at his face. 'Bitch!' The bag fell with a juicy splat into a puddle at her feet, and split open. Liver glistened; rich, dead maroon against the black tarmac. Blood diluted into the water.

She pushed past him and struggled onto her bike. He lashed after her with his umbrella; it caught in the spokes and the bike keeled over, trapping her leg underneath. She felt the unforgiving frame crack against her leg and somewhere distant the pedal scraped deeply into her ankle. He stood near her head and she thought he was going to kick her. She closed her eyes.

The spittle hit her jaw and trickled down her neck as gently as a kiss. She felt more than heard his departure, as the bridge vibrated to the blow of each of his footfalls. She lay for a few moments preparing herself for the struggle to get up. I am a fallen woman, she thought; the laughter she didn't want rushed into her and out again immediately. Her uneven breathing seemed to encourage it. She inhaled slowly and little by little let the breath out. She began to disentangle herself from the bike. Below her the traffic jam grunted on, struggling to escape its fouled nest.

She was unable in the heavy rain to tell if she was crying. She giggled repeatedly, knowing it was an aberration that Helen would stop; but first she had to travel the unimaginable distance that lay between them.

25

Helen rested Usha's foot on the embroidered cushion and dabbed at the curls of skin. Beneath the rime of blood, purple bloomed at the edges of the damage.

Usha sucked her breath in sharply. 'Are you sure this is good for me?'

'Absolutely.' The bitter smell of antiseptic made Helen feel useful. 'It isn't too bad,' she said. 'The ankle bone's a bit battered but you'll live.' The naked vulnerability of Usha's foot clenched in Helen's chest. 'You should report him,' she said.

'That'd give someone a laugh,' she said. 'Yes, well, officer, I fell off my bike.'

'He made you.'

'Okay, how about: "He made me fall off my bike"?'

'He assaulted you.'

'With my bicycle, mainly.'

'Still . . .' Helen began looking through the box of plasters. They seemed to be big enough only for cuts that wouldn't need a plaster in any case.

'There weren't any witnesses. And the police don't have much interest in crimes that happen to Asians.'

Guilt stabbed through Helen. 'I'd come with you. I could say I was there, that I saw the whole thing.'

'No.'

'Why not? Bastards like that –'

'Okay. Supposing it got anywhere: Surinder could stand up in court and say I led him on. Girls like me do that, you know.'

'He hasn't any proof.'

'There's no evidence either way,' said Usha. 'My family are ashamed enough without it going on record that a good number of other people think I'm a slut, too.'

'Jaz isn't ashamed of you.'

Usha gave her a long look. She took her foot off the cushion. 'Leave it. It's complicated.' She inspected her ankle.

'What do you mean, "complicated"?'

'My parents care what people think. I've done enough damage.'

'If you let –'

'It isn't a question of letting,' snapped Usha. 'I choose to do what I do. Doing something public is different for someone like me.'

'How?'

Usha yawned. 'Do we have to talk about this now?'

'I'd like . . .'

'Okay.' Usha winced as she began to put on her sock. 'There are good and bad aspects of a close community. One good thing is that people look out for each other; a direct result of that is one of the bad things – whatever you do is observed, and judged. When I was with Alex – and before – all that seemed petty.'

'And now?' Helen sat next to her.

'I still think that what I do is up to me. But there are other people involved and because they think all that stuff is important they get hurt.'

'Isn't that their problem?'

'Maybe,' said Usha. 'But when you're brought up on collective responsibility it's hard to get rid of the feeling. When I was a kid, I hated all the close scrutiny – I used do the round trip to Shoreham on the bus just to be on my own.'

'So this thing with Surinder would be bad news for your folks.'

'It's a points system: doing something that the community frowns on means you chalk up a certain number of points. Except it isn't only you – it's your family. And when the people without points have dealings with your family, the family are treated as having the points when they had nothing to do with the transgression.'

'That isn't fair!'

'Individualism isn't big in that framework.'

'But it means that if a person had earned ten points for doing something wrong, and there were twenty members in the family, that'd be two hundred points!'

'I didn't say it was a good system,' said Usha.

'How do you work the points off?'

'Tricky. If you're a man with an adulterous wife or unvirginal daughter, you could always kill them. That shows you are *really* pissed off.'

'Usha . . .'

'It happens. But that *is* the wacky end. Some people go around feeling ratty and embarrassed. And some people are a lot less bothered than others. It just depends.' She yawned again and rested her head on her hand. 'My parents always seemed quite cool. I didn't think . . .' She stretched out her legs and sighed. 'I didn't think. That's all.' She rested her feet in Helen's lap. 'I need a bath. I ache all over.'

In the steam-padded bathroom Usha peeled off her clothes. Helen perched on the new wicker linen basket and watched as Usha wound her hair into a bun and pinned it high on her head. She admired the long slender body and the high neat buttocks, the warm wood hue, the curved symmetry of her waist. She touched Usha lightly on her flank as she turned and they briefly embraced. Usha stepped back. As she bent to test the temperature of the water Helen saw the full extent of the bruises on her inner thighs, especially on the right leg. The sudden recognition made her want to cry out: *dark bruises, as big as a fist*, that woman had said; *the unwatched TV; the clinic loud with the suffocating silence of women.*

Resting one hand on Helen's shoulder, Usha stepped into the bath. Helen looked at Usha's perfect young body and wanted to weep for her own that had cauterized itself against her. Usha sank down into the sibilance of bursting bubbles. Her head looked disembodied in the white foam. She looked at Helen, took a deep breath and submerged completely. The foam closed over her face. Her knees shone like polished sculpture. With difficulty Helen resisted the urge to pull her back into the air and waited, holding her own breath, for Usha to return.

'You're not serious.' Maggie put down her paintbrush and wiped her hands on a cloth. Pinned by Maggie's focus on her, Helen could only nod; and continued painting the door frame. Maggie came over from the window and took Helen's brush. 'Stop. My living room can wait.' Maggie had magnolia gloss in her hair; she looked like she'd been sprinkled with pollen. 'I don't know about you but I could use a drink. Coffee you can stand a spoon up in and some jammy dodgers, that's what I need.'

Feeling like a naughty child about to be taken to task Helen sat at the table and watched Maggie making the coffee. 'You're a remarkable woman,' said Maggie, spooning granules into the cups. 'Only you could casually say, "By the way, my girlfriend is going to be a surrogate mother to a child fathered by my possibly ex-husband." Good grief.' Maggie poured water from the kettle. 'Last thing I knew we were talking about Austrian blinds.' She turned to Helen. 'Well, for goodness sake, *say* something.'

'That's it.'

'But Helen, what about . . .' She threw up her hands. 'Everything!'

Helen looked at her friend's puzzled, excited face and was filled with love for her. Funny how we feel about friends, she thought: this love is more reliable, more forgiving. 'I don't know,' she admitted as Maggie put the coffees on the table. 'But I think we're going to do it.' It was the first time she had said it out loud.

'You're mad, my love.'

'Don't give me the voice of reason,' said Helen. 'It has no sense of adventure.'

'But maybe a sense of reality.'

'Maybe.'

'How can this work? Usha's nice and everything and I'm sure you've become very attached to her but this will ruin her life.'

'This wasn't my idea!' defended Helen, prickling with fear at Maggie's reaction. She had convinced herself that Maggie would understand but instead she was using Helen's own words to dissuade her. 'Usha suggested it. Usha wants it.'

'You can't let her. Come on – don't tell me you honestly believe this is a good idea. Biscuit?' She took one and pushed the plate over to Helen.

Helen's conviction was wobbling but something deep in her gut slapped her and told her to pull herself together: this is what both she and Usha wanted. If she listened to Maggie all the effort of getting this far would be undone. 'I thought you'd be pleased,' she said.

'About my best and dearest friend fucking up her life, her husband's life, *and* the life of an innocent bystander?' As she spoke a biscuit crumb shot from her mouth and pinged against her cup. 'Give me one good reason why I would think this was a Good Thing.'

'Why do you insist on missing Usha out like that?'

'Because none of this can happen without you. You're the linchpin.'

'It can hardly happen without Usha, either.'

'Don't be obtuse. You know what I mean. I have some digestives as well, by the way.'

'Forget the damn biscuits – we're talking about a baby!'

'Fine.' Maggie sat back in her chair. 'I'll see if I have any bloody rusks.'

Despite herself Helen laughed. Maggie grinned at her and sipped her coffee. Helen took a biscuit, relieved to have Maggie back on her side, however briefly.

'Seriously, sweetie,' said Maggie. 'This is trouble. It isn't simply "a baby", is it. It'll grow into a person. What will you tell them? And a half-white, half-Asian kid is probably not going to have an easy time, let's face it. Crummy culture, but that's the way things are.'

'You wouldn't criticize a mixed heterosexual couple who were going to have babies.'

'No,' said Maggie thoughtfully. 'But there seems something ... unavoidable about that.'

'Two women who want a child together must be penalized, then, according to what you say. Most especially if they're from different ethnic backgrounds.'

'Christ, I don't know. I'm just telling you the thoughts as they come.' Her gaze on Helen was pensive. 'It has to be said that since women can't make sperm perhaps they should accept that a lesbian relationship can't produce children.'

'So lesbians don't feel the urge to become mothers.'

'I didn't say that. But every desire one has can't be fulfilled. There are gay men who want to be fathers.'

'Using your logic,' said Helen, 'because gay men don't have wombs they must accept that their relationships, however committed, cannot produce children.'

'Is that unreasonable? I think it's sad, and must be unbearably so for many. Compassion is one thing; practicality is quite different.'

'But if a female friend offered to do the deed for them?'

'Hmm ...' Maggie's agreement was grudging but sure. 'Yes, I wouldn't have a problem with that.'

'Well then.'

'But that's hypothetical. And I only agree in principle.'

'Dan's offered to do the deed.'

'I don't care. He'd do anything for you.'

The lump that came to Helen's throat made her swallow almost painful. 'Perhaps he would have, once.'

'You're on the verge of doing something stupid and I want to stop you,' said Maggie.

'It'll be alright.'

'I wish I could believe that. I don't know why you do.' She held Helen's hand for a moment and Helen was surprised to see tears welling in her eyes. 'I'll get those digestives,' she said briskly.

They sat munching biscuits, not talking. One day we'll be two little old ladies, thought Helen: sitting together dunking biscuits and complaining about our aches and pains. She couldn't imagine a child older than she was now, nor could she imagine Usha old. Maggie, though, would be as irascible and as crude, with hair as bright and unruly as it looked today. For a time Helen fled the present, wishing away forty years to be with her friend in a safe and distant bubble.

Usha sniffed and took another tissue from the box on Helen's lap. The film soundtrack began to whine again with Indian instruments that sounded out of tune to Helen. The heroine began to sing and clutched her hands together at her breast. This was the sound Helen had heard in corner shops from radios turned low as though in apology.

'Poor thing. Her heart is breaking,' Usha said.

'It's annoying that they don't give subtitles for the singing bits,' said Helen. 'What's she saying?'

'Her heart is breaking.'

The hero was shown riding away on a horse, his jewelled scabbard flashing in the sunset.

'This is so corny.'

Usha nodded. 'It's great.' She blew her nose. 'There will be a happy ending but first we have to have the obstacles and the odd death or two.'

A panning shot followed a black horse thundering up to the gates of a vast white building decorated with minarets. The rider banged on the huge wooden doors.

'This is the bad guy,' said Usha. 'He wants the girl for himself, so he's about to spin some story to her dad about the hero, not knowing he's already done the decent thing. Then the brother, who gets mistaken for the cousin –'

'Stop!'

'Never mind, there'll be another song soon.'

Helen wished she could be less judgemental and take the pleasure from it that Usha did but its pounding of sentiments wearied her. She looked through a few more pages of the sketchbook on her lap. She wanted to make a new piece but it wasn't from these pages. She felt she was close enough to it to grasp it, but she didn't know what it looked like. She tried mentally mixing colours but all she could imagine were strips of colour lying next to one another. Something else loitered out of reach.

She sharpened all her pencils and lined them up neatly in the tin. She turned to a fresh page and sat with a pencil in her hand, waiting.

'Hey,' said Usha, 'look at those hangings.'

The rider of the black horse was walking through a magnificent gallery whose walls were hung with the intricate, meditative patterns of Islamic art. They were beautiful but alien: too religious, Helen thought, I want something freer. There was a tiny flaw in the middle of the clean sheet of paper. She left the pad open at the page, thinking it didn't matter. She kept coming back to it, though, until it was all she could see on the page. She brushed at it, knowing the gesture was futile. Finally, she turned to a new page and waited for something to occur to her.

When the credits rolled, Usha sighed. 'Wonderful,' she said contentedly and blew her nose again. 'So, what now?'

'There's something we haven't talked about,' Helen said. It had lent even more unreality to the situation, this not acknowledging one of the fundamentals. Helen realized that she had wanted Usha to say something, for it not to be her; now that it was her, it would seem as though it was her fault.

'And that is?'

'This baby would be half Asian and half white.'

'And quite beautiful. Look at the mother.'

'But things could be difficult for a mixed-race child.'

'People would probably think it was Italian or something, if you're afraid of Asianness. That's what really bothers you, isn't it.'

'Don't be absurd. I'm thinking of other people's reactions.'

'Imagine if my parents had said "well we'd better not have any children because people are going to notice they're all brown" – there'd be no Usha for you to have this conversation with. I've lived through it, haven't I? You're pandering to prejudice if you start thinking like that.'

'But a half-caste falls in between stools. All I'm saying –'
'Listen to yourself – "half-caste", "mixed race".'
'I don't understand,' said Helen, feeling the sharpness in Usha's voice.
'"Half-caste" – you might as well say "half-breed" and be done with it. It's straight out of some terrible Hollywood Western. And what's this "mixed race" mean exactly? Think about "racial purity". "Pure" English – what could that mean? After invasions, settlements, emigration here by, let me see, Vikings, Romans, Normans, Saxons . . . You get the idea.'
'Right,' said Helen, feeling got at. 'Of course, what I really meant was you're a darkie and Dan's a honky and the mixing of your two sets of genes would herald the end of civilization.' She slammed her sketch pad closed. 'My mistake.'
'There are things that even you aren't necessarily aware of,' Usha said gently.
'You have a way of making me feel responsible for everything,' said Helen.
'You don't need *me* to feel that way. You were born apologetic.' Her kiss was warm and reassuring.
Helen closed the tin of pencils. 'I spoke to Dan.' It rushed out of her mouth sounding like a confession. Her heart began to beat quickly.
Usha looked at her but she was afraid to look back. 'And?'
'The man from upstairs, he say "yes",' she whispered, cursing her fatuousness. She raised her eyes. Usha's were wide: that strange, clear brown reflecting back at her.
'I told you!' said Usha triumphantly.
They looked at each other, suddenly faced with having to plan what had only been speculation. Helen saw trepidation in Usha's eyes and wanted to take back what she had said, but had the sensation of having stepped onto something that was now moving too fast for either of them to get off.
Later, when Usha came Helen held her tightly, her hand warm and slick between her dark thighs, seeing then the bright lick of blood on her pale fingers, as though, decision taken, Usha had begun to make a fresh bed for life to lie upon.

Helen closed the front door behind her. She noticed the smell of the flat now when she came in, her old familiarity tilting into a visitor's perception. She looked through the post that Dan had picked up and simply put in a pile. She opened the gas bill and the telephone bill and threw the junk mail straight in the bin.

She sat at the kitchen table until Dan came home. He looked apprehensive. 'Why are you here?' He shook his head. 'That didn't come out right.'

'It's alright. I thought we should all meet at some point.'

Dan didn't look like the prospect appealed very much. 'Oh.'

'I know it'll be awkward but I think we should.'

'What does Usha think?'

'I haven't told her yet.'

Dan rubbed his face. 'Look, I don't want to hear the details, alright? I'm trying to keep you and her separate in my mind.' He raised his hand. 'You might not think that's the right way for me to think about it but that's too bad.'

'I don't think there are any right ways.'

He raised his eyebrows. 'You've changed your tune.'

'New situations need new songs.' She looked at him. 'Did I really say that?'

His smile was tired. 'If you think it's a good idea then maybe we could do it. I'll think about it.'

'I should go. I'll see you soon, okay?'

'Okay. Oh – your mother has been trying to get hold of you. I think she thinks I've murdered you. Little does she know it's the other way round.'

'Dan . . .'

'Please don't look at me like that. That's how you look at a puppy with a sore paw.'

She looked away. 'Sorry.'

'At least you're here. God, I do sound pathetic, don't I?'

The phone rang. They looked at each other and listened through the open doorway as the answering machine clicked on. A long pause. Then Moira: 'Hello, Daniel. Hello, Helen.'

Dan got up and closed the door. 'She wants to come round. She's decided that what our flat needs is some co-ordinating touches and she's found just the thing in some little shop somewhere.' He groaned. 'She's bought something.'

'Showing her customary sensitivity to other people, I see. Mind you, you have to wonder about a woman who uses cotton wool pulled out of a rabbit's arse.' The white china rabbit sat on top of the cistern in Moira's bathroom.

'I gave her that.'

'You were adolescent, you didn't know what you were doing. What's her excuse?'

'I like it. Well, I don't mind it.'

'Just don't let her put one in our bathroom.' They looked at one another. Helen thought of the intimate clutter. '*The* bathroom.' She stood up. 'I really must go.'

She didn't know whether she should kiss him goodbye. Instead she touched his face quickly. His beard was springy and soft, like grass.

26

Dan raised his hand to knock on the door, then hesitated. He could hear their voices. Wind shook the main door at the end of the hall and the glass rattled in the frame. Clumps of dust shivered against the skirting boards. The hall seemed suddenly attractive, a place he could stay: no conversation, no complexities.

The door opened. Helen gave him a questioning look. 'I wondered where you'd got to,' she said. 'I heard the door close upstairs and you coming down the stairs. Then . . .'

'I . . . my shoelace was undone.'

They both looked down at his brown slip-on shoes.

'Come in,' said Helen. 'It's going to be okay.'

Usha looked at him with veiled eyes. 'Dan,' she acknowledged with the formal air of a much older generation.

He smiled without showing his teeth, thinking how it must look like he had a tic.

'Well,' said Helen.

Dan wanted to scream. The obvious topic of conversation was too raw to touch; but what else was there?

'The garlic bread will be ready,' said Usha and left. He and Helen looked at each other.

'This,' he said, 'is a really crummy idea.'

'It's awkward.'

'Yes, like having your fingernails pulled out is awkward.' The idea of Usha having his come put inside her kept shoving itself in his face. That's all we think about when we look at each other, he thought, that's why we can hardly speak: Helen is almost a side issue.

He accepted a glass of wine and drank it too quickly. Huge hiccups shook him. Helen fussed around; Usha watched in silence. His eyes were watering and his chest felt like something dense and malevolent was jumping around on it. The regularity of the spasm made him feel like a demented metronome. He felt Usha thought his incapacity was merely a sign of his ineptitude.

'The leg's broken on the table,' Usha said. 'So . . .'

'It was alright when Ivan was here,' Dan said. It sounded like an accusation. He hiccuped.

'. . . so we'll eat sitting on the floor,' Usha said as though he hadn't spoken. She began to push the sofa back. The thin fabric of her loose trousers was smooth against her buttocks. Dan wanted to lay his hand against the ruby silk. He looked at Helen: have you, he thought, did you, in those murmured seconds before you opened the door on the jester? She was taking the useless glass of water away and wasn't there to meet his eye.

'Ivan bought that table in Habitat,' Dan said. He waited for the hiccup; it only came when he relaxed his expectation.

'He was done,' said Usha.

'It was a flat-pack,' he said.

'How interesting.' She shoved the armchair with unnecessary force.

'What I mean is, maybe it's come unscrewed. I could have a look at it for you if you like.'

'If you want to lie under the table, feel free,' she said. 'Helen and I will be over here.'

'Well –' He hiccuped while Usha listened. 'Not now, obviously.'

'You know,' said Usha witheringly, 'it didn't occur to me to actually look at it. Gosh, you men are so wise. Hey, Helen,' she said as Helen came in with the plates, 'Dan's advice is to *look* at the table leg.'

'I was only trying to be helpful,' he said.

Usha spread a cloth out on the carpet. 'Maybe if you could explain what a screwdriver looks like we could get one of our own,' she said. 'Do you need a licence or anything?'

'For God's sake,' said Helen.

They sat down. For the next couple of hours he and Usha watched each other trying to be civil, while Helen kept an eye on them both.

'What are the symptoms?' asks Jamie, trying to make the end of the stethoscope stick to his nose.

Dan looks up at him, at his silhouette against the blue sky. He ponders. 'My heart hurts,' he says. Grass scratches at the backs of his knees. A bee came in close and saw he wasn't a flower.

'Hmm,' says Jamie. He presses the red plastic sucker against Dan's chest. As he leans down his face gets its details back; his freckles are dark as chocolate. His expression is grave. 'There's nothing we can do,' he says. 'I'm afraid you're already dead.' He crosses Dan's arms and sits back. He tries to stick the sucker to his tongue.

Dan closes his eyes against the light.

Lesley's hair ran like a fissure across the sunflowers printed on the pillow.

'I can't,' he said and rolled off her. I can't fuck you now, he thought, because I'm never going to again.

'Oh,' said Lesley politely as though he'd mentioned something inconsequential in passing.

They lay in silence looking at the ceiling.

'It isn't you,' he said eventually. 'It's me.'

'What's the matter?'

'I've got a lot to think about. I don't seem to have enough room left over to . . .' He didn't know how to tell her everything was to stop.

'It's a shame,' she said, turning to him. She was generous with her body, often throwing her arms back over her head like she'd been flung down, opening herself to him; he felt nostalgic for a past that wasn't yet history. 'Because I don't think we'll be doing this again.' He noticed that she'd pulled the sheet over her breasts.

'No.' For a moment he didn't realize she didn't know what he was thinking. 'What?'

'I've been trying to find a way to tell you.' Her leg moved away from his. 'I don't think we should go on any more.'

He thought how he should feel relieved of the burden but he just felt cheated: I thought her feelings would be hurt, I *wanted* to hurt her. She wouldn't cry now. He wondered what the fuck his problem was.

'I see,' he said.

'I like you and everything,' Lesley said, 'but it isn't going to go anywhere, is it? You were something I had to get out of my system. But we've had some fun, that's the important thing.'

'Fun. Yes.' She had used him. He had been something to get out of her system.

'Being with someone older has been great, though. Really,' she said. 'That bald spot is dead sexy.'

Bald? He was thinning, not *bald*. 'Good,' he said, thinking some kind of response was required.

'Anyway,' she said, pulling her knickers on under the sheet, 'I'm with someone my own age now. I think that's better, don't you?'

'If that's what works for you.'

'You're cool, do you know that? Sometimes I've thought you're a hopeless case but basically you are cool. Because you know I have to do what's best for me.'

'Absolutely.' He concentrated on looking cool. 'So who's the young person?' He smiled to show her he was making a cool joke. He saw her naked breasts for the last time as she swiftly donned her T-shirt. He wanted to wave.

'Dave,' she said. 'Formerly known as Bongo.'

'The drummer.'

'Yeah.' She picked up her tights and began to cover her legs with black. 'He's in a new band. They've got a gig tonight.' She looked at the clock.

'I was in a band once.'

She zipped up her skirt. 'You never mentioned it.'

'It was a long time ago.'

'They're looking for a singer – I think I might have a go. I'd make a good rock star, don't you think? Of course, you can come and see me any time when I'm famous: I won't lose touch with real people.'

'I'm grateful.'

She picked up her DMs. 'I'll give you some privacy so you can get dressed.'

The speed of the alteration was disorienting: twenty minutes ago she had opened her clean pink cunt and asked him in.

She closed the door behind her and he dressed, surrounded by her possessions.

'I know your heart was never really in it,' she said later in the car she had helped to push-start. He dropped her at a pub where people dressed like her milled around outside looking at each other. She walked around to his window. He wound it down and she gave him a last, chaste kiss. 'Go home to your wife, Dan,' she said. He lost her in the press of people feeding into the building like black sand dropping through an hour glass.

The car took him home kindly, though the engine mumbled on for a time after he took the key from the ignition. 'I wish I knew what was wrong with you,' he said wearily, but it was more reflex than emotion.

He had to do something. He couldn't – wouldn't – stand around and let Helen leave him alone. He became convinced that all he had to do was talk to her; get her away from Usha and he would be able to reason with her. He drank the last of the wine straight from the bottle and stood up. Toilet, then downstairs to rescue his wife.

In the bathroom he looked at himself in the mirror. His eyes were a bit bloodshot but he had a healthy colour. He combed his beard, then his eyebrows for good measure.

'You're not a bad bloke,' he told his reflection. 'She knows that. And she knows you're only thinning.' He combed his hair carefully.

Looking again at his beard he decided it could do with a trim. He'd do that, get changed into something smart and then go downstairs. He cheered up, now that he had a plan. He could get away with using scissors to trim his beard; it was only a little untidy.

To alleviate the slight sway of the room he braced himself against the towel rail under the mirror and cut the ends off a couple of whiskers. There was something frivolous and irritating about the snip-snip of these single hairs. He took hold of a clump of them and, holding it firmly away from his face, he cut the hairs off close to the skin. He did another one, and another. He mixed up some of Helen's shaving mousse and using her pink-handled razor made his face smooth and hairless enough to wear under the sheerest of tights.

'My God,' he said to his reflection. 'I haven't seen you in a long time.' He could see the thin scar above his lip where he had cut himself with a penknife whilst demonstrating to Jamie that it was completely blunt. His face was now bounded by angles and not the softness of hair. The skin was pasty, so it looked like he wore the pale outline of his beard. He poked his tongue out and grinned. Surrounded by skin his lips looked insubstantial, weird lines looping around the teeth-edged hole of his mouth. He turned away. It was new and he was too close.

In the bedroom he chose the Egyptian cotton shirt that Helen had given him in some happier time and the blue trousers that he had bought in what was, according to Helen, an uncharacteristic bout of good taste. He changed his underpants and his socks and dressed slowly, enjoying the cool greeting of the fabrics. He picked out his blue silk tie and placed it around his neck. He focused on his reflection. Ties were a beardy thing, he decided. He dropped it on the floor. He put on his best shoes, and had a good look at the clean-shaven stranger. He laughed, to see what it looked like. He tried serious, too. Finally, he brushed his hair again and went downstairs.

Usha stared at him.
'Dan,' he said.
'So I see.'
'I've come to see Helen.'
'She's at Maggie's.'
This wasn't in the plan. 'But I've come to see her.'
Usha regarded him with interest. 'You're all dressed up. Are you going somewhere special?' Her hair hung from her head like a cape.
'I've arrived.'
Usha shrugged. 'Sorry. I'll tell her you called.' She began to close the door.
'No.' He put his hand on the door. 'I'll wait.'
She waved a hand genteelly in front of her face. 'You've been drinking.'
'Yes,' he said. 'There are some things that one must do no matter how distasteful they are.'
'Why don't you wait upstairs?'
'I've been doing that for too long, young lady.' Did you hear what you just said? he thought. 'We have some things to talk about,' he said.
'You can't talk about anything if she isn't here, though, can you? I'll tell her, alright?'
She looked pointedly at his hand where it rested on the door. He noticed the veins on the back of his hand, blue and lumpy, twisting like roots. 'You and I have things to talk about, too,' he said.
'That's a –'
'Now would be a good time.' He pushed at the door. She let go and he stepped into the flat.
'You sit there,' he said, pointing at the sofa. 'And I'll sit here.' He sat heavily in the armchair.
She stood and looked at him for a few moments then sat exactly in the middle of the sofa; feet and knees together as though they were tied. She glared at him. 'You want to inseminate me yourself.'
'What!' He laughed, shocked.

'Isn't that what this is all about?'

'What makes you think I – good grief.'

'I can see it in your face.'

'Let's get one thing straight –'

'You think you can come in here and –'

'Be quiet!' His voice projected well, slapping her down. He lowered it. 'This is the most bizarre situation I have ever been in in my life. Do me the courtesy of finding out what I think instead of telling me. I don't want to sleep with you! I want to sleep with my wife! For fuck's sake.' He shook his head.

'I'm sorry.'

She wasn't. She just wanted him to go.

'You don't believe me,' he said.

'What difference does it make what I think?'

'It makes a difference to me.'

'Why?' She raised her hands. 'Why should it?'

'First, because it's the truth – you're an attractive young woman but that isn't enough. Second . . .' The inside of his head was fuzzy; this was too difficult. It came to him. 'Second, what you think affects what Helen thinks. She asked me to . . . donate something. Because of you. Because you're tormenting her.'

'What's between Helen and me isn't any of your business.'

'Oh come *on*! I have been asked to wank into a *jar* because of what's between you and Helen. I think that gives me some right to know what the hell is going on.'

'You've agreed to do it anyway.'

'Because of her. Not you – her. But you haven't the first inkling of what you're putting her through. Why do you have to wave this thing in front of her, this thing she can't do – you don't want a child, you're little more than one yourself.'

'So *you* know what *I* want now!' Usha's colour deepened as she flushed.

He wanted to get hold of her and shake her, make her admit to whatever it was he considered her guilty of. He tried to calm down. 'I'm worried about her. No, I don't know you – so how can I know what you intend –'

'You want to know whether my intentions are honourable.' Usha clasped her hands around her knees. 'How quaint.'

'You don't know what you're doing to her. I can see it. I've known her for so long – I can see it, don't you understand?'

'Let her go.'

'No, I can't. I can protect her. I can protect her from you.'

'She doesn't need you. She can't even confide in you – what use are you to her?'

'That isn't true,' he said. 'Above all, we've always been friends.'

'The sort of friend that you tell everything?'

'Exactly! You've known her only a few weeks. She and I –'

'If you're such good friends,' said Usha icily, 'why didn't she tell you she aborted your baby?'

He had to think about her sentence over and over again. 'What do you mean?' he said helplessly when he understood it.

'You went away and left her.'

'You went away.' Helen mumbles into his chest; his shirt is already wet with her tears.

'I'm back. It's okay. I'm here.'

'She felt she had no choice: she had no faith in you even then,' Usha said.

'The consultant said . . .' He had the feeling of the air thickening. 'It was an infection. No one's fault.'

'The tubes were damaged because of an infection. And she got the infection because of the abortion.'

All the energy had drained out of him. 'No. You're lying.' There was no conviction in his voice. He recognized she spoke the truth.

'You'd better go.' She stood up.

He had no will. He followed her to the door and let her shut him out. He went upstairs. The nausea hit him as he went through the front door. He ran to the bathroom where he vomited again and again until there was nothing left in his whole being. He lay on the floor in his fine shirt and his accidental trousers.

At some point he crawled into bed. He held his cock, wanting the comfort of pleasure: but even masturbation was denied him, it was so inextricably linked to its potential rather than its point.

Through the haze his mind clacked on. He knew he would still help Helen: he had promised; he would not take that away. She must have wanted to tell him for years: that she hadn't made him ache as though his chest were caving in. He couldn't find any tears, could only suffer the malicious, dry grip of their memory around his throat.

He waited for sleep to rescue him.

27

'He was drunk,' Usha said. She watched Helen's face; concern shadowed across it. Usha wanted to stop her. 'He threatened me.' Helen's doubt was obvious. 'You don't believe me!'

'If he was pissed I suppose it might have come across like that. But he wouldn't do anything to hurt you.'

'He forced his way in.'

'You said you let him in because he looked pathetic.'

'He did push the door.'

'I'm sorry if he upset you. I don't think –'

'You still take his side,' Usha said. 'You even apologize for him.'

Helen looked at her thoughtfully. 'I do, don't I.' She rubbed the last of the handcream into her fingers. The warm flower scent hung about her like a veil. 'He would be sorry, though.' Helen's knowledge of Dan burnt in the centre of Usha's stomach.

'Such a noble human being,' she said. 'I don't know how you can bear to be without him.' She began to get up.

'Oh Usha.' Helen didn't move. She sounded far away. Usha felt guilty, and scared. She went into the kitchen.

'What did he want?' Helen called through.

'He didn't say.'

'What did you talk about?'

'Nothing. He wasn't being very coherent.' Usha ran the tap so she wouldn't have to keep lying.

Helen snapped the lid of the moisturiser closed. 'I suppose I should go and see him. It might be important.'

'Don't.'

'I won't be long. He —'

'It can't be that urgent. He would have said, wouldn't he?' Usha sat down on the sofa. 'You were going to tell me about the new design,' she said, picking up Helen's sketchpad. When he tells her what I said, Usha thought, everything will change. For a time she could enjoy the balance.

'Oh yes,' Helen said, enthusiasm lighting her face. 'It came to me on the way home.' Usha looked at her mouth: her lips were so soft. Her kiss was like nothing Usha had known. When she sat down Usha took Helen's face in her hands and they exchanged a long kiss. Usha felt she was feeding from her, an unhappy, vampire hunger that nevertheless filled her with desire. She wanted to keep Helen there; yet wanted her to leave, to remove her bleakness.

They heard the main door open, and pulled apart. 'This isn't a healthy environment,' said Helen. 'I've been thinking – maybe we should find somewhere else. I saw a place in Ditchling Rise –'

There was a quiet knock at the door.

'What's wrong with using the bell?' Usha said, feeling invaded by the physicality of the sound: the bell gave you wires and distance, the knock was from his hand, his skin against the grain of the door.

'I'll get it.' Helen got up.

Usha wanted to have more time before everything unravelled. 'Leave it,' she said. 'Let him come back.'

Helen gave her an odd look. 'We have to be adult about this.' She opened the door. Usha set the embroidered cushion on her lap and watched her hands against its colours.

'It doesn't matter any more,' Dan was saying as he came in. 'I don't know what I thought I was doing.'

'Usha didn't mention about the beard,' said Helen. 'It's . . .' She was pink. 'I think it looks fine.'

Usha forced herself to look at him. His naked face embarrassed her. Soon he would speak. She waited for the crack she had made to split wider and bring everything crashing down.

'I don't know what Usha's told you,' Dan said, 'but I was a real wanker yesterday, barging around like someone with a testosterone rush.'

'You must have a major hangover,' said Helen.

'Strangely, I haven't. Things seem a lot clearer to me now in some ways.' He opened his briefcase. Usha felt stretched taut: why didn't he just get on with it? 'Anyway,' he said, 'I wanted to apologize to Usha.' He turned to her. 'I brought you this.' She was convinced that what he held in his hand must be a thing of violence and simply looked at him.

'You could try being a bit more gracious, Usha,' said Helen. She took the weapon from Dan and handed it to her. It was a book wrapped in tissue paper that rustled like dry skin. Baffled, she tore the paper off. Gold lettering glinted against the deep metallic blue cover. The writing formed a pretty, faintly familiar pattern but she could not read it. The crossed swords of the Sikh emblem clashed beneath it.

'It's the *Tales of Truth*,' Dan said to Helen. 'About all the hassles the Sikhs endured in the past simply because they were Sikhs. That's what the guy in the shop said. Would you say that's a fair assessment, Usha?'

She nodded. He and Helen were looking at her like anxious parents. 'It's in Punjabi,' she said, flicking through the pages.

'That's right,' said Dan. He was ashamed. He wanted to please.

She closed the book. 'I can't read Punjabi.'

'But I thought ...' He looked at Helen. 'You said she spoke Punjabi.'

'I thought she did.'

They turned to the third person.

'I speak a little, that's all. My father thought that if we were going to live in England we should speak English; it was a sign of respect. I know a few traditional things, like nursery rhymes, and phrasebook stuff. That's it.'

'But the temple ...' Helen said. 'You said the service was in –'

'Yes. But I never said I understood it. None of the kids did.'

'Like Latin,' said Helen.

'My grandmother was appalled when she came to stay,' said Usha. 'The little we did know was all wrong and she was always correcting us. It was a drag.' She wiped the smudge of her fingerprints off the shiny blue. 'Nice cover.'

'It's useless,' said Dan.

'Books are never useless,' Helen said. 'Just not equally useful to everyone.'

'Platitudes aside,' Dan said, 'this book is useless.'

He and Usha looked at one another over it. She thought about handing it back to him but he turned away and was soon gone; it was only then that she fully realized that nothing had been said, nothing had changed. He was still protecting Helen.

* * *

Jaz brought the smell of rain in with him. Water lay in little stars on his night-sky shoulders.

'I hate the weather in this country,' he said. 'No wonder the people are so miserable.'

'Like you.'

'It affects me as well.' He hung his jacket carefully on the back of a dining chair. 'A bit more sun wouldn't hurt, would it? I remember when we went to India –'

'Oh no, not that again, ' said Usha. 'You were talking about this last time you were here. You do realize that was about fifteen years ago?' She sat down with Jaz. 'So,' she said. 'What's the India thing all about?'

'I've been thinking, that's all. If I made enough money I could go out there.'

'To *live*?' She looked at her handsome brother and wanted to touch his cheek. A space inside her eased larger; brittle edges split wider than she could contain.

'Could be. It's possible.'

'You don't speak a single one of the languages, Jaz.'

'The language of commerce is English. And I could learn Hindi or Urdu or whatever. I'd be fine – I'm educated and I've got sense.'

'Why? Why would you go? This is what you know – *this* is where you fit in.' This is where I am, she thought, willing him to notice that.

'Doesn't mean I couldn't do as well – better – somewhere else.'

'All this because of a few clouds? It does rain there, you know – Punjab may be the breadbasket but you can't grow wheat without water.'

He sighed. 'I'd like to walk around and not feel I'm in a minority.'

'But you would be! You'd be English, for a start. And you wouldn't be dirt poor. That puts you in a minority straight away.'

'You fall for all that stereotypical stuff about poverty,' he said. 'There *is* money there.'

In the kitchen she looked at the sari-clad woman pictured on the box of teabags, smiling as she picked tea. 'As I said, you'd be in the minority.' She spooned coffee from an apparently unpeopled mountain into his cup.

'It's a good minority.' He leant against the door jamb.

'And I suppose you'd get yourself a little wifey to cater to your every need.'

'At least she wouldn't argue all the time.'

'I'm not arguing,' she said. 'I'm discussing it with you.'

'Is that what it is.' He took the cup from her. 'It's hard to explain.' He pulled a flat tin from where it had slipped down between the cushions on the sofa. 'What's this?' He rattled it.

'Don't do that,' said Usha. 'You'll break the leads.' She took the tin. 'It's Helen's pencils.'

'She isn't still staying here, is she?'

Usha had tried to imagine Jaz's reaction to the truth about her and Helen. She felt certain he would think it was a joke. 'Things are . . . difficult.'

'Doesn't she have any other friends?'

'That isn't very nice. "I'm terribly sorry about your marriage but bugger off somewhere else, will you?"'

Jaz raised his eyebrows. 'Her language is rubbing off on you, I see. You want to watch that.'

'How do you know what I want?'

'I've known you all your life: I know what you need better than you do.'

'Tell me,' she said. She meant it.

'I think you need other friends.' Disappointment that he could not tell her sank through her. 'What happened to Veena?' he continued. 'And that girl from college, the one from Liverpool.'

'Tracy.'

'Yeah, her.'

'I'm working now. It's difficult.'

'Helen's alright but . . .'

'She's not what I need?'

'How can I put this . . .' Jaz said. 'Do you remember the story of the donkey and the lion skin?'

'It was a tiger skin.'

'Lion.'

'Tiger.'

'Okay, tiger,' agreed Jaz unexpectedly. 'But you do remember it?'

'Yes – donkey accidentally gets draped with tiger skin and everyone's afraid of it and then the skin falls off and no one's afraid of it any more. I never could get to grips with that one: it isn't very plausible, is it, having a skin fall on you like that?'

'But the point of it was?'

'Watch out for falling stripey things?'

He drank the last of his coffee. 'If you look like something you're not but it impresses people, you'll get on: until the tiger skin falls off.'

'I don't understand what you're trying to say. That I'm not being enough of a Sikh for you?' She hadn't seen his almost unfriendly expression of criticism directed towards her before. 'I'm being what I've always been,' she said quietly. 'You can look at your own life; mine doesn't have to be the same.'

His voice was gentle. 'I'm just saying, Ush, that –'

'I remember now what Mum said about that story – if you look like a Sikh you'll command respect; otherwise you'll get oppressed along with everyone else.'

'I suppose you can use any interpretation you want.'

'According to your purpose.'

Something was shifting between them. Usha wanted to put her arms out to balance but kept her hands in her lap where they fidgeted with the soft blue wool of the jumper she had borrowed from Helen.

Rani bustled after her. 'Sit down, sit down. I'm so glad you've come. At last – you're a naughty girl, Usha.'

'I've been busy.'

'Too busy for your auntie? What a terrible thing to say.' Rani's sensible cardigan was grey; through the knit Usha could see the yellow sprinkle of the silky fabric underneath. The cuffs were turned up but still Rani's fingers only just poked out; the jumper had been Uncle's.

'I know. I'm sorry. I'm here now, though, aren't I?'

'And you must tell me everything about everything.' Rani leant forward, cocking her head like a curious bird. Fairy lights hung soft splashes of colour around the fireplace. When Usha was eleven they had been put up at Christmas, and had stayed ever since. When Uncle died they were turned off but Rani had stood up one day while Usha and her family were visiting and switched them on, and no one said a word. 'How is this job?' asked Rani, nibbling at the information Usha had given her.

'Okay. It isn't difficult but you do have to pay attention.'

'Mm. I bumped into Surjeet Singh the other day. She was telling me you've done very well to get that job.'

'She thinks so.'

'She seems like a nice girl.' Rani was looking at her, waiting for a reaction.

'She's alright.' Usha grinned. 'No, she isn't.'

'Ah,' said Rani with satisfaction. 'Now you're talking to me.'

'She thinks I think I'm too good for that place. That I'm a snob.'

'And are you?'

'Maybe a bit. But I don't show it. *She's* the snob: she can't accept me at all.'

'She's probably jealous.' Rani was looking happy. Usha realized how much Rani had missed her, and regretted her miserliness in denying her.

'You're smarter and prettier,' Rani said. 'That'll be what's upsetting her.'

'She knows about Alex.'

'*Everyone* knows about that.'

'She doesn't approve,' said Usha.

'These middle-aged young women worry me,' Rani said. 'They don't know how to move with the times. Their times.' She shook her head. 'Such a disappointment.'

'It isn't only her,' said Usha. *Her father's closed face, having ejected all its anger.*

'Your mother loves you.' Rani held her hands. 'She does.'

Her mother, looking at her father.

'She let him . . . me . . .' Her throat tightened around her voice. Her eyes thought about tears.

'And he loves you, too. He's got a temper, your father, but it won't last forever. You made life very difficult for them, you know.'

'And them for me.'

'You haven't been to see them.'

'I have orders not to.'

'Hah!' Rani rolled her eyes. 'His orders, of course. But your poor mother . . .' She patted Usha's knee. 'Things will come right.'

Rani's platitude grated on her. 'Why – praying for me, are you?' she asked sarcastically.

'I prayed for your Uncle's life and look what happened. No, I wouldn't bother with it.' The hurt in her eyes made Usha want to look away. 'Trust Rani. I know about these things. If they didn't love you they wouldn't have made sure you had somewhere decent to live, would they.'

'Jaz is the one looking out for me. He's done so much –'

'He keeps an eye on you, yes.'

'And he's paid the rent on the flat.'

'Physically he was the one who did that. But it wasn't his money. It was your father's.'

'What?'

'It's true,' Rani said.

'Jaz lied to me?' Although it sounded like a question Usha heard it inside as a statement. It didn't make any sense: you might as well say up is down, she thought, or yellow is red.

'He's very clever,' said Rani. 'He would have let you believe something and not corrected you.'

Usha was struggling to grasp implications. 'If Dad's doing it, why pretend he isn't?'

'Where do you think that Dhillon pride you have comes from?'

'He *told* me to leave. He *told* me that I would be outside the family.'

'He was angry. You *had* offended him. But Usha, for such a clever girl you can be very silly.'

Usha spread her hands in incomprehension. 'Tell me.'

'He had no reason to believe you were going to do what he said, did he? You'd spent all your time doing the complete opposite!'

'You mean it wasn't . . .' Usha absorbed what her aunt had said and made it into a question. 'Why didn't Jaz tell me?'

'He said you should make up your own mind about whether you would try to heal the argument.'

'But he knew!' She looked at Rani. 'You knew, too. You didn't say anything.'

'I never saw you.'

'You had my phone number.'

'And you had mine. Much as I love you, Usha, you can't expect to have everything done for you.'

'You've all . . . cheated.'

'No,' said Rani gently. She put her arm around Usha. 'We've all been waiting.'

Helen took the thermometer from Usha's mouth and looked at the reading.

'Well?' said Usha, wondering that she could speak.

'We haven't been doing this over a long enough period to be certain,' said Helen. 'But I'm as sure as I can be that you're ovulating. Your temperature's up.'

'Maybe I'm coming down with something.'

'Maybe.' That physical blue of Helen's gaze pushed down on her. 'You look fine to me.' Helen's hand was on her shoulder and Usha wished it away. Since she had decided Usha was serious, Helen had acquired a focus that frightened Usha, that was completely independent of her; she was central to a plan but, primarily, one part of many. Helen had described methodology to her, had pointed to paragraphs, had shown her glass dishes and pipettes, all as though they were nothing to do with Usha personally; as if Helen were simply describing a meticulous recipe. She had stopped asking if Usha was sure.

'I'll go and see Dan,' Helen said.

Usha knew she should speak but her tongue had been disabled and she could only watch Helen leave.

When she came back they thought about what Dan was doing and tried to pretend they weren't. Helen told Usha about something Maggie had done in the office but she didn't listen. Eventually, the phone rang. Helen answered it without looking at Usha.

'Hello?' A short pause. Then, 'Okay. I'll come up.' She looked at Usha but there was nothing behind her eyes. She left and seemed to return in the same instant. She held something small wrapped in a white cloth. 'Here it is,' she said unnecessarily. She showed Usha the small glass dish sealed with a plastic lid. Her hands were shaking. Usha's stomach turned over when she saw the unremarkable white substance.

'Next,' said Helen, following the invisible list, 'we have to –'

'No.' Although she could feel Helen looking at her Usha couldn't take her eyes off the container. It was obscene. 'No.'

Helen didn't exactly laugh but it was as if she had started and someone had grabbed her throat. 'But I have it,' she said. The container was moved a little closer to Usha, who backed away a little. 'This has cost me everything.' Her dead voice was weighted with anger. 'Everything.' She enunciated each syllable.

Usha shook her head. 'I can't,' she whispered.

Helen stared at Usha with a wild expression. 'You drag me this far and then . . .' The movement of her head was like the repetitive motions of caged animals. 'You promised,' she said firmly. 'You're going to bloody do it.' She thrust the container towards Usha, who stumbled in her haste to avoid it.

'You're crazy,' Usha said.

'And who the fuck is responsible for that? Hmm?' She gestured to the container. 'You made me get it. *You* use it.'

'Keep away from me.'

There was a calm in which they looked at each other, then Helen made a move towards her. They struggled for a moment, each an obdurate mass. Then Usha struck the glass from Helen's hand and it crashed into the sideboard and fell onto the carpet in three neat pieces. Helen let out a wail. They looked at the damage lying before them.

'I can't,' said Usha.

'You bitch. You evil little bitch. How could you let it go this far? How *could* you?' Helen clutched her arms to her stomach and made a small keening sound.

'I . . .' Usha had nothing to say. She touched Helen's shoulder. Helen's recoil was swift.

'Don't!' A frigid stillness was carved into her features. 'You have no real notion of what you've been doing, have you? I don't know what you wanted to put me through this for.'

'I wanted to help you.'

'You went on and on at me until I had no resistance left. Is that when you knew you were lying? Or was it before that? Did you ever have any real intention of . . .' Helen ran down, as though she was talking to herself.

'I think I –' began Usha.

'You don't bloody think at all, that's your trouble. I tried to get you to see, but it's like you're incapable of it. You can't see what's right in front of your face, the most obvious things . . .'

'Don't –'

'Things anyone can see. Like . . .' Her smile was ghastly. 'Dear brother Jaz.'

'He has nothing to do with this. With you.'

'It is clear to anyone with two brain cells to rub together that what you most want – what you *really* want – is to fuck that overbearing brother of yours. What a pair you'd make.'

'You're disgusting. You're so bitter it makes you –'

'Oh come on,' Helen said silkily. 'Imagine him inside you. All that forbidden flesh. Smooth,' She drew out the vowel, her lips pursed into a kiss.

'I don't have to listen to this.'

'No, but you are, aren't you? Usha, Usha, don't you see? Alex, me, Jaz – we're all forbidden fruit.'

'You don't know what you're talking about. Only a mind as perverted as yours could even think these things up in the first place.'

'If I'm a pervert what does that make you?' said Helen. Her arms were still sheltering her stomach. 'You are more barren than I'll ever be. At least I can admit what I want; I'm not ashamed.' She fell to her knees and with a neat, efficient action wiped up the pathetic spill and wrapped the glass tenderly in the cloth. Wordlessly she departed, leaving the last vestiges of her plan soaking into the carpet. Usha felt battered; unable to think clearly. She tore off the jumper of Helen's that she had been wearing and flung it on the floor in the bedroom, then pushed it under the bed. Going to the wardrobe to find something else to wear she saw the dark blue suit hanging on the door. She touched it, remembering the catch in her throat the first time she had seen Jaz in it; now, though, it smelt only of the perfume Helen had given her and of the faint, stale odour of women's cigarettes.

28

*H*elen opens the box and looks at the rich colours of the silks inside. She picks out a handful and spreads their thick hair on her lap where they lie under her fingers as smooth as water. She looks at her drawing, then chooses a honey gold and the deep glossy black and puts them side by side on the table: they lie like plump, lustrous fish readied for gutting. She adds a fresh red, bright as a blade.

She can hear the new people moving in downstairs. She had watched Usha and Jaz moving Usha's possessions; many journeys to and fro she watched them, Jaz's turban a dark tarmac grey, Usha's hair loosely tied back and as thick as clothing on her back. To and fro, and in all that time Usha never once looked up; the last journey from the house was no different. Helen knows she wouldn't have looked either; and knows, too, that Usha knew she was there.

She selects a pale frosty grey, and a yellow rich enough to melt. Her palette is suave against the shine of the bay table. She looks at the colours, letting them take their place in the pattern. After a few moments the doorbell rings. She hesitates, thinks about ignoring it: it can only be the new tenant. She has their sounds; she doesn't want any more reminders. Social obligation drags her from the table.

The woman has very short, very blonde hair; her roots are dark. She wears a loose black T-shirt with Same Shit, Different Day printed on the front. She has eyes the colour of stone. 'Hi,' she says. 'From downstairs?'

'Hello.'

'No milk, you see. For coffee?'

'Oh.' Helen isn't going to elaborate for her. If she wants something, she can ask for it.

'Oh right.' The missing link falls into place for the young woman. 'Could I borrow some milk?' Usha only left disgusting soya crap in the fridge. I need cow juice.'
'Sure,' says Helen. 'Come in.' She leads the way to the kitchen. 'So you're a friend of Usha's.'
'Kind of. I more sort of –' Through the open front door they hear a crash, like a cymbal being struck against the wall. 'Oh god,' says the woman. 'What's he done now? I already stopped him from trying to carry five boxes marked "Fragile" at once. He can read. I don't know what his problem is.' She shakes her head and grins. 'Why do we put up with them, eh?'
Helen thinks about Dan. 'Maybe because they put up with us.'
The woman snorts. 'I know who's got the raw deal in that one.' She takes the carton of milk from Helen. 'Cheers. Hey, you have a pasta machine.' She looks at it like it's an artefact from an alien planet. 'Is it difficult? I love pasta.'
'It's easy.'
'I know this is a bit cheeky, but will you show me how it works one day?' She is genuinely interested and pokes a none too clean finger into a spotless metal orifice.
'If you like.'
'I do like.' She sighed. 'Back to the grind, I suppose.' At the door she says, 'Don't forget about the demonstration.'
'I won't. Maybe you'd like to eat the results, too.' Helen has issued an invitation before she realizes it. She wonders what she and Dan and the girl and her clumsy boyfriend can possibly find to talk about.
She closes the door and goes back to her silks. That grey is too pale; instead she chooses one that reminds her of pebbles. She is ready to begin.

The skin on his hands is dry; it looks thick, his fingertips textured like bark. When he touches her arm she wants to pull away but it is only professional interest.
'Seems a shame,' he says. He has a crumb stuck in his moustache.
'But you will do it?'
'It's nice work.' He shakes his head. 'But the customer is always right. If that's what you want . . .'
She looks down at the colours on her arm. They are clear and bright and meaningless. 'Yes.'
It hurts much more this time though she still wishes it was worse. The

tattooist whistles under his breath as he works and the crumb trembles. Behind her someone comes into the shop and stands for a while looking at the flashes on the walls. They approach the tattooing area and watch wordlessly. She turns her head. The young man looks at her. He has long hair and wears tatty denims. 'Death,' he says. 'Cool.'

'Take a seat,' says the tattooist. 'I'll be with you in a few minutes.' The gun growls on, burying its teeth deep in her skin. In the pauses where he loads more colour she can hear the large clock in front of her ticking and every second sounds like the previous one.

'There,' he says. 'Done.' He holds a mirror up so she can see. The black bird's wings still stretch into fingers but it looks too heavy to take flight. Tethered, blinded, it will always be there.

'Thank you,' she says and covers it up.

'I think I got everything,' said Maggie as they walked, crackling with carrier bags, back to her house.

'I don't know how you can shop without a list,' said Helen. The thin handles of the carrier were giving a confusing sensation between numbness and pain. She shifted the bag slightly and it found new flesh to crush.

'It's a gamble,' said Maggie. 'Sometimes I do forget stuff but when you're cooking that just gives you a challenge. Though I do admit using custard powder in that casserole was a mistake.'

'It was certainly different.'

'Is Dan coming over?'

Helen shook her head. 'I want you to myself. We haven't done this for ages.'

'How are things now?'

'Difficult sometimes.' She shrugged. 'A lot happened.'

'How are things at work for him? He was doing silly amounts of overtime last year.'

'It's much better. Summer term starts on Monday. I think he's actually looking forward to it.'

They rounded the last corner. 'Nearly home,' said Maggie. 'I wonder if my fingers will fall off before we get there.' She stopped at the gate and put the bags down. Helen did the same, and examined the purple creasing on her palm.

'Don't you dare!' Maggie shouted, startling Helen into a pounding heart. A small dog in mid-leg-cocking looked at her. Maggie and the dog looked at each other in the high-noon atmosphere; a curtain twitched to Helen's right. The dog wasn't wearing a gun; he turned and trotted off.

Maggie gestured at the potential piss site. 'Now, isn't that beautiful?' she said. She and Helen stood together and looked at the chunky motorcycle. Its tank was metallic green, chrome glittered everywhere; fat tyres were snug against the road as the machine slouched insolently on its shiny footstand.

'It's been parked here every day for a week,' Maggie said. She stretched out a finger and ran it over the gleaming handlebar.

'Do you know who it belongs to?'

'I can't stand it any longer,' said Maggie. She slapped her thigh. 'It's me! It's mine, do you hear, mine!' She leapt on it.

'Maggie, don't. People are so possessive about their bikes.' Helen looked around worriedly.

'Don't I know it.' She pointed aggressively at Helen. 'So keep off it, bitch.' She burst out laughing. 'Really, Helen, sweetie, it *is* mine.'

'But you don't know how to ride a –'

'Oh but I do. I got my motorcycle licence before I went to university. And not a lot of people know that,' she added in her best Michael Caine voice. Maggie's charged-up enthusiasm was infectious and Helen found she was smiling and couldn't seem to stop.

'Can I sit on it?' she asked.

'Absolutely.' Maggie climbed off. Helen sat astride the soft leather seat and put her hands on the handlebars.

'Hold on,' said Maggie. She pulled a key from her pocket and put it in the ignition. She pressed a button by the right handgrip and the engine started politely, clearing its throat first, and turned over like a outsize purr. 'Turn the throttle this way,' said Maggie, twisting it back towards Helen. The bike raised its voice a little. Helen did it herself, revving the engine crisply but gently. The machine was alive and she was part of it.

'I'll take you for a ride,' said Maggie. 'I've even had some refresher lessons.'

'You kept very quiet about all this.'

'I did, didn't I? It was bloody difficult, I can tell you.' She turned the key in the ignition and the engine fell quiet. 'Come on,' she said. 'I want to show you my leathers.'

Maggie had a one-piece black and green leather suit with padding on the parts she might fall on should she come off the bike. She had special reinforced boots and fat padded gloves. Her helmet was black and full-face and made her look like an astronaut. 'You think I look funny,' she said. 'Have a look at yourself.'

Helen looked in the mirror. She was decked out in an old leather jacket, thick leather gloves whose insides felt like putting your hands into someone elses's pockets, and had a large pair of jeans on over her own. Her helmet was red with a white stripe, and the foam inside pushed the flesh of her cheeks up towards her eyes. Maggie winked at her. 'Sexy or what?' They walked bigly out to the bike and Maggie put the pillion footrests down. She got on the bike, kicked up the footstand and started the engine. She motioned Helen to climb on behind her.

'Hold on to me if you like,' Maggie said loudly. 'But not too tight. The important thing is to relax. Don't move about, but pay attention to what the bike is doing.'

Helen rested her hands lightly on Maggie's hips and then the bike was moving smoothly away. She could hear her own breathing inside the helmet and a little patch of condensation formed on the visor. In front of her Maggie's hair blazed between the blacks of her helmet and leathers. The streets slipped past like a movie. After a while Maggie pulled over.

'What would you like to do?' she said over her shoulder. 'We can go back home or we could go out of town for a way.'

'I love it!' Helen said. 'Let's keep going. Let's never stop.'

Maggie laughed. 'That's my girl. Devil's Dyke, here we come!' They sealed themselves back in behind their visors and set off again.

Once out of town the road surface was smooth and there was hardly any traffic. They were going much faster now. Helen wanted to laugh. She felt restricted in the helmet, cut off from the roar of the engine. She raised the visor but the wind howled noisily around the plastic so she lowered it again. They got onto a straight stretch of road and Maggie opened the throttle; over her shoulder Helen could see the speedometer creeping up towards seventy. I should feel frightened, she thought, but behind this window I feel too sheltered from everything. She wriggled her hand out of the glove and into the rushing air and undid the helmet's chin strap. Steadily, so as not to distract Maggie or wobble around, she pulled the helmet off.

The air slapped into her face and took her breath away and she could barely keep her eyes open. Maggie saw what she had done and whooped and kept them hammering into the distance. The wind and the engine roared in her ears and it was hard to take all the sensations in. A sound was born somewhere deep inside her and began creeping out of her mouth. The moan built through a shout and blossomed into a scream that was as loud as she could make it. Just as she ran out of breath she felt something in her throat, and coughed.

'Oh God,' she bellowed. 'I swallowed a fly!' Maggie shook her head a little and Helen knew she was grinning.

Helen laughed and, holding onto Maggie a little tighter, she rested her head against her friend's back and watched the blur of road as it fled away beneath their wheels.

29

'*It's that you could tell her and not me,*' he says.
  'I didn't know how to tell you,' says Helen. 'And then it got too late.'
  'Sometimes I feel like it means all our years have been false.'
  'They weren't! You and I –'
  'I said "sometimes". You have to give me time. But when I think how easily you told that manipulative little . . .'
  'That's not –' She bites her lip and regards him with eyes of darkened blue. 'I'm sorry.' Her voice is unsteady. She holds his hand and her fingers fidget with his. He wants satisfaction from her misery but her contriteness is a physical pain to him; he can't feel entitled to it, despite wanting to punish her, despite feeling she deserves to suffer for withholding for so long. But he suspects it is somehow his fault, and his righteousness flags under its own fraudulent weight.
  'After what I've done, I shouldn't have come back.' She regards him with puzzlement. 'Why did you –'
  'Oh, Helen, Helen, enough. Maybe we're two sad bastards who can't cope without the other sad bastard.'
  'I've . . . damaged you.'
  'Then I'm slightly sadder than I was before. And anyway,' he says, 'the damage has been spread around pretty evenly. What about Usha?'
  Helen lets go of his hand and sits back in the chair. 'She'll live.' The skin around her eyes looks so thin.
  'You see?' he says, collecting her hand from her lap and returning it to his hand. 'It's too much, this talk, talk, talking about things that we can't change.'
  'I want to make things better.'

He grins. 'That's not exactly going to be difficult, is it.' Her smile is weary but at least it's there.

'I want to make it work.'

'Good. Then we both want the same thing. And there is something we can both do.'

'And that is?'

'Stop keeping secrets. From today we try to do things right. No more secrets.'

'No more secrets.' She leans and kisses him on the cheek. He looks admonishingly at her and she adds a firm kiss to the lips. He feels an unfamiliar optimism: it is possible, he thinks, wishing them months hence.

The doorbell rings and the tension of the conversation breaks. He feels lighter. 'I'll get it,' he says.

'It's probably the new people again,' says Helen. 'This'll be the fourth time: they've had milk, sugar and Sellotape so far.'

'SuperDan to the rescue,' he says. 'I'll just pop my underpants on over my trousers.'

He hums as he goes to the door. Everything can start again; they both want that. He opens the door. He and the young woman with the short blonde hair stare at each other.

'Oh fuck,' says Lesley. She crosses her arms. 'Your beard's gone.'

'So's your hair.'

'You live here?' she says accusingly.

'I'm afraid so. You dropped me off here once, remember?' The old pit was gaping again.

'I didn't realize it was here,' she says pointing at the floor between them.

They regard each other with hostility, then Lesley shrugs. 'Never mind, it's only till the end of next term. The band are going on tour after that.' She folds her arms. 'I'm the singer.'

'What are you called?'

'Polly Cotton.'

'Catchy name for a band.'

'No,' she says. 'That's my name. We haven't got a name for the band yet.'

'What about Viscose Blend? The Mixed Fibres?'

She looks at him coldly. 'I think we can come up with something ourselves.'

He has the urge to close the door in her face, the only disadvantage being that he wouldn't be able to see her expression. 'Oh well. So, neighbour, what did you want?'

'I need a match for the gas.'

'Just the one? I think I can manage that,' he says, turning away before she has a chance to reply. He fetches a box from the kitchen and she takes it wordlessly. 'Bye then,' he calls and closes the door.

'You took your time,' says Helen when he returns to the kitchen. 'What were you talking about?'

'Old times,' he says. 'She's a third-year student. Lesley . . .' He pauses for effect, despising himself. '. . . Markham – that's it.'

'Her roots need doing,' says Helen, turning the page of the magazine she has begun to read.

'I didn't notice.'

'Oh, and I meant to tell you – I've invited them for a meal,' says Helen. 'Thank goodness you know her, that'll make things easier.'

Dan removes the lid from the coffee jar. All the storage jars have a yellow frill around the top now. Helen thought Moira's contribution to the decor was hilarious and insisted that the frilly things be kept.

'These are getting grubby,' he says.

'I know,' says Helen. 'That will really piss her off, won't it.'

'Why don't we ditch them?'

'Absolutely not! And under no circumstances must she be allowed to take them away for washing. That would spoil everything.'

She's looking thinner. In their platonic bed there are new, awkward angles to accommodate; like Lesley; so unlike Lesley.

Helen puts a cardboard box on the kitchen table. She lines it with tissue paper and lays the piece she mounted yesterday in the box. It is striking: a bold, graphic representation of a golden key; the key lies on a red background made of layer upon layer of fat stitches. It looks soft enough to lay his head on. The red is cut with jagged black lines whose shapes are echoed in yellow; groups of gentle grey stitches the colour of cobwebs spatter across the whole like stars, like rain. For all the sumptuousness there's a rawness about it; he's seduced yet unwilling to relinquish something he can't quite identify.

'You're sending it to someone?' he says.

Helen nods. 'Duncan.'

'Duncan? Are you sure it's his kind of thing?'

'I want him to have it. He can shove it away in a cupboard if he doesn't want to look at it.' She folds the tissue paper down; the colours disappear and he doesn't have to look at them any more. She closes the lid and fetches a roll of *brown paper.* He watches her wrap the box, puts his finger on the string when she asks; it closes tight around his fingertip then slips off into the gnarled knot that keeps the string taut. She takes the parcel out into the hall and puts it by the front door. 'So I don't forget to take it with me in the morning,' she says. It looks abandoned.

Later in the kitchen Dan sees the top of the bin is full of torn paper. It is Helen's preparatory drawings; crisp, confident lines and beautiful colours, dismembered. He takes out several pieces and tries to make one drawing but the pieces are too muddled. He ties the liner firmly closed, then takes it out to the dustbin and shuts it in the dark.

'What are you doing here on a Saturday?' Mick asked. The photocopier chuntered on behind Dan as he collated the last lot of copies.

'Same goes for you,' he said.

'Getting some peace and quiet. I love my children dearly but why can't they be appealing *quietly*?'

'How's Caroline?' Dan asked as he stapled the course notes together.

'The more children she has the more serene she gets.' Mick shook his head. 'Philip's sleeping a bit better at night now, so that's something.'

'Has the jaundice gone now?'

'Yes, he's fine. We don't need to toast him under the sun lamp any more. He's got a great tan, too.'

The photocopier stopped whirring and clunking, breathed a long sigh and fell silent. The copies felt like they'd been lying in the sun. Dan began the next lot of collation.

'You can get the copier to do that,' said Mick.

'It hates me,' Dan said. 'I don't ask it to do anything complicated, and then we get on fine.'

'How's Helen?' Mick laughed. 'That hasn't got anything to do with what you just said, by the way.'

'She's okay. Things are less fragile than they have been.' Last night, for the first time, her body had welcomed his in the warm dark of their bed; quiet tears bound them in the breathless clutch that followed.

'Good.' Mick drank his coffee down. 'Well, I suppose I'd better go and sort myself out. Why is it the beginning of term always catches me by surprise?'

'You're usually too busy impregnating your wife.'

'True. But rest assured, once I've figured out what's causing it I shall stop immediately.' Mick looked over Dan's shoulder at the papers on the table. 'You are disgustingly organized,' he said. 'You should be ashamed of yourself.'

'I am,' said Dan. 'Believe me.'

Mick wandered off singing a surprisingly tuneful rendition of 'Hi ho, hi ho, it's off to work we go . . .' that faded and finally disappeared as he went up to his office on the next floor.

Dan gathered together his papers and went back to his own office. Outside his window the magnolia's creamy flowers looked stiff and waxy in the increasingly confident sunshine. He opened the window a little and sat at his desk. He looked over the lecture timetable and put the photocopied notes in order. The feel of Helen's skin under his fingers and the clasp of her around his cock hovered behind his actions and he found he was enjoying the administration involved in preparing for a new term. Possibilities seemed to proliferate around him and he allowed himself a cautious happiness; he and Helen had begun again.

His heart sank at the knock on the door. He wanted to finish his work and get back to the home that was feeling normal again. 'Come in,' he called.

'It's only m-me,' said Lesley. Her surprised hair was freshly rebleached. She'd had yet another couple of holes pierced in her ears. 'I was hoping to find you here.' She came into the office and stood there looking uncomfortable.

'Well, sit down,' he said, staying seated at his desk. He rubbed a hand over the returned comfort of his beard.

She perched on the edge of a chair. 'Helen said you'd come into the office.'

'You called at the flat?' They had seen each other very little; it had been surprisingly easy.

She shook her head. 'No, she was on her way out and I asked her if you were in.' She looked at her bitten nails. 'I wanted to see you.'

He could feel the pull of her need. He didn't want it. 'So, what's up?'

She laughed nervously. 'It's a bit d-difficult . . .' She crossed and uncrossed her long thighs which were clad in ragged black leggings whose holes revealed another pair in psychedelic colours underneath. 'The thing is . . .' From her bag she pulled a white plastic strip with a blue band on it and held it up. He stared at it but it continued to have no meaning.

She tutted. 'You don't understand, do you?' She shook her head. Her eyes were bright, and sad. 'This time,' she said, 'I really *am* pregnant.'

30

They sit amongst the debris of Usha's freshly moved belongings. Jaz takes one of the biscuits Lucy has provided. 'I think I'll come here often,' he says. 'You never give me chocolate biscuits.'

'You never asked. How you expect people to know things without telling them? It never stopped you eating all the fruit shortbread, did it.'

'Hmm.'

They sat in silence for a while. 'I think you should know,' says Jaz suddenly, 'I'm thinking of getting married.' He's looking embarrassed. Usha feels like there's something jagged pressing from the inside into the skin between her breasts.

'Don't be stupid,' she says faintly.

'No,' he says. 'I am.'

'Who?'

'I don't have anyone specific in mind. Mum and Dad –'

'Arranged?'

He nods.

'But you always said that was a custom from another culture, that it had nothing to do with life in England.'

'I can change my mind. We don't all go on thinking the same things all our lives, do we? I've thought it over and –'

'You've decided some submissive little miss who can't even speak English is the one for you. Even though you haven't actually met her yet.'

Jaz puts his cup down too quickly and coffee slops onto the carpet. 'I knew you'd jump to conclusions. Why don't you let me finish before you start on your . . . analysis.' The word obviously tastes bad. He dabs at the spilt coffee with the pristine, tie-co-ordinated handkerchief from his breast pocket. 'No,

I don't want to marry a girl from India. We wouldn't have anything in common.'

'She'd be handy, wouldn't she, for when you emigrate to Punjab to become an employer of servants.'

Jaz ignores her. 'Mum and Dad have friends in Leicester. There's a couple of girls up there who look quite suitable.'

'You should hear yourself, Jaz Singh Dhillon – "quite suitable"? Pension plans are suitable; walking shoes are suitable. People – women – aren't to be chosen like jeans off the shelf in your shop.'

'It isn't like that. They've agreed that this is what they want, too. I'm as much a pair of jeans as they are. And you know it isn't like we don't get to meet – if one of us isn't keen then –'

'Call that meeting? Hah! Half an hour in some strange front room with the girl's auntie listening to every word. I can see how you'd find out a lot about each other in that situation.'

'As if I'd be happy with that! This is only arranged in the loosest sense – the modern way of doing things. All the parents are involved and I think that's a good thing – they want the best thing for their child, they want them to be happy.'

'And love, Jaz. What about that?'

'Love! Hasn't done you much good, has it. Alex –'

'No! Not again! You bring him up every –'

'Ush, all I meant was, leaving things to chance isn't the only way. Love doesn't have to drive everything from the outset. Look at your neighbours – I bet they married for your romantic love. When two people are well matched, well chosen, it follows naturally. Look at Mum and Dad. Look at Auntie and Uncle.'

'Their lives, their experiences, were totally different from ours.'

'So,' says Jaz, 'we take the things we can use and adapt them to a different situation. What is wrong with that?'

'Do what you like. You always have done.'

'Don't be a kid. Getting married is natural – don't you want me to be happy?'

'Of course I do.'

'Then be pleased for me.'

'But you'll leave me!' She feels her life unravelling and all the threads whipping through her fingers, burning to the bone.

'No, I won't.'

'You will. You'll marry some awful woman and I'll never see you any more.'

Jaz is at her side, putting his arms around her. Bloody Helen: Usha is too aware of the closeness of his body yet she would not have him further away. 'No, Ush,' he says. 'It won't be like that. I promise. And I've always done what I've said, haven't I?' She nods. 'Well, then.' He holds on to her for a little while longer. 'Silly Usha,' he says, then ruffles her hair as he stands. 'I've got some business to see to.'

Suddenly he is gone and she is by herself in a new room.

'This had better work,' says Usha. 'If Jaz knew who was in the house . . .'

Lucy grins. 'Don't worry. We'll get it sorted out.' She pats the seat next to her and Usha sits down. 'He'll be back soon.'

'I'm sorry it didn't work out —'

Lucy waves a hand dismissively. 'It's okay. I've had enough, though. And I don't see why I should move out.'

They hear the sound of the front door opening and closing, and exchange a look. Alex comes into the living room, looks at them, turns on his heel and leaves.

'He —' begins Usha but Lucy silences her and motions her to wait.

Alex reappears in the doorway. 'Ah,' says Lucy. 'There you are. Meet Lesley's replacement.' Usha's heart is pounding; Alex is so familiar yet now so far away.

'Hello, Alex,' says Usha.

Alex doesn't quite squirm but it's close. He nods at her, avoids her eyes. 'Very amusing, Luce,' he says.

Lucy raises her eyebrows. 'It's true. Usha needed a place to live, Lesley was wanting to move out — perfect timing.'

'You can't expect me to put up with this.' Alex's anger is gathering. From this distance, Usha sees it for the petulance it is; this rumbling of rage once had the power to silence her.

'You're entitled to your say,' says Lucy. 'That is the house policy.'

'I don't want her here. It's bad enough that you —' He pauses. 'We should have all talked about this.'

'The house is very democratic. Cara and I agreed. You're outvoted.'

'Then I'm out of here.' He leaves the room. Lucy scoops up a couple of video cassettes from beside the armchair and dashes to the door.

'And you can take these with you!' she calls and throws them with a clatter *into the hall. She slams the door. 'Yes!' she exclaims and smiles triumphantly at Usha.*

'What are the films?' Usha asks.

'Oh don't worry about those,' Lucy says. 'Just one of Alex's hobbies.' She pats Usha on the shoulder. 'I'll make us some tea.'

She walks down the path and around to the back door. Through the clear vines twisting across the frosted glass she can see the back of her mother's head as she stands at the counter. The mandala Usha made in a Religions of the World class at school is still fading on the wall. The clock with the ridiculous happy sunflower face beams across at it. Usha's throat feels tight as her mother stands for a moment with her hand at her left hip; Usha hasn't ever really noticed the gesture before yet it is at once familiar and full of comfort.

The key to the front door has grown warm in her hand and now her palm is scented with metal. The smell of the cooking food is creeping out through the squeaking ventilator fan and the spices lie heavy in the damp air. Usha stands looking in on the silent activity, feeling that there is no place for her there. She has broken something. She will draw away quietly; this is not the time. As her decision is made it is taken from her. Her mother turns and they look at each other through the tangle of transparent stems and leaves. There is no hesitation: Mum is at the door and the air rushes over Usha and folds her into its warmth. They embrace and Usha can feel the tears in her mother's breathing. This is the first woman she has touched since she last held Helen and the absence of the burden of desire is a sudden loss, a sudden relief.

'Too long, Usha, too long,' says Mum pulling her into the kitchen and shutting the outside away. 'What has taken you so long?' There is no chance to reply, which suits Usha as she has no answer to the seam of hurt running through her mother's voice. Mum bustles with tea, with the chopping of vegetables, firing questions that hang necessary and unfinished all around them. Mum's hair is greyer than she remembers, seething with a silver that arches over the black.

With a plunge of guilty dismay Usha remembers something Jaz said. 'Those headaches,' she said. 'You've seen someone?'

Mum waves her hand. 'They pass.'

'But you should see someone. You should —'

'Don't you think I know what is wrong with me?' The knife is sharp, so close to her fingers as it shreds through green.

'You're not a doctor. And Dad can't treat you; he doesn't see you properly.'
'Anyone can see what has been my problem, silly child. Since Rani told me that you went to see her, I have been waiting. But without my headaches. Your father –'
'I suppose Dad explained them away like that but –'
'Your father –'
'He's so self-opinionated it –'
'Your father,' says her mother, her voice laddered with exasperation, 'is standing behind you.'
He has his arms folded. 'You should have come to greet the head of the house,' he says. 'But that is only my opinion.' His voice is Jaz's smoothed out, laid over with the sounds of the continent he left behind. 'As a doctor, of course, I would have to say that you must seek a second opinion.'
'And you'd listen?' says Usha.
'If it were correct.'
'What about my opinion?'
'Is it correct?'
'Possibly.'
'Then I may listen.'
The pressure cooker begins its edgy hiss and Mum hurries to the gas. 'You two,' she says, 'must stop this at once. I will not have my table filled with arguments. No one will pay any attention to the food.'
'There are some basic rules that need to be established before you come back here, young woman.' He pulls out a chair and sits down. 'Sit.' He gestures at the chair opposite.
'Come back? Here?'
'Exactly. But I don't want to have to look up at you like this.'
Usha places herself level with him. 'I can't come back.'
'In my house you will behave in a way that will not upset your mother. Do you understand?'
'Dad, I'm not coming back here. Not to live.' She is surprised to hear her voice so calm, so certain. 'But I'd like to visit, often.'
'What kind of offensive life will you lead then? You have made us suffer enough.'
'I'm living in a house with three other girls. The house rule is that no males are allowed. Relatives are okay but that's it. Jaz has been spying on me for you – I expect he'll keep it up.'

'Your brother is a good boy,' says Mum as she stirs a steaming pot and bangs the spoon hard on the rim.

'He's a man.'

'He will always be my boy,' Mum says.

'He isn't perfect, you know.'

'There's an English expression for that,' Dad says. 'About pots and kettles. Very appropriate, don't you think?' He stands up. 'Where you will live will be discussed,' he says. 'Help your mother.' He leaves the kitchen.

'It's good to see him happy,' Mum says. As Usha takes a lid from a saucepan and peers inside Mum slaps at her hand and moves her firmly out of the way.

'Happy? He seems just as bossy as usual,' Usha says.

'That,' she says, 'is how I can tell. Now, you help me with these onions. I want to hear all about these new friends of yours Jasbir has told us about.'

'They're old, used-up friends now,' Usha says pushing away the ever-near eyes of Helen, of Dan. 'I'll tell you about life at Sainsbury's instead.'

Together they move towards the first meal.

'Mum's been singing again,' says Jaz. 'I knew there was a good reason for you to stay away.'

'It's sweet.'

'It's awful.'

'She loves to sing.'

'And especially when she's happy. But I wish she heard it the way we do – she'd hum quietly to herself which is where it belongs.'

'I am so hungry,' Usha says, tapping impatiently on the counter. 'Are you ever going to be finished with those bits of paper?'

'These "bits of paper" are invoices. They're the things lawyers produce for doing nothing at all very slowly. I, on the other hand,' he says as he clips the invoices together, 'have a business to run and the paperwork must be done.' The top invoice has gold embossed lettering laid on high quality paper that looks woven: 'Gill Enterprises: supplying the best to the best'.

'I think you can leave paying this one for a while,' Usha says fingering the thick paper. 'They're obviously doing alright.'

'I know they are.' Jaz takes the empty till drawer out and sets it on the counter where it can be seen from the window. 'That's why we're joining forces. We had our differences for a while but I sorted it out.'

'That's what you said about whoever arranged to have you attacked at

the back of your own shop.' She sees a small smile on Jaz's face. She knows suddenly what it means. 'Oh, it isn't. Jaz, tell me it isn't them.'
'The best way to defeat your enemy is to get him on your side.' He goes through to the stockroom and checks the rear doors are locked.
'Which guru felt compelled to share that nugget of wisdom?' she says when he comes back.
'I just made it up. Not bad, eh?'
'How do you know you haven't simply changed sides and all you're doing is convincing yourself that it's the other way round?'
He pauses, then shakes his head. 'No, too metaphysical for me. Anyway, I have the contract to prove it. Signed this afternoon.' He pulls a folded document from his inside pocket. 'See?' He hands it to her. 'This is the start of the First Fashions chain. And the first in a long line of bigger and better cars for me.'
His signature is an indecipherable scrawl in the shape he has made his own. The solicitor's writing is a tentative blue. Gill Enterprises' signature is clear, the letters carefully formed with a childish intensity. 'Surinder Gill'.
Gill. Of course. She had known it on Veena's wedding day and stored it away until now.
'Why didn't you tell me?' she says.
'So you're going to run my business now, hmm?'
'You can't. Not with him. He's . . .' Jaz's face seems suddenly silly to her: she wants to slap him. 'I've had some . . . trouble with him. I didn't say anything as it –'
'I know,' says Jaz. 'He told me.'
'He told you?'
'Yeah, he said there'd been some kind of misunderstanding in the pub but it's okay – he apologized.'
'He apologized.' She sounds alright but her tongue feels unco-ordinated.
'If you're just going to repeat everything I say I might as well only take myself out.'
'I don't believe it. Why did he apologize to you?'
'He was being up front, I suppose. A good way to start a partnership. Of course I didn't tell him it was me who drove through the puddle that drenched him and his imitation Armani. That would be a bad way to start a partnership.'
'But it wasn't you he'd . . . the disagreement wasn't with you.'

'No, well, it's been sorted.' He claps his hands together. 'Right. I'm off. Coming?'

'Do you know,' she says slowly, 'what he did to me?'

She has Jaz's attention. 'What do you mean, "did"?' he says.

'He . . .' She sees the choice. When she realized the connection between Lesley and Dan, she had to decide. She sent Lesley to him but said nothing. He was lucky only to get discomfort when she could have done so much more. And Helen: it would have eased her to know. Usha didn't want to help. All she can feel is a blankness that presses in on her whenever she thinks about it. She hadn't been able to provide what Helen wanted and Helen had blamed her. It's simple. But she misses the soft nights, the pale silk of her hair, the laugh that lightened her eyes.

Jaz is waiting. 'Ush?'

She can't take the step, though it means she never will. 'He interfered with my bike,' she says lamely.

He takes the contract from her and puts it back in the dark of his warm pocket. 'Why the drama? I thought it was something important. What did he do, let your tyres down?'

'Something like that.'

'I don't want you behaving like a kid, you know. This business is going to work.'

As he locks the door she looks through the grille at the till drawer whose future contents will benefit both Jaz and Surinder and at the racks of clothes arranged expectantly around its spotlight. Jaz checks the door and pockets the keys. 'It's a shame you missed Subash,' he says. 'He's dropped the turban and is now tying a scarf around his head like a pirate. He reckons it looks cool but it makes you realize just how small his head is in relation to his body. No wonder he can't cope with anything complicated: his brain isn't big enough.' He looks at his reflection in the window of the shop next door and straightens his tie. 'He isn't very fond of Surinder, either,' he says. 'That should make you wonder about your own judgement, don't you think?'

'Mm,' she says, thinking that maybe Subash isn't so bad after all.

'You're looking very cheerful,' Usha said.

Surjeet smoothed her overall; her expression was not far off a smirk. 'I hope you're not implying that I'm usually miserable,' she said.

'No. But today you look especially lovely.'

'Very witty,' said Surjeet.

Why is it, thought Usha, that however much I promise myself to try to be nice, she always rubs me up the wrong way? She tried to compose herself. 'I hear you're moving to the deli counter.'

'It's about time. That Monica Evans – you know, the one with the squint and the stringy hair – is going upstairs to work on the computer stocklist. Good job, too – putting her on public view with food was a big mistake. Of course, her dad knows the assistant manager so you can work that one out for yourself.' Surjeet laid her left hand ostentatiously over the right. She and Usha looked at each other. Usha thought about resisting the implicit demand but it seemed more unkind than Surjeet deserved.

'That's a beautiful engagement ring,' said Usha. Surjeet kept her triumph muted but she sat up a little straighter.

'Thank you,' she said, as if Usha was a small child who had done the right thing. She held her hand out and admired the effect. 'All the women in my family have nice hands,' she said. 'Made for wedding rings, my granny says.'

Her hands looked perfectly ordinary to Usha. 'Mm,' she said. They spent a few moments watching Surjeet make the diamond twinkle. 'So,' said Usha. 'When's the big day?'

'Five months today. September is Surinder's favourite month. He says hello, by the way.'

'Surinder Gill?'

'Of course, who else? Mrs Surjeet Gill,' Surjeet said and giggled. Clearly it wasn't the first time she'd tried it out. 'Jaz says you'll give us a hand at the reception. That'll be alright, won't it – you helped out at Veena's wedding, too, didn't you? Always the bridesmaid, never –'

'I was a guest.'

'Oh. That's funny. Surinder mentioned you running out of samosas.' She sniffed. 'Oh well, if you don't *want* to, then you mustn't, but Jaz did say –'

'I'm sure he did.' But he didn't mention your fat bum wobbling around after Surinder, she thought. 'Oh dear, look at the time,' she said, standing up in a hurry and banging her shin on the coffee table; a sheet of pain flashed through her. 'Tea break's over,' she gasped. 'Congratulations. Give my best to . . .' She couldn't say it. She dropped her gaze from Surjeet's and walked away quickly, forcing herself not to hobble.

* * *

As she changed out of her overall she examined her shin. Her tights were stuck to her leg with a sticky bead of blood.

She put on her jumper and tied her hair into a pony tail with a matching yellow ribbon. Instead of putting her overall in her bag she left it hanging on the rail with her name badge – 'Usha Dylan' – still attached. In the moment that she cracked her leg on the table she had decided that she wasn't coming back. She wondered if the deli counter knew what they'd let themselves in for.

Outside it was mild and the sunshine made everything look more interesting than it really was. She walked into the town centre to buy something nice to wear: it would be completely unlike anything she had. Today, she decided, was a beginning. If things were to change she would have to do it herself. Helen would make a list at this point, she thought, but I, I have made a decision.

She paused at The Little Dutchgirl. A poster of a fat black woman dressed as a fairy was displayed in the window; in a cloud of chiffon, topped with a blonde wig of impressive proportions, she shimmered with sequins and the end of her wand was a big silver star with *Help!* written on it. Across the bottom of the poster, in twirly gold handwriting, was written *Staff wanted – apply within.* Usha walked on, then stopped in the middle of the pavement, alive with possibility.

She turned around and returned to the poster. She stepped back and looked at the front of the building, then went up to the door with its lion-head knocker: it was ajar. She could hear a couple of women's voices inside. She pushed the door open and followed the sound.